DOCTOR BLOOM'S STORY

Doctor Bloom's

A NOVEL BY

DON COLES

ALFRED A. KNOPF CANADA

PUBLISHED BY ALFRED A. KNOPF CANADA

Copyright © 2004 Don Coles

All rights reserved under International and Pan-American Copyright
Conventions. Published in 2004 by Alfred A. Knopf Canada, a division of
Random House of Canada Limited, Toronto. Distributed by Random House
of Canada Limited, Toronto.

Knopf Canada and colophon are trademarks.

NATIONAL LIBRARY OF CANADA CATALOGUING IN PUBLICATION

Coles, Don
    Doctor Bloom's story / Don Coles.

ISBN 0-676-97602-6

I. Title.

PS8555.O439D62 2004   C813'.54   C2003-905521-3

FIRST EDITION

www.randomhouse.ca

Printed and bound in the USA

10 9 8 7 6 5 4 3 2 1

For Alice and Jack Coles

THERE'S AN IMAGE I OFTEN HAVE OF MYSELF, MY *ur*-self before I began to elaborate and embellish it, an image I retain from the last seconds of sleep or recover in a reliable daydream. I'm sitting in a corner of a remote upper room, casting brief glances about me and then tilting my face downwards as though to meditate on what I've just seen. In fact I have seen nothing because no one else is in the room and there is no furniture. It may be, it can hardly be anywhere else, the unused attic room of my childhood home in Amsterdam, that tall narrow Leidsegracht house—the attic room where I would go in late March when the weather turned a little warmer, to check on the dead flies at the window ledges. They meant, that random spatter, another winter gone, and in my rudimentary way I was taking note of this sort of thing even then.

If this is interesting at all it's because the passage of time is by far the deepest thing I know about life, and, in an inverse way, about art. Also because everything's connecting. I am a doctor who is abandoning medicine for literature, fitfully convinced that I have access to enough interesting words to justify this abandonment. (Doctors do this, I don't know if you've noticed. Maybe they do it because time keeps on defeating life: no matter how diligent or technically cunning they are—the impossibly delicate filaments, tiny cameras travelling bloodstreams—their defence of life is brief, is never enough. So they're tempted towards something with more stamina. *Ars longa*, etc. Though maybe not.)

In my own case the "abandoning" could involve a thought confided to me a long while ago, almost certainly by my mother, who died when I was too young to benefit from such confidences—confidences which are only now (and only imperfectly, haltingly, her voice after so long silence is wind-blown, is guesswork, Delphic) revealing themselves. Be that as it may, any physician or ex-physician who presumes to stray close to the making of literature has special ghosts to do battle with, in this respect I don't feel even marginally original. The roster of ex-doctors who have brought their stethoscopes, as some of them with such risible satisfaction have told us, to that larger study of humanity which prose fiction proposes! Maugham, A. J. Cronin, "that charlatan" Axel Munthe. And many more. All vastly over-rewarded in their second careers.

So I thank the Fates for Chekhov, the one gifted exception to this inventory of physicians-as-kitsch-authors. And I take to myself his advice to his brother, who had scratched out a single short story and thought he too would now be on the same high road that Anton had travelled to fame, fortune and, of course, actresses: "You must drop your fucking conceit."

OK, Anton. I've made a note.

Remains only to tell you that in what follows here, my "story," less of me will come forward to be identified (applauded or excoriated) than some might wish. Others will be sorry that this modesty was not carried a lot further. In any case, things are missing, you'll find—some of these due to a spasmodic tact, others simply because they've sunk too far down in the historical *oubliette* to be retrieved. There are many consequences of this, all of them good. At one stroke you are relieved of the self-serving spectre of the *Bildungsroman*. Hurray! This does not mean that I'm a completely inert observer, nose pressed to window pane, passing intimate newsflashes like bouquets behind my back into the gloved anticipatory hand of some uniformed messenger-boy while the front of me goes on goggling and eavesdropping. I do have a role here. I speak, I move about, towards the end I engage in a significant "act." But that is, as they say, it.

Time to start.

I am Nicolaas Bloom. Dutch by birth (my mother, mentioned above as a secret-bestower, was a Scot, ours was a bilingual family), surname until I left Holland, Blom. Born 1944 in Amsterdam, an only child. Local schools until eighteen; accepted in 1962 by the School of Medicine at the university in Leiden. Left medicine halfway through my studies to re-enroll as a Comp. Lit. major (I had unexpectedly fallen in love with poetry and drama and above all with short stories and supremely with Anton Chekhov, and have never regretted a day or a word of all that) but my parents, by this time father-plus-stepmother, were so distraught that after the three best years of my life (such word-vistas!) I re-entered Medicine, my place in the program having been kept for me. Graduated *doctorandus. med.* University of Leiden 1973. One year before that I had married (for the solemn quiet look she accorded me in the general office of the hospital in her hometown of Breda, where I was doing my internship, also for the whispery times we soon began having in my intern's cubicle there) Saskia van der Velde, a nurse-in-training at the time of that look, born 1952, of

Breda, in the province of Brabant. Began a general practice in Amsterdam but developed an interest in the heart shortly thereafter and went back to med school until 1979 when I was anointed *cardioloog*. Emigrated to the U. K. in 1984 (my wife, a small-town girl as I have mentioned, never felt at home in Amsterdam, which I loved, but at the time I loved my wife more, so off we went as though we were of one mind). Tried, for that small-town girl's sake, the Border Country for just over a year, a village on the Northumberland/Yorkshire county line, but the moors' unresting winds blew us south (a frivolous remark, obviously: what really happened was that there was very little welcome up there for yet another cardiologist), so we settled in Cambridge, choosing Cambridge because, as a direct result of two papers I had published on paroxysmal tachycardia during my involuntary leisure time on the moors, Queens' College offered me a fellowship, thank God. We were together there for nine years, living on one of the world's privileged streets, Barrow Road of that town—it had almond trees lining both sides and its semicircular private drives were surfaced in rust-coloured gravel, the little stones of which uttered small crackling sounds as your car pulled up to your front door. How we both loved that town! and that road! And then that ended too. Halfway through those Cambridge years there was a stillborn child, a daughter she would have been. Not "would have been," we both rejected that formulation. She *was*, we *did* have a daughter—although one who, no reason for it, decided against light, air, even her own uncried cries, before we could steady ourselves. Three years after that, Saskia died. She had developed breast cancer, although according to her doctors at Addenbrooke's the odds on her surviving this were good to excellent, she being both young and fit. But she defeated them. She did finally permit the mastectomy, but the subsequent and expected weight loss just went on and on, I think she ate nothing when I was not at home and I could not always be at home. When it was over I found a letter in which she explained why she wanted to die. She had stopped liking anything, the letter said. In just those words: *Ik heb nergens ʒin meer in.* What I once knew of that language flees further from me each year but those words nestle close. In fact we had conceived, in both senses, our child as a means of saving the marriage, even though I doubt if either of us, by that time, believed such saving possible. I forget what had gone wrong. No, I don't forget, but since I don't nobly take all the blame, the only sensible way for me to behave now is to keep as quiet as Saskia does. I did try explaining things once, late at night after an increasingly careless (too much wine) dinner at my house with a Cambridge couple we had been fairly close to. I had been living in the house alone for just over a year by then. I could not merely sense, I could see both their faces freezing in distaste as I tried to finish my several minutes' explanation. We said good night in the dark beside their car out there on Barrow Road and I watched their shadowy silhouettes gesticulating contentedly at each other all the way down to the brightly lit intersection at Trumpington.

Not long afterwards I came here. I'd sold the Barrow Road house for indecently more than we had paid for it— five times more, to be exact. Acquiring a licence to practise in Ontario, whether as generalist or cardiologist, was at that time not the problem it is today, but thanks to my Barrow Road windfall I was in no rush to start. I rented a small furnished house on a short street a little north of Eglinton, east of Mt. Pleasant, and looked about. It was mid-October and the city glinted with huge stacks of pale yellow leaves, half of them on the ground and half still aloft. Those massive yellow flickerings as I walked or drove about did me, as they say, good. I had with me a briefcase stuffed with letters of introduction from former colleagues at Addenbrooke's and at Queens', from Amsterdam naturally, even from the local hospital in Breda, where I had interned for eleven fateful months and where—I think I've mentioned this—my scrolling eyes had paused, no, halted at a carelessly beautiful nurse called Saskia who seemed willing to be halted at. But I was in no hurry to use these letters. I had never been in anything like these circumstances before—alone (that is, wifeless) in a strange town, a new country, no friends beyond those who might, it's true, begin speaking out of those briefcase letters if I opened them; and with enough money to keep it like this for a long while. It wasn't the best of times, but it wasn't that other thing either. I was not looking for consolation, as far as I knew. I would see what I would see.

What I saw before the year was out was, though nothing as big as a shock, a middling surprise. I saw that although my entire grown-up life had, up to now, directed its attention to the physical body and its discontents, this direction was no longer of much interest to me. Saskia would have laughed or cried to hear this. Whichever of those she might have opted for, laughter or tears, it would have been soaked in irony—irony that now, just now when she was no longer there to debate, then to argue, finally to rail against my notionally idealistic dedication to patients, my many absences (whether demonstrably justified or suspect), the reported late night sightings in the Queen's Head or the Little Rose with proscribed colleagues or, worse, students, I should now all on my own be renouncing these commitments. How typical, how unbearably unsurprising, I can imagine her crying out (although she'd more likely have contented herself with "*handig Nicolaas,*"* not meaning it). But the harsh laughter, the bitter calls down staircases, these I can hear, not merely imagine. They flit, thin unwanted lightnings, through so many of my memories of the last years of our marriage.

(Some people don't believe this sort of thing, that a few basic sounds can characterize a relationship. Still, there it is. I won't come back to it.)

What I wanted to say is simply that doctoring, my *levensgezel*, life companion, during thirty years, was now sidling off. I would not formally divorce it, but I wouldn't fully cohabit with it again either. It could stay, but on sufferance. Something else was on its way to replace it.

And, well, since I have no wish to insult you, best to curtail the posturing. What is "on its way" is what you're looking at. This is it, it is this. It is what follows.

* clever Nicolaas

the Story

No question this was one of Larry's bravura performances. The overweight young man who'd been on a collision course with him all evening, Giorgio, surname unknown, was insisting on the crucial importance of reading aloud to us every word of his story, in spite of the fact that this would take him easily past the workshop's agreed five-minute limit. We absolutely must, Giorgio said, hear all of these pages. It would be a crime to shortchange them, he felt. What they represented, or, he said, what they *presented*, was an epiphany, and to cut the reading short before we got there would be to render the whole exercise pointless. Would James Joyce have tolerated abridging that scene, Giorgio demanded, where Stephen watches the unknown girl standing with her lifted skirts in the rivulet by the sea? Would he have aborted it before its natural and perfect end, with Stephen striding off along the strand in his ecstasy? *No,* Giorgio said, *way*. As for the story he was currently working on, when we heard that next week, we would see that it ended kind of similarly, Giorgio predicted. With an epiphany. If he could put it that way, he said. For the epiphany's sake bear with me, he said.

Nobody wanted to bear with him. Larry said, "Giorgio"—giving it four syllables, the extra one or two not really added out of generosity—"do you have any idea what the fuck an epiphany is?"

Giorgio was impressed. Larry has a coarse tongue, everybody knows that, but as a rule he keeps it for his drinking pals. So *what the fuck* got some attention. Still, Giorgio tried to fight back. "Sure, Larry," he said. "Moment of beauty. That's what Woolf calls it. Moments where things stop. We're doing Woolf in my Monday night course, Dr. Kilachand's course. What a great course. Everybody loves that course."

Larry was giving him his well-known death-stare. Giorgio may not have noticed this. "Moment of beauty, Woolf calls it," he persisted, sounding, however, rattled. "You collect them, right? Then when you notice you've got a flat patch in your story, you pull one out, stick it in there, perks the whole page up. Sits there and glows. That's Dr. Kilachand's idea, anyhow. Mine too. Epiphany, Larry."

Larry got up from his chair, apparently to check some discolouration in the ceiling. I know he doesn't like hearing any other course praised, I've never known any lecturer who does, but this didn't seem to be it. (Why should I defend him, at that point it wasn't at all clear how I'd feel about him—but Larry's a popular fellow who packs them in every year, so reactions like this one wouldn't have much to do with vanity. More likely it'd be knowing that the praised colleague, whoever, hadn't had a novel idea since his or her long-ago doctoral thesis and only had two then, both of them untraced plagiarisms. Awarenesses like that can chafe.)

When he had finished inspecting the ceiling Larry sighed, not quietly, and sat back down again. The room was noticeably still.

"Next Monday check out Dr. Kilachand's epiphany definition again, big guy." Not quite death-stare now, more life-weariness. "If he said what you say he said, I'll personally screw his tenure application next month. Which I intend to do anyway, come to think of it. And reconsider your Woolfies. Who's next?"

And whoever was next cleared her throat, crouched lower over the table and began reading.

I'd been in the workshop for three weeks at that stage, and was just beginning to get the hang of it. To explain how I got there will take a minute. I had been living in my house for two years BL—before Larry—taking the Yonge subway downtown for the three afternoons a week I'd committed myself to at a downtown clinic. (My patients there, I'd better say, I was seeing not as a cardiologist but as a generalist, having decided to cut back on the other thing. This was because I didn't want to become necessary, *the* heart man, *the* anything special man. More on this later.) On my way home I'd usually spend an hour or two idling in Indigo, the one just north of Eglinton, reading *The Guardian* or *The Independent*, sometimes even buying *The Guardian* or *The Independent*. If I felt really nostalgic I would also read or buy *de Telegraaf.* I was buying, at that time, a dozen books a week, not the Russians because I've been reading their millions of words ever since the Leidsegracht, but other things at or near that level, by which I mean books that were probably not on Indigo's *What's Hot* table. I wasn't buying much that was new, in other words—only, as you were already thinking, snobbish things. Point is, I was keeping to myself, not bent upon change or novelty, and as far as talking goes, indifferent to anything beyond the most utilitarian of conversations. I'd often go weeks at a time without speaking a syllable outside the doors of the clinic. The anchorite's life is simpler than it has ever been, I don't know if you knew that. Aside from a grunt at the cash when I was lugging the President's and my own choices out of Loblaws, I was close to mute. This felt all right, this felt even better than that, it felt exactly right. Heinrich Böll has a story about a man called Dr. Murke* whose job is interviewing culture-celebrities for the Bavarian *Rundfunk*, and whose hobby is snipping the pauses, the silent bits, out of the tapes of those interviews and then re-splicing them into a tape of their own, a tape which he then, by preference and out of his disgust with his job and the culture it pimps for, spends his free time listening to. Thing is, I was about as undevoted to the human voice as Dr. Murke will forever be. The only words to enter my consciousness were the ones that rose, night after long night, out of my books, out of the noblest pages in the world, and they required no gloss from me. There are plenty of such pages, I knew I'd never run out. And I knew also that no matter how long I lived, they would stay close and their words would keep faith. When Pushkin was lying on the couch in his study, bleeding to death from the bullet that that prancing moron d'Anthes had fired into his stomach, and was asked whether he wanted to say goodbye to his close friends, he looked around at his books and said, "Goodbye, friends." I could list my own special titles here but it would be invidious, it would also be a syllabus, and who needs that. Well, almost everybody does, but let's get on. I regarded myself as the votary of a purer stratum of intelligences than I had ever before been this alone with, islanded with. Was there

* *The Collected Silences of Dr. Murke*

anything to pity myself for in this? All, I'd have said, if you had asked, was well.

In other words I was narrowing things down a bit. I was browsing the brink.

What saved me was Larry Logan moving into the next-door-but-one house just after he and his wife split. He came to live on my short street because, he apparently told the real estate agent, he couldn't afford to live on a longer street just then. Marianne stayed on in the nearby marital home with their two children, and I didn't get to meet her right away. For a while Larry and I met randomly (drinks at one or another neighbouring house, short-street people do that), and I'd begun to notice, without really registering them at first, certain behavioural tics, party-pieces he seemed to favour, e.g., interjections along the line of "Whatever will they think of next!" or "Kids today!" into ongoing conversations, these usually delivered in a pious, head-wagging Obi-Wan Kenobi manner and often instantly subverted by blatant starings-about as though to identify worthier interlocutors than those currently standing near him. There was also, once, I remember this one with some clarity, a series of unnaturally intricate yawns during a lengthy you-must-change-your-life harangue from the street's Rilke-enthusiast. This was all I knew about Larry, aside from what I tended to hear from the neighbours. "Writer, or something," was what I tended to hear. The real estate agent told me he was a popular novelist. OK, I would look him up. Otherwise I'd stick to my observed view that he was a tolerated eccentric, funny on his good days but normally not. Then one afternoon he asked me if in my medical capacity I had any thoughts about insomnia, he said that he wasn't sleeping and he hated not sleeping. To which I replied with the usual bromides but also handed over a sampler of lorazepam which a drug rep had left with me at the clinic an hour earlier. It was a casual basis on which to prescribe anything but in the short term, at least, it seemed to suit Larry. Several months later when he learned that I was more devoted to Chekhov than to med journals, and that I had an idea, well or ill founded, that I too might have a story to tell—a memoir, possibly, a novella, something that could be worth a reader or two's attention—Larry offered himself as mentor. He taught a creative-writing workshop at Ryerson, he said, some people had found it helpful. It was not the easiest workshop to get into, he wanted me to know—in fact, his was always the first course to close enrolment, so I oughtn't to suppose he was beating the bushes for additional students. But I could join his workshop if I wanted to. For a wise old bird like me, he said, chap who might have a headful of decadent European experience to build stories out of, he would make an exception.

"That's what you do? Teach writing?"

"When I'm between novels."

"How does it work, may I ask?"

"Dozen people sitting around a table, everybody's into a story or family history or whatever. They take turns reading a page or two aloud, bit of discussion, we're done."

"So. I don't know if I would really like that, to be honest."

"Then don't do it, forget I said anything. Your pills aren't worth shit, by the way."

Several more months went by before we progressed beyond that. About half past three one afternoon, subwaying north from the clinic earlier than usual, wondering as

I'd lately begun to wonder where I fitted into the obscure scheme of the hurrying world (I was at that time fifty-eight years old, not old for a GP with rusting cardiology competencies, nevertheless hearing the distant drum a bit—and I was getting nowhere, *no where*, with my interminably delayed ambition to write, *scrivere*), I saw Larry Logan further down the subway car in earnest colloquy with a tall and slim young fellow, student, whatever he was, in a navy blue track suit. The latter had his hood up so I couldn't tell if he was having much to say. Larry was of course in his black leather jacket and all-weather Oakleys, looking an almost exact double for, I belatedly realized, Zbigniew Cybulski. Zbigniew Cybulski was a Polish screen actor of whom you may not have heard but who was an icon of sorts, a European James Dean, in the 1950s and '60s, forever sloshing about in Warsaw's underground canals beneath a luminous cloud of *Weltschmerz*. Both Zbigniew-Larry and the student kept glancing at a few loose pages which they were passing back and forth between them. The station I always leave the train at is underused at that hour, so for reasons of discretion (it was almost certain that Larry and his companion were aimed at the same station) I left the train one stop sooner, at Davisville, and started walking those longish extra blocks towards home. Somewhere in the third block, having reflected enough on those two in the subway car— writers, obviously—also wishing to sidestep the depressing thoughts I've just mentioned concerning my own non-place in the pantheon, I invoked (an almost guaranteed rescue operation for a low-spirited Bloom) the dazzling seven-letter name again. Specifically, as I headed over towards Mount Pleasant, I began thinking about that little herd of antelopes that are the last images in a dying man's mind in my favourite Chekhov story. The antelopes are running through a clearing and the man knows that the only reason they're in his mind is that he was reading of them the day before. He finds them "extraordinarily beautiful and grace-ful," and then they rush past him and somebody at his bed-side says something he does not understand and he dies.

Thinking about that story, and feeling that if I could have written only those final few paragraphs I would have lived to more purpose than I had lived so far, but then advising myself that there was more to it than just antelopes in a clearing—for instance, I was thinking, one of the mis-takes you could make if it were your story would be to go on and on about how much the dying man loved having that rush of antelopes in his mind, imagining that your readers would find this every bit as transfixing as you did and that they would want to prolong it in their minds for another half-page at least—whereas Chekhov just gives you the one glimpse and then, with his terrific sense of timing, gets out of the way . . .

That's the line of thought I was following when I finally turned into my short street. The student in the navy blue track suit was thirty feet away and advancing towards me, coming from the direction of Larry's house. Obviously I'd walked slowly enough, obsessing about antelopes, that the two of them had beaten me home and finished whatever they'd had to finish. The person approaching me was, though, as it took me no time at all to decide, neither man nor boy. With the hood down, dark hair so short that it looked like a fine fur, small oval face, the girl, young woman, female person definitely, passed by me just seconds before I turned in at my house. I didn't look closely at her although I did notice that she paid no attention to me as she passed: this is always a small nail in the heart, as any man who is my age and was once undepressing-looking will know. Joyce's friend Italo Svevo said it best: *When you are old you have to stay in the shade, however witty you are.* That was going too far, I told myself, dappled days are not yet out of the question for me. But for how long, I wondered.

It was not because of the young woman, though, it was more due to the antelopes that I made the next change in the grand plan (*sic*) of my life. Partly also this was because it was, as I've said, at this same time that I was admitting to myself that my story, memoir, whatever it was or would be, wasn't going anywhere. The fact that I wasn't sure what genre I was working in might have tipped me off earlier, but it hadn't. The reason there was this confusion between novel and memoir was that my narrator/protagonist, although much younger than I and engaged in a different profession, and happily married and admired by all—in other words representative of all sorts of extreme variants on my own condition, hence plainly a character in a story and not at all related to a memoir—this fellow kept on covertly directing his steps towards me, he kept on disclosing minor interests that were quite close to mine, now and then he would even lift his face into a shaft of street light which would have made it easy for anyone within half a mile who had known me thirty years ago to start saying to whomever he or she was with, "Don't look now, but—" or "Isn't that—?" You see my problem. I had tried to correct this, I kept on trying to dislodge myself from the text, but I wouldn't go. Maybe, I thought, I *am* too much on my own. Maybe conversation and relationship *are* better than inner delirium. It was beginning to feel as though something should be done. I consulted the only colleague at the clinic whom I suspected of having even a small interest in a non-medical text, a fellow cardiologist called Sherin. To his credit Sherin did not mutter anything evocative of physicians healing themselves but merely asked if I had ever considered getting expert writing advice. Preferably from some established writer, he said. He thought that this sort of counselling was "around," was available, was perhaps a fad, but might be worth a look. But "established" was key, wasn't it, he asked. Don't consult some doddery neighbour who when he was a lot nimbler almost sold a story to the *Sunday Star*, was Sherin's advice.

This was not and could not have been a description of Larry Logan, whom Sherin, anyway, had never met. Sherin had heard I had a writer for neighbour, that's all, and was probably taking the sort of random shot at somebody better known than himself which we all like taking. Larry had published a half-dozen quite successful novels, one of which had become a movie of no special merit, and perhaps the novels were not of any special merit either. He was a professional though. I'd bought a copy of one of his novels shortly after he had mentioned the low value he put on my "pills," hoping of course that the novel would prove to be kitsch of the worst order. But to my chagrin it wasn't. Not only was it not kitsch, it wasn't bad at all. It didn't invite me into any deep cavern of the psyche and it didn't remind me of any really first-class novelist, but I hadn't expected it to—I mean, how many are there of those? When Iris Murdoch tells a gushing interviewer that she, Iris, is a second-class novelist, you begin to think about these things, and if you're like me, i.e. somebody who has had weeks and weeks of immense pleasure from *An Unofficial Rose* and *The Sea, the Sea* and *The Black Prince*, but who

still in the back of his mind and in the front of it too knows
that there exists a class of novel that's even better than these
three wonderful books . . . Anyway, long story short, the
most anybody could have expected from Larry was third-
class, and that's what I got. It can be very readable, you
know, third class. There's plenty worse. Anybody who
could do this, I reasoned, could be learned from.

So: if my cardiologist-colleague's tip about looking for
expert advice was worth following up, the solution was only
two houses away. I rang, I asked, and a few lives, all but one
of them still unknown to me, rotated a little. A week later
I was lining up outside a seminar room at Ryerson
University along with eight other people, all grown-ups, I
was relieved to see, waiting for the *Maître*. I should say,
before he arrives, that Larry's agreement to my joining the
workshop had not been given without a one-fingered lift of
those black Oakleys and an appraising stare before the
Oakleys dropped down again—a reminder, I was sure, that
I'd rejected his offer before. When he came, though, he
paid no attention to anyone but went straight on in, flicking
light switches as he walked down the room towards what
was, as we came to know, his invariable chair at the front of
the oval table round which we all sat.

And that's how it started. Also how it went on. Larry at
the front, slouched and seemingly comatose, biding his time,
listening to whoever among us was reading her or his work
aloud, and knowing that whether he liked it or not, his was
the only comment that that reader had any interest in hearing. In such ways the workshop's proceedings were hieratic.
Watching the just-finished reader's face while the rest of us
were stammering out our blame or praise, you could count
on that face to be watching only Larry, trying to intuit

whether he was approving or despising what we, these
nobodies, were saying. And when the nobodies were done,
into the pent silence Larry would come, setting all straight.

Well, he had the credentials, didn't he. He had *seven*
credentials and all of them novels, straight-up A-to-Z nar-
ratives, none of them showing the smallest taint of what
one member of our group, a returnee from the previous
year who plainly knew what our leader's biases in this matter were, castigated during an early session as "this feckless
postmodernist arseing-around." Who cared whether those
seven novels were third-rate, fourth-rate, lower-than-that-
rate? Everyone there would have given all he owned, all she
owned, to have done as much, to finger forth from a book-
seller's shelf, someday, a book with the world's most magical
name on its spine—her own name, his own name—

You must drop your fucking superiority, O'Bloomov.

Right, Anton.

One tidying-up before going on. Not everybody "read"
that first night. Or the second night, a week later. And no,
I am not speaking of myself. The tall, slightly gawky, track-
suited young woman did not read in either of those first
weeks and seldom commented on anyone else's reading.
Only once, on the second of those Thursdays, did she say
anything at all, and it was so quietly offered that I heard
only the last of it.

Something about "waiting," I decided. And "paying
attention." Waiting for or paying attention to someone or
other.

Not Godot, I was pretty sure.

Everybody, full of goodwill as they seemed to be, sat in
silence a full half-minute, as if they wanted to assure her that
her contribution merited all that undisturbed meditation.

Then Larry said, "Good place to end," and headed for the door. I soon learned that this was, by his standards, an unusually dignified exit. And even here the dignity didn't last. A quite austere elderly man, perhaps of East Indian extraction, apparently called Wewak, made the mistake of hurrying after him with a question, one which obviously didn't slow Larry down for long. By the time I reached the corridor he was halfway down the staircase, calling back up to Wewak the optimistic benediction to "Keep it moist."

That was an early October night with a hint of mist in the air, and on my way home I thought I was noticing a smell of burning leaves, probably an illusion since that's something this country has pretty well stamped out, if I can put it that way. Mist-plus-burning-leaves brought England to mind, specifically Cambridge , where the homely custom continues unabated and unembarrassed—those generous gardens on Barrow Road used to keep their late autumn bonfires burning all day, a small smouldering far off behind the house, a familiar appearing-and-disappearing blob of orangey light back there under its wavering wisp of grey smoke. Leaving the subway at St. Clair that night, doing this because I wanted to use up more of the interminable evening, and walking up Yonge breathing that illusion of smoky air, I remembered standing with Saskia in the "wild" part of our garden behind that Cambridge house watching our little fire towards the end of an October afternoon, and remembered how, just a few feet from us, a robin flew to perch on the top of a long-handled spade which I'd stuck into the earth there. How my wife loved those robins! She watched for them, set out cake crumbs, admired their fearlessness and paid close attention to what she felt sure was their utter individuality. These were, of course, the smallish redbreasts of Cock Robin song and verse, a genus quite distinct from the North American version, which might better have its own name. Hard to say what that name would be—Robin Dimbreast, Dunbreast, either of those would do. That late afternoon in our garden we stood watching our visitor for as long as he chose to rest there, flipping in tiny precise gestures his tail feathers into a series of attitudes and angles, and cocking and recocking his head at us. We were ready to leave, but I needed that spade to douse the fire, and there was no way I would have been allowed to make a move towards it. Not that I wanted to. When the robin, careless of all this, flew off, the energy of that afternoon went with him. I remember staring into the red-gold embers in search of a comment Saskia might enjoy, or might, at least, endure listening to. Although maybe all I was doing was scanning for an odd-coloured flare of flame, anything to distract me from the arriving shadows that must, though I can't be sure about this, have seemed so fitting that late afternoon.

Wild garden, domestic wilderness.

It was unexpected, though, that little pulse in time as I walked up Yonge Street. Saskia coming back and standing so close, I mean. Did I miss her? Often. If I had a wish, would I have wished her back? Back in the world and in my life? I'd asked myself that question so many times, and had come up with such evasive answers—but the poll, which (for the sake of putting an end to a uselessly resurfacing *angst*) I had for a year or so been keeping an informal count of, had been hardening towards No. Even though, when I thought about it, two lines in a favourite Pushkin poem often glared out at me—

> Yet she was someone I once loved with passion,
> With daily tension and anxiety . . .

This time, anyhow, in spite of those lines, I left my poor revenant standing there and went into the house alone. The Barrow Road house in Cambridge, for a few haunted seconds. But then this one, on my short street in Toronto.

Big crisis at the clinic Monday morning. My bad luck to have been there, I'm never there mornings as a rule. But an elderly patient had pleaded that if she was to get her Wheel-Trans ride, it must be before noon, couldn't I make an exception and be at the office early? Longer story than that, but too trembly to be going public with.

How had she gotten my home number, is what I was wondering.

Brèf, I arrived at the clinic about half past eleven and walked in the front way because it was raining, which was why I had driven down in the first place instead of using the subway, and had parked out in front because it's closer. Normally we don't use the front entrance. Using the front entrance means you have to walk through the waiting room en route to your consulting cubicle, and while you're doing this every single one of your own patients who's in that room tries to catch your eye and let you know that here he or she is and they don't want to hassle you, or anything, but on the other hand here they are waiting for you, so as soon as you can manage it, that will be great.

I'm not sure they are thinking all this but that's what I think they're thinking.

Only this time I didn't walk straight through the waiting room because I couldn't. Even as I was opening the outer door I could see a man's black shoes, with his feet still inside them, on the carpet, pointing upwards instead of flat on the carpet as they ought to have been, and part of his trouser legs, also horizontal when they shouldn't have been. And there was some bustling roundabout. Whatever this was, it had obviously happened only seconds before I arrived, because no doctor was on the scene, the main response from the clinic's bureaucracy so far was that one of our office ladies was leaning over the counter looking exasperated, and the man with the incorrectly positioned black shoes, who looked to be in his fifties, my age or close, was lying in the middle of the room and was unconscious. In the same moment that I came in, Margoles, a recent recruit to the firm, very agile, luckily, although in the end agility wasn't enough, raced in from the corridor followed by two nurses and another doctor, and fell to his knees and began CPR while the rest of us milled about. I looked for a pulse and the wrist was already cold, cold. Wrists know when the game's up before anything else does. The waiting-room patients were advised to retreat to their chairs and sit down, and did so, perhaps not disappointedly. The concentration around the fallen man thinned out to an efficiently functioning core.

Right up until the emergency crews arrived I was kneeling at the fallen man's head, keeping it steady. Not that he was attempting unsteadiness. His eyes were closed and seemed content to be so. Looking down at him from so near, the dignified Italianate face and those perhaps-contented closed eyes, affected me strongly, though I didn't know why. The firemen arrived, a minute later the paramedics and the ambulance, and minutes after that the man was borne off. We had a ten-second conference and agreed to get people out of there as fast as we could. A half-hour later the waiting room's witnesses had been dealt with and an entirely new bunch were turning the pages of the outdated copies of *Maclean's* and *People* and *Your Doctor Advises*.

It was only that night, sleepless as usual and lying in the dark, that I understood why those patiently closed eyes had affected me as they had. My early morning reading that week, by which I mean the book that I was reading most mornings between four and six, was a history of the Medici family in its power century, the sixteenth. In the second-last chapter I had come across and then reread and been made thoughtful by an anecdote concerning Cosimo de' Medici, the oldest and proudest of the Florentine lords of his day and long-time head of his famous family. Being observed sitting with his eyes closed for quite a while one afternoon in the immense gallery of his palazzo, the Pitti, in Florence, and being asked why he was keeping them closed for such a long time, the old man had replied, "To get them used to it."

I had tried doing this for a while even though, old as I am, I was not nearly as old as Cosimo had been and did not think that in my case there was any urgency.

The man with his shoes pointing upwards on our carpet, however, whose eyes had been so firmly closed, and who because he was so much younger than Cosimo de' Medici had probably not had time to "get used to it," died. Sherin, who arrived on the scene only seconds after me, thought that he might have been dead when he hit the floor.

He had had a bypass the year before, which Sherin had done. This had been a success, but apparently there had been a new blockage that had shut things down with a speed and an efficiency that gave neither the patient nor us any chance to react.

Unhappily it soon developed that death was not the end of this affair. It turned out that the bypass the previous summer had not been conducted exactly as had been scheduled. When Sherin had gone in there and had, as it was testified he had said at the time, "had a good look around," he had made an ad hoc decision to up the scheduled double into a quadruple—there had been two additional suspect-looking arteries, so why not anticipate future trouble and deal with them now? That's what Sherin had asked himself. In his place I would have asked myself the same thing and answered as he did. In any event Sherin had gone ahead. And Bob's your uncle, because everything had seemed fine, and the patient, a Mr. Salvioni—that Italianate face had been honestly acquired—had been grateful and had been permitted to return to the summer fairways, although no more than the first nine.

After that waiting-room death, though, what had been fine was no longer so. The Salvioni family was now threatening to bring a suit on grounds of irresponsible and unconsulted conduct. There wasn't a chance of such a suit getting anywhere and any halfway responsible lawyer knew this, but you can always find one of them who scents a fee, and such a one crawled into the light to get this underway. Sherin wasn't universally loved in the firm, it turned out, feelings were hurt and a common front had not developed. It was a nasty time.

How this affected me was at first easy to say. *Not at all* would have covered it. I told Sherin I would support him and let this be known, which perhaps helped him a little and certainly helped me, since it meant his enemies stopped dropping into my consulting room for diminishingly amiable chats. But two things then began happening. One was that I thought more intently of discontinuing practice altogether, on the ground that all this was demeaning, did I really want to continue in a profession/practice which showed so little loyalty? so little courage? And there was a subtext I hadn't even thought about until then, namely, my seemingly fireproof bank account: if I gave up doctoring, how long would that Barrow Road coup last? And just one more question: would my romantic notion that the only province I really wanted to explore and to bring back interesting news from was not science, not medicine, but was "art," was "writing"—would this notion, one on which nobody had ever tested me—no one had ever patted me on the back and said, *This is you, Bloom, étonne-nous!*—would this stand up, how long would it last now that I could see the possibility of it rushing upon me?

Shuffling upon me is all right there too.

A lot of questions. Reader, if you are there, I did what I think most would have done, in the circumstances. Nothing. This is not quite accurate. I did not leave the practice, that's true, but I did mutter discontentedly up and down a few corridors concerning the likelihood of cutting back on my already sparse office hours. Rodent leaving the leaky ship, one of my colleagues told me he had heard another of my colleagues saying to a third of my colleagues. Wonderful, I thought. One more reason for plotting an early exit.

The other consequence of it all (the lawsuit never materialized and the Salvionis retreated into internal dissensions of their own) was that I committed myself much more fully to that subject which I am sure you would be happy to hear a lot less about—Bloom the unprecocious author, that literary late-Bloomer. And committed myself more, also, to Larry Logan's little group. The two seemed to go hand in hand. At least, in Larry's group, nobody was bringing suits.

Last night the topic of discussion centred around "soul," whether this could have any place in the novel of the New Millennium. I mentioned that Strindberg regarded soul as "a storm of interruptions," meaning that you couldn't fit the idea of "soul" into anything merely rational, or understand it in any daylight way—but you couldn't ignore it either. Not if you were in the habit of making use of it whenever it suited you. Or when it spoke. When it interrupted.

When it—when soul, that is—interrupted what? Well, your life.

Giorgio thought this was great. "Ginsberg, right?" he cried. "Ferlinghetti, right? Or how about William Blake? Lightning bolts from the soul! You're dead on, Nik, dead on! Give me one of those bolts from the soul any day"—and Giorgio leaned across the table-corner offering me a high-five, which, in spite of my low, subterranean in fact, regard for two of the three names he'd mentioned, I had no problem accepting.

Larry shifted in his chair a little, which was why, everyone knew, Giorgio instantly retrieved his hand from the high-five. But Larry wasn't the next one to speak.

"'Storm of interruptions' is so good. I'm going to go home and think about that. But I—I believe you're very wrong about one thing."

It was the young woman in the track suit. Which she'd replaced with another uniform tonight, I noticed. Instead of the track suit, black tights, long black skirt, thin black turtleneck. The existentialist uniform of post-war Paris, approximately, and before all others, of Juliette Greco, who when I was seventeen I had determined to seek out as my personal tutor and initiator into the rites of Eros. Of which I had known nada at the time. Forty-one years on, some things had changed, but for Juliette and me it was too late.

Her impersonator was looking at me.

Very wrong about one thing? "What's that, then?"

"What you said about the soul speaking. Soul doesn't speak."

"Really."

"No. I mean, yes. 'Making use of it whenever it suits you,' you said, which was right. Making use of it was right. But then you mentioned speaking."

"Which was wrong, in your—" I was headed in a rude direction, but Larry saved me, bless him. Not that saving me was on his mind.

"Which screwed the quote totally," he said, grinning happily at us both. He'd been somnolent, as so often, but now he was up and alert. "Soul doesn't use words, Strindberg was implying, isn't that right, Nico? This interestin' thing in each of us that we call soul—it has the sense not to speak. Which reminds me of somebody. Some heavy ponderer. Some voice out of the deepest and *dunklest* cellarage. But who?"

A stare around the table. Giorgio sat up for a second as if he knew, but then re-slouched. He wasn't going to be Larry's punching bag again. Not until next week, soonest.

A brief murmur from somewhere.

"Sorry?" That was Larry.

". . . No . . ." This was Juliette Greco. Not really, alas. Impersonator again.

"I thought I heard a short, potent name. The sage of Zürich. Didn't I hear that name? Sage of Zürich? Don't be shy—"

"Yes. Jung. Perhaps you are thinking of Jung." There was an accent, slight, so slight I hadn't heard it before, made more evident by the persuasively exact Germanic enunciation of the proper name.

"Eureka! Yes! Sage indeed! Thank you! Soul! Very like Jung's anima, don't you agree, in the sense we've been speaking about it here? Also like the same guy's unconscious? Eh? Big-time power floating around, but nothing you can pin down? The way you can pin down the spoken stuff? Terrific. Glad somebody here has some answers for us."

Juliette wouldn't look at him. She was looking at her notepad and pencil on the table before her.

Larry hunched forward. I knew he was about to damage the silence again. Before that happened, though, still looking down, false-Juliette said, in a down-looking voice, "They are not my answers. My husband."

"Ah. Husband."

"He knows about Carl Jung. Everything." The accent might not have been German. Looking, as she spoke, at a blank wall, passing her hand briefly across her dark head-fur. The piece of wall she was looking at was well above Larry's head.

"Ah," Larry said again. "Good for him. That's the gentleman who calls for you here every night? After class?"

She was examining her notepad again. If she nodded, I didn't see it.

"OK," Larry said. "Some other time." All at once he was bored. He needed another object to talk at. *At*, not *to*. "Dr. Bloom. You agree with the lady? Tell us you agree with the lady. Tell us something, OK, Doctor?"

"*Hou je kop toch, smeerlap.*"* This was more Larry's style than mine, but the style was infectious. As for speaking in Dutch, I'd learned that if you speak an inferior tongue very rapidly and without looking around, nobody minds.

"Dr. Bloom is insulting me, folks. What can I do? I know only enough German to understand that Dr. Bloom, right now, is insulting me in Dutch. It may well be double Dutch, for all I know. OK, Dr. Bloom. I know when I'm out-*sprached*. I leave the field to you. Good night all. Don't forget next week's epics."

There was the end-of-class exchanging of pages—our homework for the following Thursday—and off we all went.

Larry waited for me down in the lobby. "Up for a drink, Dr. B. ?" We went off to Cruddy's, nice pub if a bit shouty.

That was the night I was brought up to, as Larry would say, speed on his love life. Not a subject I was anxious to be informed about, but no matter. Larry's unburdenings care nothing for the restive eye-roamings of a bored companion.

"Congratulate me, Nik. I'm *homo naturalis* again."

"Good to know."

He was eyeing me, an ironic eyeing, the while beginning a gentle counter-tenor rendition of one of his cherished

---

* "How about shutting up, you—" (Dash represents an untranslatable Dutch rudeness.)

Victorian music-hall ditties. "*When there isn't a girl about, You do feel lonely—*" He cut himself off. "You'll never guess who it is. Well, of course you wouldn't, how could you? Her name's Terry. Assistant in the department office. Girl of outstanding intelligence. Even you must have noticed her. I feel sure we're going to be firm friends."

"I've never been in the department office."

"I keep telling you, life's passing you by. I was picking up my mail after class last week and she made a big point of leaning across her quite wide desk to hand it to me. Scoop-type blouse and no bra. What a child I still am, Nik. I was greatly moved."

We had a pitcher of Rickard's Red which Larry went at not quite singlehandedly but almost, meanwhile praising Terry in unoriginal ways. I soon retired into my own thoughts, and before long Larry must have been doing the same. We finished our first pitcher of Rickard's Red, after which I noticed that each of us had his own pitcher.

My thoughts-in-retirement were about Juliette Greco— the real Juliette, the long-ago one, not the false one of tonight's workshop. The false one, apparently due to her black turtleneck (and in spite of her buzz-cut hair, so disappointing if what one had in mind was the real Juliette's uncontrolled mane), led to the thoughts, but the thoughts did not concern the false one. For two years in my early teens I *was* French. And existentialist, naturally. In my imagination I frequented those *caves* that the adolescent Blom, so callow that a whisper from a shadowy canal-side doorway in his hometown could enthrall him for a week, never saw but that he was certain the true Juliette lived in, in her dark arrogance would inhabit forever, defiant wanderer in one of the micro-galleries of his mind. That smoky voice, the tiny underground stages, all those imagined shabby places permanently full of—of who? Of writers, *bien sûr*. Glow of writers' cigarettes in the dark. Writers' lipstick-smeared wineglasses. Writers' brooding or provocative glances. The bar Tabou on the rue Bonaparte, the Flore and the Deux Magots so close together in St-Germain-des-Prés. I'd searched out all the echoing names and printed them carefully in the little book I would certainly take with me when I was finally able to travel there, aged whatever, even nineteen, even as old as twenty would probably still be OK, stepping down from the Copenhagen–Amsterdam–Paris express onto the platform at the Gare du Nord . . .

Such injustice, never to have been there when I was new! I feel it still.

But about this false one. Not her fault, of course, black turtlenecks are still sold to the general public. But if I could learn her name, I thought, she could shed Juliette's and go her own way, in or out of this story.

"Larry, that girl, that one in the turtleneck—I've never heard her name, and I—"

But Larry's thoughts hadn't left the wide desk in the department office. "Surname, you mean? Don't know it," said Larry. "Haven't asked her, have I. Terry and I may never hit it off quite to the surname degree."

It started him going again, though. Complaints about his publisher, his soon-ex-wife ("forty-year-old big-mouth broad"), the *nomenklatura* at Ryerson and their insistence on idiocies like office hours, and, inevitably, "that wanker Kilachand." He'd got his second wind and so, among the frequent blurry stretches, a lucidity could break the surface.

"Bloomster, you've been in the group over a month now. Month, easy. So what d'you think? Worth your while? Breaks the monotony? Y'know? Worth it?"

"Wouldn't come if it wasn't."

"Glad to hear it. Not the, you know . . . sharpest. This group. In the drawer."

"No need to apologize."

"Wasn't. Not even dreaming of. You misunderstand me. I think you do it . . . deliberately. Wilfully, I will add. When the mood hits, you head back into your soaked, your—flooded—your Zuider Zee, waving your finger about, case you glimpse a handy hole to stick it in. Dike, y'know? Pardon my Dutch."

"I wasn't asking about what's-her-name. Terry. Asking about someone in the workshop."

"What do you care?" Larry looked around the room resentfully. "Goes for everybody. Not the sharpest." He stared off again, catching the eye of one of the four bikers at a nearby table. I detest this sort of thing. Drunks staring about in bars. I once, years ago, had to pretend to be ready to punch it out with a fellow who looked very much like a well-known Dutch middleweight and who was sitting up at the bar in an Amsterdam café. De Spiegel, that's the one. And this was about to happen why?—because a woman at our table who'd had too many Absolut vodkas-on-ice was staring about in this same irresponsible way. She made some comment about the middleweight, I forget what, not a compliment though, and her eyes kept on going back to him, and finally the middleweight picked up on this and started showing interest. At which point this woman looked at me with a look that said, *What are you going to do about this?* I hadn't the smallest idea what I would do (although I don't mind letting slip here that *nothing* was definitely one of my options) and still don't know what I'd have done if the middleweight hadn't fallen off his bar stool trying to get at our table. The Spiegel's stools were unusually high, he obviously forgot that and fell awkwardly and sprained something and had to be helped away, what a relief.

But this time the biker broke off the stare of his own accord.

Larry roused himself, and went on, meditatively, "Of course there's Wewak, weird old Wewak. He the one you're thinking of? In the workshop? Weird old guy. Wewak. Know who I mean?"

This wasn't getting me anywhere. "Everybody knows Wewak."

"Weird. Picked out of a Papuan jungle by some dipshit Brit major just post-war, fellow wanted a cheap batman I expect. Or worse. Somehow bobbed up here. Bobbed up, y'like that? The creating imagination never stops. He was asking me the other night about—what was it?—immigration. Now what do I know about that? Immigration? God's sake. Wants his brother to come visit him here. All the way from Papua. Shock of his life if he ever came."

"*Pourquoi?*"

"Obvious. Fellow'd certainly be a cannibal."

"Course."

"Shock of his life. What I meant to say, back there, all I meant, how would you feel about subbing for me if I should vanish, if I should—" His mind wandered off.

"You were saying?"

"—if I should go walkabout for a week or two?"

"Walkabout?"

"Terry's got some holidays coming up."

"Excellent."

"Don't be like that. This subbing, now, the way I see it—"

"Subbing? You serious?"

"Why not? You're even older than I am. They'll respect you."

"Larry, come on. I'm unpublished, I'm—anybody else would be better. How about Giorgio?"

"And you're a foreigner, makes you exotic. They respect that, too. *Who* did you say?"

It was late and finding out the real name of the unknown woman I'd dubbed Juliette hardly seemed to matter any more. One last try, though. "There are a couple of people in the group who seem, to use your word, plenty sharp enough. One of these was sitting about mid-table across from you, the one who—all that about Jung—that young person, you know, she has a bit of an accent, which—"

Larry was now leaning far back in his chair holding his glass in one hand and his empty pitcher in the other, and clinking them together. A waiter waved from afar. " 'Young person' is terrific, Nik," Larry said. He turned to me with an ersatz smile. "Descriptive. I love it. I really do. *Young person*. Never believe how much I adore that phrase."

"I've been wondering. She's the only one who hasn't read to the group yet. Any reason for this?"

"*Young person*. Rolls right off the tongue."

I pried my jacket off the back of the next chair.

Alacrity was not the word, but Larry did sit up. Sitting up seemed to allow the last of his straying resources back. "Take it easy," he advised. What followed came heavily but with a remnant of clarity. "Not your type, Nik. Trust me. Moody. Excessively moody. Not much fun at all. Forget her, Nik. Much better bet, now, is that slightly, oh, roundish, I admit, but still eminently—still very perky, I would say—Mrs. or Ms. Madell. The first week, you weren't with us yet, I mispronounced her name as Model. Not important, of course, but she took note of it. Pulled herself together immediately. Posture-wise, y'know? Her name's really Madell. Mrs. or Ms. I don't know if you knew that."

Mrs. or Ms. Madell would probably be "very quick off the mark" if I were to "evince interest," Larry maundered on. But when he gave me an opening, I repeated my question.

"Oh, that one. *That* one. Well, I dunno. I don't know why she won't read. Retiring, I suppose. Bashful. Did read once, actually. But not to the group. Came to my house with me once, read for a few minutes on the back porch. She'd asked me after class if I might have time to see her the next afternoon, why not I said. I mean, I wasn't going to grope her, was I? Was I? I was not. Not my type. Teacups under her turtleneck, know what I mean? If that." All at once he looked sad, or perhaps only thoughtful. "Have their own charm, of course.

"Anyway," he said, "she came, read, went away. No eye contact the whole time. Didn't smile once. Dead boring."

"And what was it like?"

"Told you. Boring."

"I mean her stuff. What she read."

But Larry hardly remembered. Boring. Couldn't tell what the hell it was about, really. Not much there, he'd say. Same as her. "Demitasses would be more accurate," he said. He was looking sad again.

"Larry—"
Longish pause. "Yes, Nik."
". . ." Whatever it was, it was gone.

Here's a postscript to that Cruddy's session. I'd thought it could be omitted but I've changed my mind. Just before we left, Larry said, "That girl, you know. That young person." He was gazing at me with a false radiance. "Since you're so interested, she did mention one name. Some woman, writer, French. Whom she admires *beaucoup*, I got the impression. Simone somebody."

"De Beauvoir."

"No, Chrissakes, not her. Some other boring Frog writer. She claimed that some people called this woman a saint."

"Saint?"

"Saint."

Neither of us spoke for a while. I watched as the radiance faded off.

We rose heavily.

We walked out of Cruddy's with deliberation.

We rode home on the subway together. I made sure Larry got safely inside his house and then went to mine.

I got safely in too.

Her name is Sophie Führ. She's Swiss, thirty-four years old, married to another Swiss (don't know if he's Führ too or if the name's all hers). For some reason, probably relating to the regulations regarding foreign students, Ryerson's records note that the husband is doing a doctorate in this country, but does not note where or in what discipline. Nor does it identify him other than as its own student's husband.

I found this out at great personal cost, i. e. by agreeing to sub for Larry in the workshop while he and the secretary with the wide desk frolic in the sun. Dumb thing all round, but it did lead to what it led to. When I was passing the department office, Terry's substitute called out that the class printouts had finally come. Phoning the records office with the student-numbers attached to the names of various women in the workshop, and eliminating as I went, I was able to learn what I now know and what you see up there— her name, nationality and the bit about a husband.

Truth is, I'm no better off than I was before. If anything's crystal clear it is that I have not the slightest intention of intervening in Frau Führ's existence. Still, I apparently needed to know her name.

The Thursday night meeting, one of the two I'll be presiding over, started high but ended, I suppose, low. We heard a short piece from the woman Larry was maligning the other night as Ms. "quick off the mark"—a first-person account of a trip to Israel, by no means terse but, people seemed to think, good on local colour. The reading was even applauded, first time that's happened, and Ms. Madell told me afterwards that it had been by far the best night of the course. I'm aware that being applauded can encourage anybody to decide that things are the best; still, it was a positive start to my career as creative-writing instructor. Wewak was next and read a canto from a long poem, although if we hadn't each had our copy to follow along with, it would have been an indecipherable chant. He has trouble with his *ch*'s and his *th*'s. Also—this business of the chant—his voice tends to move unpredictably up and down a limited musical scale. The group got through what would have been an awkward critiquing time by asking him things like, "How wide *was* that beach, anyhow, Wewak?" I then tried to persuade Ms. Führ to read but she said she wasn't ready, could she read next week instead?

At the end of class I hung about for a minute tidying chairs, helped by Wewak. I was doing this chiefly so I could form an opinion of Ms. Führ's assiduous doctoral-candidate husband. The latter was waiting just outside the door when she left, but I didn't see him clearly, as an event it was therefore not much. Wewak accompanied me on my way to the elevator, chanting softly as we went, and by listening hard I thought I made out the word "immigration." He must think I'm Larry, I thought. I was feeling sorry for the confused old chap and asked him where he had come from, and he said, "Wewak." I explained that I was not asking him his name and he explained that he was answering the question I had asked. He came from a village on the north shore of his island country, which was Papua New Guinea. This took a while to get clear, but eventually I was understanding him better and there both those identifying words came, *Papua* and *New Guinea*, no problem with either of them. Wewak went on to tell me that when he had decided to emigrate and had applied at a temporary Canadian information bureau in Papua New Guinea, a consular official there had told him that his tribal name would not translate and he must adopt a new name. This had upset him so much, he said, that he had been unable to speak. It was clear that he was finding it a little hard still, telling me this. The consular official had then told him he would henceforth have the same surname as his village, and entered this on his passport application. The name of his village was Wewak.

I went off hoping that, if I had been in Papua New Guinea at that time and had eavesdropped on that episode in the consular office, I would have invited the Canadian official to bloody start over again with this particular application.

I also had a pointy admonition for myself about Wewak.

Ms. Führ had definitely caught my attention with her comments on my "soul" remark. True that the comments had not all been complimentary but she had said she would go home and think about it, hadn't she? Yes, she had. I admired her discrimination for selecting, out of the night's babble, that one word together with its "storm of interruptions." I also remembered her modesty in acknowledging that this would necessitate further solitary thought. Obviously there were better things about this woman than the page or two she had read to a bored instructor on his back porch.

The next afternoon, just back from the clinic, I was resting in my living room when the phone intruded and a voice which, when I thought about it later, had no business being so recognizable, spoke my name. Of course it was she, my existentialist. My pseudo-Juliette. My first reaction was that my thinking about her had caused her to call. In fact I had been daydreaming, a condition which had bulked up into a dream proper, and within the dream I—in the guise of a short man, which as you know I am not—walking with a hampered and inexperienced, because short-legged, gait through a wide and smoky landscape such as I have never, short or tall, walked in, was seeking Saskia. I found her but her outline melted and became that of Juliette Greco—the real Juliette Greco, not the false one of the workshop and of this present phone call. I asked Juliette Greco if she would sing a song for me. What I had in mind, I said, was my all-time favourite Grecoesque love song. When she agreed, asking which was my favourite, I replied, "'Les feuilles mortes.'" Everybody knows that this is Yves Montand's song, so Juliette gave me a scornful look and began to leave the dream. When the phone rang and my mind began to clear, she hadn't quite left, so for a moment all three women were very near, Juliette and Saskia and now Ms. Führ. This was too many even for the dream's naïveté, and very soon only the last-named remained. It was then I realized I was listening to her voice on the phone.

She said she was not sure she should be phoning but there was a question she wished to ask and the college had finally, after considerable resistance, given her my telephone number. She had been thinking, she said, of what had passed between us at our last class, and was hopeful I would tell her the source of my Strindberg quotation. She would like to look it up, she said. It was the finest metaphor she had heard all year.

"But I don't know where it's from," I had to say. "I heard it long ago. I was at a conference in Stockholm . . ."

(. . . that conference, held at the Karolinska Institute in one of Europe's most beautiful capitals, was one to which all of northern Europe's leading cardiologists, and some, I among these, not so leading, had been invited, but Strindberg was not mentioned at the Karolinska. He was mentioned in bed on Friday night after the conference's concluding session. The bed was in an apartment overlooking the broad and black-glittering Malar, which is a river flowing into Stockholm from the Baltic—overlooking, also, the Västerbro, a bridge which connects the city's northern and southern parts, and which at night, when I saw it, its string of white lights against the remote dark sky, seemed to me as loneliness-enforcing a sight as any human being ought to risk seeing. Beautiful, though. (Is everything beautiful lonely? Hmm. All loneliness beautiful? I don't *think* so.) The woman in whose apartment and bed I was was not a cardiologist, not a physician either, but the Karolinska's "special events coordinator," a title which amused her on this particular evening—and among her books was a complete set of Strindberg's plays, bound in dark green leather with titles in small-print gold on the spines. I remember how, from its unobtrusive shelf and although its contents were in a language I understood hardly a word of, that elegant set of dark green books sent forth a tense and singular intelligence. Unlikely but true. At some point in the night the special events coordinator read aloud from a preface the playwright had written to one of his plays, though whether the play was *Miss Julie*, called *Fröken Julie* in Swedish, or another of Strindberg's plays I cannot remember. The soul, the preface declared, though it is for the most part "reclusive," can under certain conditions emit "a storm of interruptions," a metaphor by means of which, in reading it to me, propped on one elbow and turned towards me among our rumpled white sheets, the most glowingly white sheets that my life story, even when it is complete, will have to show, the special events coordinator became responsible for the imprinting on my mind and memory of a scene I have secretly watched, watched with passion and despair for a while, later with disbelief (was I really ever there? in that room and that bed? were we even *nearly* as, oh, tireless, as I have for most of my subsequent life believed we were?) and a sort of rueful affection (affection for myself for having been, in such an orthodox fashion, so happy), watched all this as it lifts out of my laconic, poker-faced past how often?—at a guess, two or three times a year ever since. It is one of some half-dozen scenes that by now must be admitted to be integral to O'Bloomov's most adored and private archive, scenes that he will still be guarding even as the last sputtering nanoseconds of his life are speeding out of control and past him— leaving far behind that last diminishing bed with its harmless cargo)—

"You have no idea where I could find it?"

"An idea, of course. One of Strindberg's prefaces. But, listen, it may never have been translated into English."

"No matter. It will have been translated into German. He is beloved in Switzerland and Germany. His plays are very often on the stages of Zürich and of München. I will find it. I will . . . track it down." Did the expression change, lighten for a second, below those serious eyes? Hard to tell, over the phone. "That is correct? 'Track it down'?"

"It's fine. You are from Switzerland? Zürich? Then we are both immigrants here."

"Yes. I will start with *Fraülein Julie*. No matter if I do not find it there. I am certain that anyone who writes that wonderfully in one of his prefaces must have wonderful things to say in all of them."

"Why are you here, might I . . . are you a student?"

"My husband."

"I see. Your husband is a student. And you, you are—"

"I think I have kept you too long. Goodbye. I will be there on Thursday."

Thinking of this aborted phone conversation and of better things too, the Karolinska Institute for one of those better things, I'd like to explain, if only to myself, why I never went back there—never back to Stockholm, never back to the Karolinska, never again to that apartment with its windows looking down on the Malar's impassive, glinting flow. A hapless enough reason, I can see, and far from original. Never going back seemed crucial to my pitiable attempt to erase ever having been there. *If I don't go back it will fade from memory, Saskia's, mine, unborn generations', sooner. Before we know it. Next week.*

Well, of course it didn't. Fade in any hurry, I mean. It was our marriage's first infidelity and it made, as things will, an impression. I've forgotten how Saskia came upon it, found out about it—she may simply have had a few more unbooked days at, as they say, her disposal than I had, and it may be that during one of these she came upon what looked like a trail. And what, when she dallied, turned out to be one, too. And I had less time in which to strew sand, jungle fronds, lies, whatever was handy, across that trail. But I'm guessing, since we never talked about it. *Because* we didn't talk about it and because this untalk was quite conscious on both of our parts, not only that Karolinska conference but all of Sweden, the entire north of Europe, of the world, almost, became for us a taboo topic, an unacknowledged but glimmering subtext to whatever was text—a signal, if it ever got mentioned in company, for small hesitations, for the hasty subverting of probably harmless drifts in the conversation, for a smile or a glance. Cold smile, lengthily averted glance.

There was also, to draw to an end here, the reverse canonization which time confers upon such things. Demon-guarded images! I might be crossing streets to avoid them still—even now, long after Saskia's relinquishing of trails, of demons, of her life—if it had not been for the appearance in my story at about this time of one of the least likely, you'd have thought (and so would I have thought), candidates for the role of . . . for any helpful role whatsoever.

I may find a better description of this phenomenon soon. I do know her name. It was and is Marianne Logan. Wife to the frolicking Larry. Estranged wife, as she more than once took the trouble to make clear.

What Marianne hoped to accomplish through me was at first more than I knew. Even at second or third it was still more than I knew. One of these days I may ask her. (*Nothing*, she'll say, and I'll believe her.) We had met two or three times on the street between Larry's house and mine, the first time when she introduced herself while en route to stoke things up with her ex by uttering in his presence, as she blandly acknowledged, a few well-tested inflammatory phrases. These several sidewalk meetings had left me with the impression, common to male friends of a troubled couple, that this was a thoroughly intelligent woman who was obviously far superior to any of the wife-substitutes her husband was continuously and mindlessly calling up. "Calling up" as in sports-page argot, i.e. "from the minors."

(This behaviour pattern is so commonplace as to need, you would think, no footnoting. Just one footnote, though, from a familiar source. If the footnote sheds no light—and I think it *does*, I think it sheds all the light that's needed here— at least it comes with the saving grace of its author's wit.*)

What Marianne thought of me I had no idea. Not much, I supposed. Ageing hanger-on of below-standard husband, probably. Also over-tall, which under-tall people like Marianne often consider tactless. Why should she think anything more?

This was a freezing cold Saturday morning, and as I had nothing unusual and no duty-hours listed for that weekend, I had risen late and was now returning from a fast walk to Mount Pleasant carrying a bag of fresh-ground Costa Rican coffee—how's that for an aromatic scene-opener? I intended to spend most of the day working on this. You've no doubt figured out what "this" is, I suppose. I don't mean the coffee.

Marianne waylaid me, no other word for it. "Off for a pirouette on the canal? I don't see the silver skates. This *is* Hans Brinker I have the honour of addressing, is it not?"

"Hello, Marianne. Bit late getting up."

"Yes. I've been wanting to talk. We've surely had enough of this peremptory sidewalk banter. A real chat. What have you got there?"

"Coffee."

"Perfect."

---

* "I promise to be a splendid husband," Chekhov wrote to a friend who was as slow to marry as he himself was, "but give me a wife who, like the moon, does not rise every night in my sky."

Once in my house, I went into the kitchen to do the coffee. I could hear her in the front room collecting the dishevelled *Globe and Mail* Saturday multi-sections from one chair or another in order to have a place to sit down. But when I came back, she was standing by the bookshelf reading spines. Marianne is a foot shorter than some people whose height has been a topic here, and looked misleadingly vulnerable beside those crammed ceiling-high shelves.

"I don't have cream, I'm afraid. Milk OK?"

"Hate 'em both. When I was lactating, or just about to, which means, in case Larry hasn't informed you of our domestic situation, that this happened twice, I was given the choice of drinking a quart of milk every day or a half-pint of cream. To compensate for never ever having drunk the stuff, you know? To ensure that the tiny new bones would be up to scratch. Or that my tiny bones would be up to carrying the even tinier ones. I opted for the drink that would go down fastest. This was the half-pint of cream. *Yech.* Have you ever tried to drink cream just *comme ça*, Nik?"

"Can't recall doing that." At least she remembered my name.

"So anyway, black is fine. Many thanks. Oh, this smells fab-u-lous."

We sat down with our coffees, she on a window seat, I in my favourite chair, which was big and stuffed and well experienced in embracing, unhappy gerund, my needs.

"I was looking at your books. Brilliant taste you have, Dr. Bloom. Brilliant. Truly. I could hole up here for a very long time. Sending you out now and then for Costa Rican coffee. Which is, by the way—"

"Brilliant."

"Yes. There's only one thing I've noticed about your

library that I don't quite get. This book by Thomas—D. M., that is. Doesn't fit, I'm thinking, with all the good stuff that's here. Do you think it might be lowering the tone, possibly?"

"Well—" I began. I was thinking, What is this, somebody who actually notices the books in a house?

"Tactless me, of course," Marianne said.

"I could explain, if you're interested."

"Please."

Marianne, I should tell you, is, in private practice, what is known as a psychoanalytic psychotherapist. She also is head of psychotherapy at a downtown teaching hospital which I will not identify further, at least not until I'm sure it will not be libelled somewhere later on in these pages. Not really central to what's going on right now, in any case.

"I read a review once upon a time of a book in which the author, so the review told me, had made use of the life of Osip Mandelstam. You know Osip Mandelstam?"

"Oh, dear. I'm not sure. I wish I did. No."

"Best poet of this century. I mean the last century, don't I. Poems clear as water. As a stone in clear water. Title of one of his books, *Stone*. A Dutch translation of *Stone* came out in 1957, which was the year I was discovering poetry, and for a month or so I went around calling out those pure lines over the little slapping sounds of the canals. *We will meet in Petersburg as if we had buried the sun there.* I guessed there was more longing in that line than in anything else ever said or written. I haven't even mentioned his imagination—deep as the ocean, high as the sky. Died *circa* 1938, *aetatis* forty-seven. Cause of death, Stalin."

"Bastard."

"Anyhow, I bought this book that was supposed to be about Mandelstam and started reading it, feeling more and more baffled because among the prescriptive soft-porn passages—one every dozen pages or so—there wasn't one single clue to the fact that here had been not only a marvel of a poet but a man worth, what will I call it, *veneration* is what I'll call it. *Love* would be all right too. God was I mad. Went through the last half of the meretricious puke in a blur. The only reason I've kept it all these years is because I like to read aloud some of its many unintentionally comical paragraphs to anybody who comes in here and admits to admiring it. It seems you're not an admirer. Good. The book's called, well, you've obviously found it on that shelf there—"

"*The Flute Player.* I'm now losing it on the shelf again. Who is it who comes in here and admires things, Nik?"

"You got me there. Nobody, actually. Don't know why I said that."

"Why shouldn't you. Anyhow, enough of stinky-poo. I see that on the next shelf here you've got . . ."

At some stage I went out and walked the seventy-eight steps to my Mount Pleasant bakery, right next door to the coffee-importer, for one of the better baguettes you can find anywhere on that longish street. Then seventy-eight steps back again and we ate lunch, this was about two in the afternoon. With our lunch we each had a couple of glasses of wine. Marianne had nice brown eyes. At four she left. "I have to go irritate Larry for at least a few minutes. He *is* back from wherever he was, isn't he? Some island?"

I said he was. I hadn't spoken to him, but he'd hurried out of a taxi the night before. By himself. I didn't go into all of that with Marianne, I just said he was back.

"If you and I hadn't run into each other, Nik, I'd have been much tougher on him than I'm going to be now. For one thing, I'd have stayed longer at his place than I can now.

Can't stay long at all now, kids'll be home. This is good news for Larry because the longer I'm in the same room with him, the more I remember what a wuss he is. And another thing— I was all geared up for him before. I usually get all geared up on my way to his house, just thinking about him as I walk. It's wonderful how pathetic he is by the time I get there. Now I'm not feeling that way. It's a good thing his house is all of two doors from here, Nik. It gives me time to work myself out of the genial state of mind I'm presently in. I'm quite genial now, Nik. Am I using your name rather often?"

"S'fine."

"Oh, good."

A nice hug. And off she went, stepping extra carefully, as befits a woman who is wearing a narrow skirt and who has lunched well, down the porch stairs.

AFTERNOON AT LAKE LUCERNE

(from a work in progress)

For lunch she thought she would make, as usual, sandwiches, but then this seemed not special enough. I'll buy us both lunch at the Berghof, she decided. She could afford it, the boss had given her a year-end bonus, it would be a surprise. In fact he hadn't finished the sandwiches she had brought the last time, and she tried now to remember exactly what he had said when she asked if they weren't good. Perhaps it was, "What are you worrying about?" Something like that. Perhaps the sandwiches had been all right.

When the train came to a standstill, there was the usual rush for the buses which took people to either the lake or the hotel. Blue bus for the lake, yellow for the hotel. Most people always headed for the blue bus. He took her hand and wanted to start running for that one, but she held back. She hadn't told him about the Berghof yet. It was to be a surprise. "What's wrong?" he said. (This was in German. *Was ist's?* is what he actually said.) He was not quite shouting, but almost. "Can't you see we've got to—" He was pulling and she thought she might fall, so she had to tell him.

He was surprised, all right. "Well," he said. (*Na ja,* he said, or perhaps it was *Na gut.)* "I wish you'd said so. I could have enjoyed thinking about it all the way here." And then he said, "Look—the Berghof bus is filling up. I could easily have got us the window seat beside the driver if you'd told me sooner. Nobody beats me at this sort of distance, you know that."

Yes, she knew it. Nevertheless, there were still seats halfway down and they got two of them. He took her hand after a while. Maybe everything would work out. She hoped that the Berghof's *terrasse*, where she had booked their table, would be close to full. He didn't like to be sitting where nobody else wanted to be.

For Professor Logan's Writing Group,
meeting of December 5.
s.f.

It was a surprise, though, catching myself looking forward as much as I was to Larry's return. Whatever Marianne felt about him, his stock had obviously risen on the Bloom exchange. So his first night back, which coincided with the night in which Sophie Führ gave her first reading to the workshop—a single page from a story about a young couple on a day trip in Switzerland—was one I'd been looking forward to. Not just Larry, but Giorgio, who'd had the flu, would be back also. Even Wewak's reedy contributions had begun to verge on the tolerable.

Given all that soppy sentiment I will not bore you with details concerning the session. Everyone was present, four of them read, including, as you know, s.f., and at the end of the evening the quick-off-the-mark lady gave me a look which said, clear as anything, *This was not as much fun as when you were in charge.* With that accolade tolling in my ears, where else, I went home. I had been there only minutes when the doorbell rang and it was my neighbour.

No, he wasn't there to thank me for having looked after things. He wouldn't sit down, either. One question and he'd be gone.

"How about that, then?" The look on his face meant that the next meaningful words, which he could hardly wait for, would also be his. For this reason I didn't spend much time weighing my response.

"It was good," I said. I felt like adding, *Not as much fun as when—*

"Good? Good? Chrissakes, Nik, everybody either read or had half- to fully decent comments to make! And most notably, Miss What's-'er-name read. How did you arrange that? Been having lots of casually attired breakfasts with her while I was gone? Nik? Thought you were past that sort of thing. Up to no good, Nikki babe?"

This was beneath his standard. I mentioned how fine it had been not having any underbred conversations the last while. I was just enough put out to also ask how Terry was.

"Terry's still down there. Probably get fired when she finally makes it back to her job, poor kid."

"She didn't come back with you? Crikey."

"Crikey?"

"How come?"

"How come? How come? How do you fucking think it comes, *Doctor*?" Italicized *Doctor* was always an insult. He was walking about my sitting room. "She chose to stay on, something caught her eye. Will that appease your so evidently frustrated, long-suppressed, not to say silted-up, not to say constipated curiosity?"

"You're pretty excited, Larry. There are some interesting new remedies around for this sort of thing. Say the word."

"Oh, balls. Nik . . . let it go. OK? It didn't work out. With Terry. You know how it is."

"I've forgotten how it is. You just pointed that out."

"Yeah, well. I was a touch tender there. We were at a club one night, I thought it was bedtime, she didn't, I left, she didn't. It happens. I have a couple years on her. Who gives."

"Better luck next time."

"You bet. Where were we?"

"What did I think about something."

"Right. Well, obviously, now I remember why I lost it there. Pretty annoying when somebody as observant as your good self plays as dumb as that. Obviously I was asking for your wisdom vis-à-vis that reading. The Swiss miss. That account of a bus-trip to wherever." By now we were in the hallway, an involuntary transition as far as I could tell. Larry's eyes were shining particularly darkly in the weird hallway lighting. I had to do something about that.

Replace a bulb, OK.

"I don't know, Larry. I haven't had time to think about it. Pretty concentrated, it was. Just the two of them. You know."

Can't remember what he said to that.

In the morning, noting unseasonable warmth when I opened the door to pick my *Globe and Mail* off the porch, I decided to go for a run. I'd started doing this in Cambridge and ended up running almost every day there, making promises to myself never to miss two consecutive days. "Run" is misleading. A steady jog. On with my baggy grey cotton top and bottom, on with my Nikes, off into the ravine. Cold but bright, a Canadian pre-winter day. Lots of crisping multicoloured leaves on the path, some packaged into clumps, some chancing it on their own. As usual when I'm running, especially in the first minutes, I'm impressed by myself. Deep breaths, nothing rattling, buoyancy in the chest. Knees, no problem. Well, now and then the left one . . . no, not really. Needs a tensor, is all. Could be thirty years ago, feeling like this. The only times I think about my age are when I'm running and when I'm making love, which I have not made for years, who knows if I still can. Fifty-eight is not young, *lieve Heer*—and yet this is good, this is all right. These almost carefree strides.

Well done, me.

Sometimes I puff that out between strides.

I don't know if *onze lieve Heer** is looking, by the way. In fact, why bring up *onze lieve Heer* in the first place? If I now eliminate Him from the discussion, I can jog right on past the entire Sunday-matinee cast of Almighties and Lords and Highests and Demi-urges—all the multifarious titles of the Former Incumbent—and just get on with my day.

* our dear Lord

Sparing only, on account of his elegant name, Blake's nominee, Old Nobodaddy-in-the-Sky.

Speaking of getting on with my day—what a day it is! These packed cinders with their covering of glued-down orange and yellow and brown leaves, really wonderful. Thumpety-thump. Above all, the orange ones, frail tint I'd never seen until I landed in this country. Make somebody millions, some *fashionista*, that tint.

I would pick orange, wouldn't I.

Where was——? Oh, right, the Former Incumbent. What's really going on when people say *onʒe lieve Heer*, I wonder. I don't mean people like my father and my hyper-pious stepmother, that's not a mystery. Yes it is, but they've never noticed it. For them it's just some non-observable entity with, apparently, causal powers. Can't put it more genially than that.

Could just as easily have been, for those two, all kinds of things, whatever the neighbours happened to favour, they'd have gone right along with it—cargo cults, voodoo dolls, curse tablets, astrologically calibrated cornfields, take your pick. Whatever was in their immediate environment to be sucked up.

But I'm thinking more about, just now, people like me. Thumpety-thump, heavyfooted Bloom running pensively along a quilted orangey path.

When I say *lieve Heer*, I'm really, I suppose, thinking "Endlessness!" Or, "Soaring infinite things!"

Nothing original there, Blomski. Nothing interestingly banal, either. OK, understood.

Although I should admit to detecting a pious upward-casting of my eyes back there a few seconds ago. Somewhere between *onʒe* and *lieve* is when I detected that.

Put it down to a brief inner stirring of the Former Incumbent. Bound to rustle about in there now and then.

When I was fifteen, I encountered my first no-nonsense philosopher, and loved him. Spinoza—whom else should a fifteen-year-old Nederlander encounter and love? Endlessness is an idea Spinoza had no problems with. Soaring things, ditto. Why not stick with that, when I get the urge to send a word or two in a vast direction?

Thumpety-thump. A green space opening up ahead. A small park. Isolated persons here and there in the small park. Small park probably has a name. Why don't I know it? Gone through it fifty times, pig-ignorant not to know. I'll correct this, first chance I get.

Not today though, can't stop.

No, if I'm going to move "endlessness," or "infinity" away from its abstract hum into something that might uncouple my mind and lift it up to somewhere more lively, which I know Spinoza would approve of, then—well, then what?

Start with the thousands of years before I entered the scene. Good start, O'Bloomov, plenty of boundlessness implied there. Upper Pliocene days of high empty skies before *Homo erectus* walked into view. Small white clouds inching across blue skies on many of those long-ago days, obscuring the sun for a minute and then releasing it again— out it dazzles—behaving just as those small white clouds up there are doing right now.

All still going on. A dazzle's edging its cloud.

But all those millennia ago there was no tiny unimportant figure moving slowly along beneath those even more slowly inching clouds. Nobody to notice the dazzle, or to pause and look up and intuit pictures of fate and mortality among the clouds.

Nobody such as we find here, this tiny unimportant figure who is me. Who is I.

No great loss? Of course it's a great loss. If nobody was watching these clouds and their inchings, why would they bother?

I ask this although when I imagine them freed from my watchfulness—just continuing their solitary small motions in a pre-mankind, millions-of-years-ago unwatched universe—then I'm at once even more awed than I was a few seconds ago. Even though, metaphorically speaking, I was on my knees already.

Sentimentality looms, Bloomovitch. Yes. I do seem to be relishing this in a rural kind of way. Over there Spinoza's edging away from me, shaking his head.

He's got stuff to do downtown.

Just another dozen thumpety-thumps, down past this next bend in the path, and I'll be done.

That couple over there standing by the red car—if I still want to know the park's name, I could ask them. Do I still want to know . . . ? Only up to a point. They're a bit out of the way.

Where was I? Vastnesses. With nothing "personal" about them. Although who can be sure about that? Consider my father and my real mother, their naive accomplishment fifty-eight years ago. Such a bedraggled frail creature emerging from that union. All of it in order that that creature might now be thumping along an orange-leaf path in a ravine in a town in a country those two people never saw.

Although they did "love" it, this country. As all Dutchmen did who were sentient beings in 1945.

I was a sentient being in 1945. More than half the present world's population was not.

Canadian soldiers smiling from flower-garlanded tanks rolling into the Lowland towns.

Dutch girls in old news photos smiling back.

Thumpety-thump. All those smiles couldn't have had anything to do with my being here, could they? Hardly. Never occurred to me until this minute. Still, nobody can pronounce absolutely concerning all the coalescing micro-events that have led to a fifty-eight-year-old man running by himself along a quilted—

What's going on? That's not someb—that's never somebody crying over there, is it? Somebody's crying over there. *Jezus Christus!* A child? No, a woman! *Jezus!*—was that a shove, or—? A man close beside her. What's he—? Jesus Christ! I think he just hit her. Another burst of crying. *Wat een klootzak!** I better—Jesus—"Hey! You! Hey—"

But they saw me coming, must have, or heard me. Heard me shouting I don't remember what-all. They must have heard me shouting. Not that I knew what I would do if I caught up to them. Something, however. Words, probably. Big help.

They hurried to a car, a red car, he was holding her hand now (perhaps I should say "*they* were holding hands," except that I can't believe that. Would she hold the hand that had just—?). He, solid, mid-size, she, hard to say. Small red car parked only a few feet from them, door open, she's in, pushed in or not I can't tell, he's around to the other side, car quickly into reverse, cinders spurting from under the back wheels. And up the small incline and a left turn and off, gone, behind those trees. Neither of them looking back. All I could do was stop running, thirty feet

---

* What a shit-bag!

away still, and stand there, breathing hard. Perhaps I shook my fist—would I do that? I think I did, what a comic-strip thing to do.

I have never been able to bear seeing anybody cry. When I can't help seeing it, it's terrible. My mind just falls down through my body. Nothing special about this, I'm not describing anything special! My mother cried just once that I ever saw, and I wasn't old enough to even ask why, but I remember it was terrible. I thought about it all night in bed and cried now and then while I thought. This is probably never a good thing—being unable to bear hearing or seeing somebody else's tears, I mean. I once saw a play, it was at the Engelenbak Theatre on the Hes in Amsterdam. What was the play called? Don't know. The protagonist's mother said to him—he was a tall, skinny sixteen-year-old, which is probably one of the reasons I was so struck by this, being the same age and same freakish size at the time—she said, "My wish for you is that you will learn to bear a woman's tears." I didn't know what that meant, hearing it, although I knew it was a folk-tale wish all right. The boy inside the play didn't know either. But although I didn't know what it meant, I was disgusted. I was really upset. Later I thought I knew *exactly* what it meant. It was the advice of a mother who wanted her son, when he grew up, to inherit all that the world might be getting ready to offer him—and who didn't want some nobody to come along and spoil things. Especially she didn't want some younger woman, who hadn't been anywhere near her and her son during all of those years of getting him ready for his life, to come along and distract him, prevent him from seeing how special he was now. How wonderful he was now. That was why the mother in that play didn't want him to worry about it if some girl started to cry. She wanted him to keep on. Keep on being as he was, no matter who might be crying.

Still. If your mind falls right down through your body when somebody cries, then that's what it does.

I've strayed a bit.

That couple beside the red car—I had a bad feeling I knew who the woman was.

When I used to run in Cambridge during the years we were living at 11 Barrow Road, I would exit from the house's side door and in seconds I would be running under a canopy of white almond-tree blossoms. This would be late March or April. The almond trees lined both sides of Barrow Road from its beginning down at Trumpington High Street right up to the semicircle at the top. I would run down under the almond blossoms, ducking my head often but even so always finding a blossom or two on my shirt or sweater or in my hair when I got home again. At the bottom of the road I would turn left into Trumpington High Street, a street full of traffic and fumes, but also lined with chestnut trees, so that the chestnuts, in the right season, lay thickly on the sidewalk in their green cases or, if these had split open in the fall, just in their own effortless dark brown glossy newness. The town's two leading junior-grade boys' public schools were on that street and the boys in their grey trousers and white shirts and striped ties would collect the chestnuts and take them home and get their mothers to harden them in the oven and then they'd drill small holes in them and work a longish string through the holes and call them conkers and use them like small fighting animals, swinging them to try to hit and smash the conkers of their friends. When I had run along Trumpington for about a hundred yards I would turn off to the left and run up Porson Road, which was lined with cherry trees, not almonds, so here the blossoms were not white but pink. From the top of Porson Road it was only a short distance back to our house again, but just before reaching our house I would have to pass the house of George Steiner, the ace polymath professor, and his wife. Sometimes I would meet one or the other of the Steiners when they were out walking their large dog, who towered over them, they being, both, short. Since I am, in the Dutch fashion, ridiculously tall, communication between us might have been awkward, but this was never really put to the test. Steiner's wife would murmur what might have been "Hello" while straining upwards in a friendly manner, meanwhile trying to control the dog. Steiner would stay down where he was and nod, apparently to himself.

Barrow Road is the shining address of my life. Nietzsche said of Turin that it was "the first place where I am possible!" This is how I still feel about Barrow Road, and how I already felt during our early years in Cambridge. I lived there only eleven years, so most of my fairly long life has been spent elsewhere, but Barrow Road, although it did this without announcing what it was doing, chose me in a final way. This has more to do with Saskia than with my preferred running routes, of course, but if what we are speaking of has to do with that which is uncomplicatedly positive, then those streets and paths and the many misted mornings in which I ran along those streets and paths win out over all the alternatives the world has showed me. There were those misted mornings and there was also the

grey light of the winter afternoons, when I would sometimes take a longer route home after my day at Queens' or
at Addenbrooke's. Often that longer route would be one
that runs beside a small stream behind the houses and from
there through the allotments. Allotments are small plots of
land which people are, yes, "allotted" by the town and on
which they grow vegetables or flowers and erect small
sheds to keep their rakes and shovels in, or to sit on a fold-
up chair in front of on a spring day or even on a grey winter day and look in a quiet and possibly reflective way at
their rows of cabbages or at where the rows of cabbages
will be. There are also small fenced-off green fields, and
when I used to run there each field would have two or three
horses grazing in an absent-minded sort of way—the
horses were usually brown, but there seemed always to be
one white horse among them. This path, once you had run
through the allotments, would take you to the Botanical
Gardens, which are very extensive and well cared for and
have trees (beech and oak and alder and pine and hornbeam
and yew and one cedar of Lebanon that in itself is almost a
small woods) which are, some of them, hundreds of years
old. In certain moods I used to think I could wander about
very slowly in those gardens for the rest of my life without coming to the end of the many moss-covered fragments
of seventeenth-century paved pathway that I, bending or
kneeling to do this, liked drawing my hand over or pressing
my hand against. I'd try to decide, while doing this,
whether this was a fragment my hand could remember having been in touch with before or whether it was, in some
significant private sense, untouched. I always felt, with my
hand on one of those tightly greened paved pieces, that I
was a very brief passing shadow in this place, but also that

I was not nearly as disconnected from myself as I had felt before I got here and settled my hand where it now was.

There were no streets in Toronto that were bordered along their entire length with almond or cherry trees, but I had very soon found, just steps from my house, a ravine that you could run in for days if you wanted to. I had been running there as often as I could ever since I arrived in the city, and had met no one I knew, although I would nod at and get nods back again from a few other regulars. But two days after that scene with the red car, which I'd been thinking about a lot without deciding what to do, I was running in the ravine and heard someone coming up to pass me. When she did pass (turning her head slightly to show she knew she had just passed another human being—some people don't bother to do that, I think it's only polite) I recognized her. It was Marianne Logan. We ran together for twenty minutes or so, which brought us into the park area where the police stable their horses. The area's called, as I didn't know then but have known for a long time now, the Central Don. Marianne was wearing a black-and-white track suit and a black bandana over most of her dark curly hair, and looked, I couldn't stop the thought, very little like what her ex had called her, a forty-year-old big-mouthed broad. We sat down at a picnic table with Cokes and I told her what I had seen two days before. This took a while and when I finished I basically didn't feel like speaking any more, but I pointed back towards where it had happened. Towards where the red car had been. And the woman and the man.

"Jesus, Nik," Marianne said. "I'm so sorry."

I was wondering whether to explain how I'd been feeling these last two days. But how I'd been feeling didn't seem really important to the story. Having done all the talking, though, I was feeling tired or empty or both, so when Marianne said she was sorry, I didn't answer and probably just gave her a strange look.

"Sorry that it happened," she said, saying this as if she felt she needed to explain something. "But also that you had to see it. You must have felt terrible."

"Well," I said, "I did."

I was wondering whether I'd go on or not. Then I went on. "But the worst thing is—I haven't told anybody this, but—" She kept on looking at me, not saying anything. "—I think I know who the woman was. Is." Marianne's eyes didn't budge. "Well, I feel—I'm not sure I should say. I mean, I did, yes, see someone I think I know. Just seeing anybody like that, crying and getting punched, I think it was two punches, one right on top of the other almost, although she was crying—that was already a tough thing, not a good thing. But then, when I thought I knew who she was—then it was worse. I haven't told anybody who she was, Marianne."

I had to take about four very short breaths right there, which amazed me, I'd had no idea that would happen. But I looked away in time, and after all nothing did happen.

"I wouldn't tell anybody either, Nik. Not unless it seemed I had to, you know."

"Her name is Sophie Führ."

Marianne said, "Let's go again, shall we?"

We ran a long way, all the way to Serena Gundy Park and then along the east side of the Don River, stopping to sit on a bench a couple of times and gaze out and around and upwards at things, not saying much, and then we headed back the same way. When we got close to my house, Marianne said she would like to come in, and she did. I started to make drinks and she asked if she could have hers in bed. I agreed that she could. She asked if I would have mine there too and I agreed to that too.

One of the interesting things Marianne said to me over the next few days, days during which she had quite a few chances to say interesting things, was about Sophie, as I had begun to call her (not to her face—I had hardly seen her face). I told Marianne—this was just about getting-up time on our first morning—that Sophie and her husband had come to Canada from Switzerland, from, to be exact, Zürich. What got said next was this. Like many psychotherapists, Marianne sometimes used literary sources in her counselling, she had found useful parallels, she told me, between a patient's frequently blurry self-scrutinies and one or another much more lucidly articulated relationship in a novel or short story. And one of the texts she'd made occasional use of was a collection of the stories of James Joyce, that famous old Züricher. Well, he did live there for some years and he died there and is buried there. His stories, which are in fact not called *Zürichers* but *Dubliners*, as I know you know, occasionally were, Marianne said— as well as being the other things that they were (e.g., she said kindly, "almost as good as Chekhov's")—quite particularly helpful in her counselling.

Lately she had begun to feel that she owed it to this involuntarily helpful genius to learn something about his life. So she was, "even as we speak," she said (in the literal sense this was ridiculous), reading Richard Ellmann's biography of JJ, a book in which she was finding numerous references to a Küsnacht family (Küsnacht is not quite Zürich, but is a sort of high-end village on an outskirt of the city) which had been a great help to the Joyces in their times of indigence, their unnoticed years of poverty and wonderful achievement there. And now comes, she said, the point. "This family's name was, *da-dum*—Führ." And she looked at me expectantly.

"Führ?" I said. "So?"

"Well . . . ?" said Marianne encouragingly.

"Name's common as dirt in Switzerland," I said. I'd no idea if this was so, but inaccuracy, as I've said, was in the air.

"In Zürich?" asked Marianne. "Your friend's named Führ, she comes from Zürich, she wants to be a writer, and one or two generations back somebody of that same name lived in that same town, or close, and knew a couple of people named Joyce, one of whom was, I believe, a writer? And all this is a *so*? A *common as dirt*?"

"OK, OK. But listen, Marianne—she's not my friend. When she walks past me on the street, she doesn't even look. Besides," I said, "she's married."

"Meaning?"

"Meaning that this could be her husband's pedigree we're tossing about here. Not hers. Führ could be her husband's family name. In which case it's her husband's grandparents who succoured the great man and the great man's wife. Nothing to do with hers."

Marianne was by now on the way towards her shower but paused and came back towards me with an expression on her face intended, I'm sure, to convey a serious impatience with the line I was taking on all this. And it *was* a dumb line. Point is, though, that directly below Marianne's seriously impatient expression, standing there as if it had no idea it could be competing for my attention in such a moment, was a recently very affectionate small soft undressed body. It was Marianne's body, the one she had had for quite a while though not, in my opinion, even close to too long a while, but which I was only beginning to get to know and was far from taking for granted. "Well," the unselfconscious creature said, "maybe. But might it not be a neat route for you, dear obstinate Nik, into this lady's confidence? If you were to admit to knowing these several things about this name she now bears, whether she's always had it or not? I can hear you now: 'So tell the class, Ms. Führ, did James and Nora know which fork to use during mealtimes at your grandparents' home? Or your husband's grandparents' home? Or some other folks' home the Joyces were cadging meals from?' Wouldn't this give your friend a reason for lightening up a bit? For giving you a special hi next class? The benison of a private smile?"

I didn't answer. Partly I didn't answer because of that deliberately provocative repetition of "your friend." Partly because I wasn't listening carefully (I had, as I admitted a minute ago, other stuff in my mind, all of it heartening beyond anything my mind had given room to for years), and no blame attaches for that. Should have paid a bit more attention, though, because a while later, when we were heading out towards brunch at a place a little north on Yonge, Marianne enquired, out of a clear blue sky, holding with both her hands on to my upper arm and looking up at me out of eyes that although not blue were as innocent as that sky, "How do you know she didn't look at you when she walked past you?"

I must have spent at least an hour sitting in my cubicle in the clinic later that day wondering what to do about this. Not what to do about Marianne, thoughts of whom kept interrupting and improving my day, but what to do about . . . you know. What I'd seen in those blurry few seconds in the park.

By four o'clock, when the last patient had left, I had made up my mind. I had Sophie Führ's home phone number. I used it. A man's voice answered. His wife wasn't home, it said. Neutral voice, Central European accent.

"This is Nicolaas Bloom. I know your wife through a Ryerson creative writing workshop."

"Yes, Professor Bloom?"

"No no. I'm not the professor. I'm just—"

"Excuse me, Mr. Bloom. I understood you were calling from the college about a student. A student who is my wife."

"Doctor, actually."

"*So.* Dr. Bloom. Is there some trouble? Is my wife in some trouble? If so, tell me at—"

"No no." This was terrible. She must have been hurt, damaged during that scene in the park beside the red car, mustn't she? In which case her husband—supposing he was *not* the man doing the damaging—would have been told of this, or would have seen it, signs of it, and would hardly be in any doubt about the "trouble," would he? And if this were so—

Slow down. There were other possibilities.

"Do you have a message for her, Doctor? I shall make sure to pass it on."

"Nothing urgent." This at once felt untrue. "Do you know if she will be at class tomorrow?"

"That is entirely the—what did you call it, Doctor?—

creative writer's choice. Yes, that was it. I am only a poor thesis-scribbling husband." A chuckle.

"Then I will hope to see her."

"It has been a pleasure speaking with you, Doctor."

The next night was our class. Sophie didn't come, which might or might not confirm my more-than-guess that she was the one I'd glimpsed in the park. Either she had been hurt enough, bruised enough, marked enough that she was staying home, or . . . some harmless other reason.

Back to that park scene. I'd had, of course, to consider widening the net a bit. If the man I'd seen there *wasn't* Sophie's husband, there was a staring-me-in-the-face explanation for just about everything. Chiefly, for that husband being as much in the dark about it all as he'd been, or played at being, on the phone.

But I didn't believe this explanation, it could stare me in the face all it wanted. It didn't bother me that all I really knew about this woman was that she liked Strindberg's soul-talk as much as, until she came along, only I in all the world had liked it. I knew what I knew, it would do until I knew more. I still couldn't let things rest until the next workshop, which was a whole week away, and my brief telephonic exchange with her husband—whether he was a Mr. or a Dr. Führ (probably Mr., since he was still doing his doctorate, wasn't he?)—hadn't given me many tips or clues. True that I had seriously *not* enjoyed his voice, but I had no history at all of penetrating insights based on timbres. Put it this way: I had to find stuff out. A way of starting was to call Student Programs at the U of T's Graduate School.

"You're certain of the spelling, Dr. Bloom?" the secretary asked.

"Yes. Well, I think so. He's Swiss-German, you see, so maybe there's an umlaut hidden in the shrubbery."

"Gracious, Dr. Bloom, wherever are you calling from?"

"No no, just—little joke. I mean that perhaps his name may be spelled differently. He'll be in your files somewhere. Swiss, about forty-five, doing a doctorate in Psych. Let me think, do I know what his topic is?"

"Ah. Ah. Swiss, Psychology. That rings a bell, Doctor. Yes. We do have such a person. But—you said forty-five years of age?"

"A guess."

"Your guess is incorrect. And his name isn't Foor. It's something else."

"Yes?"

I waited. After a while I understood she was not going to continue. When I mentioned what I had understood, she told me I had no right to any information at all from the Graduate School's files about this person. Or about any other person.

But then, an afterthought. "Unless this is a health inquiry, Doctor?"

"Health inquiry?"

"A medical matter involving Mr., um . . ."

"Ah. Yes, well—it is, as a matter of fact. Confidential, of course."

"Of course, Doctor." A minute later I knew that the Swiss man who was registered with the Ph.D. Program in Psychology and whose dissertation title was "Fetish and Phallus: Sexual Ambivalence in the Autobiographical

Writings of Carl Jung," and whose listed address in Toronto was identical with the address which I knew concealed the presence of the ersatz Juliette Greco, a.k.a. Sophie Führ, was named Walter Rollo Maggione.

OK, no umlaut. His home address was Wasserschöpfi 43, Zürich, Switzerland, an address with an umlaut. And the year of his birth was 1944.

There were a few surprises here. For one, Maggione was a little more than ten years older than I'd supposed. For another, this made him exactly my age. A disheartening thought, perhaps.

And one more item of late-breaking news. James and Nora Joyce had never been to dinner in the house of the forebears of a man who was currently being arraigned by a thinly informed immigrant Dutch ex-cardiologist as a might-be wife-abuser. The Joyces had, though, it was now clear, dined at the home of persons whose granddaughter (great-granddaughter, more likely) would, many years later, forsake that home for an address in Zürich and thence an address in Toronto where what would befall her would surely seem to them, if some malicious sprite were to post the information down to them, like one of the darker and crueller of the grim old tales of Faery.

That's if all this wasn't my private fantasy.

Which it wasn't. I *knew*.

Marianne was made for this. Jung was somebody I had sidled past in my autodidactic relationship with the extra-medical world, but Marianne was right at home with him.

"Funny thing is," she said, "professional psychologists don't read Jung any more. Haven't for eons. He's become the preserve of the lit-crit people, Frye-folk among others—archetypes and so on. His stuff is full of exotic views, no, brain-whirring views of remote cults and practices. But in the cracks of those books of his you find a thousand ideas we lesser folks can feed on. Which your guy's undoubtedly doing too. In his thesis. What's for breakfast?"

I hadn't planned to involve Larry, who had got himself involved elsewhere. He was in a shootout, an increasingly public one, with the Creative Writing Program at Ryerson. They wanted him to extend his office hours for individual consultations with his students, which he was refusing to do. His grounds were unusual. They were that he had never had any office hours, and that that which had not existed could by definition not be extended. He was going to lose this one, but not before he had caused the Program's executive committee to lose a few things of their own, mostly time-related things. Hours that were intended for restful inactivity or for their own creative works would now be dedicated to wrangling with this articulate pest, who happened to be (a) tenured and (b) the most popular instructor in the place.

In addition to this, he had reconciled with Terry, who, sunburnt and somnolent, had unapologetically made it back from Antigua.

And another "in addition." He had picked up a rumour somewhere, and was come to quiz me on it.

"I don't know anything for sure, Larry. Not for sure. I'm working on it."

"OK, OK. Not really OK, but if that's the way you . . . at least tell me what you know about this guy?"

"His English isn't as good as hers. Hers is—"

"Better than yours, I know. I accepted her for the work-shop, after all, didn't I?"

"You want me to go on talking?"

"Go on talking."

"I know his thesis title." I reeled it off. Fetish and Phallus, etc.

"Titles like that," Larry said dreamily, "charm the shit out of ya, don't they?"

Sophie did come to the workshop on Thursday and although that impassive face showed no sign of damage, she'd come so early that she was in her chair when Larry and I, the next to arrive, came in. Her early arrival only made sense later on. Watching her slowly finding her way into her coat as the class was ending, turning her body to try to fit the second arm in without raising it, was as painful as—no, not *that* painful, certainly. A bad sight, though. I can't say whether we'd have noticed if we hadn't been primed. But we were, in our different ways, primed.

Her husband was waiting at the door to collect her when the buzzer sounded. Down the stairs the two of them went, he on her left with his arm round her body, his hand grasping her right arm. She was keeping that arm close to her body and pointing straight down. I asked myself, if I were walking as she was, what would it say about my pain centres? That I was trying to shield my ribs on that side?— or further down?—or—?

"Scumbag's got a fetish of his own, Nik," the articulate pest said as we stood at the top of the stairs watching.

The other event of that evening was the second of Sophie Führ's readings.

———

THE RETURN

She feels thankful to have the compartment to herself. It will be dusk in less than an hour, about the time the train will be running through the suburbs of Munich, and by then she hopes to know what she will say to him. About this, of course. About a wife absenting herself for three weeks in order to understand what is going on with her.

("How unoriginal," or "How unnecessary" . . . she's trying to remember which of these is closest to what he said when she first told him this was what she wanted to do.

The first one, probably.)

The lights in the compartment have just come on. Not needed, really—through her window everything's still daylight. It's nice that no one else is here, though. Just the quiet of the compartment, the generous, helpful look of the five unoccupied places. And has anyone at all passed along the corridor?

Such a serious face that the inside lights are causing, now, to be reflected against the rushing Bavarian country-side!—a seriousness that's there, she guesses, because behind it are the first stirrings of what's probably going to grow into remorse. *Why* the remorse is there is . . . well, she doesn't *know* why. They'd agreed on Basel, after all: she had chosen it and he had agreed to it. And both had felt that three weeks would be the right length of time. To her those weeks had at once begun to glow, to shimmer. *How* they had beckoned her! Brimming with—well, with solitude, she had hoped. She had agreed with him that, yes, there would be days, and nights too probably, of loneliness, but surely there would also be, she had said—wouldn't there?—times when she would be free to concentrate *purely*, reading and thinking in this "pure" way, upon the new thoughts, the new words, that were now mattering so much to her.

(There were those words *pure, purely,* again—borrowed words, of course. And of course *they* were the problem, weren't they. Yes, they were. The words and whom they came from. Could anything ever be done about this?)

What had he said? That to take with her as her primary companion during this privileged solitary time the work of a writer who knew (as a little research of his own had made abundantly clear to him) "so little, so almost nothing" of the world, and whose passion for that "almost nothing" was so unreasonable—

"This is not a *philosophe* you are inviting into your mind, *Liebchen*. This is no thinker. This is a *believer*. A very different sort of being. A different sort of woman. Altogether foreign in nature to the woman I am married to."

That was it. Almost exactly recalled, the intonations exact too.

In all this he may have been a little severe . . . but at least he had allowed her to go. Finally, smiling, he had said that yes, he supposed he could manage on his own. The current stage of his thesis—he supposed she knew at least that much, that he was finally close to the penultimate chapter—need not suffer unduly.

MINDELHEIM. The familiar pale yellow brick of the station house flashing past. Gone in sight's instant.

The most she had ever expected were glimpses, one or a few, a very few at most, into whatever it might be called—wisdom, perhaps. Wisdom certainly existed, she knew it did, this was undoubted; and during her first days in Basel, in her room or on a long walk by Basel's river, she had felt an occasional shudder of possibility that some part of wisdom might be about to show itself. Not just from her books, this was to be expected, but also from certain unregarded and normally inaccessible places within herself. Glimpses into abysses, yes, into heights beyond belief, these were the metaphors she was accustomed to. But now that she was aware of these other places, inside, she'd begun to imagine that if any sort of harmony or unison between metaphors and "inside" were to show itself—

The earliest sign of anything special, she had thought, might be a kind of calm.

Something that might then slowly, over years, inhabit her. And grow beyond calm.

This had not happened, but the reason was not that the books she had had longest and trusted most had fallen short. Those books had lifted and stirred better minds than hers for hundreds of years, it was not for her to say there was any failure in them. Jakob Boehme, for instance, whom she had long ago confessed to herself she loved, such modesty and joy was in him. Those two things together, modesty and joy—what could bring more of a sense of rightness? And Teresa, chosen and loved before all others until a few days ago. And the Englishman called Law, meaning *Gesetz*. Unusual for a name, even in England, surely. Three hundred years ago he had written *A Serious Call to a Devout and Holy Life*. A "serious call." How strong and right that was.

If these had been all, if nothing else had happened . . . but it was too hard to picture that, now.

For a moment, minutes from her journey's end, Basel's river rose up in her mind again, and she felt she was walking beside it as she had walked beside it every single afternoon, those late grey afternoons, windy and grey almost every one of them. How temporary and provisional she had felt while walking there. Due, she had told herself, to the Rhine's massive, patient current moving beside her, seemingly keeping time with her. Due also to her realization that this same great flow had moved beside and kept pace with so many, many generations before her.

River and words together. A huge presence and a prosaic, she was sure, thought.

That was how it had been, the walks and the Rhine and the anticipation of the calm that might be waiting, until out from this *Kreis,* this serene circle of familiar voices, the new companion had fallen upon her. Exact metaphor—she *had* been "fallen upon," a falcon out of the innocent sky. Though hardly a "companion" at first. Hardly a "companion" even now.

(In spite of the strange thing she had discovered, the discovery about their ages. That she, thirty-four years old, should be the exact age of Simone at her death. A sign of some sort, she had at first thought. Of closeness. Or of no such thing, she had then thought. Vanity to think so.)

But that this falcon-mind should have given her the most truth-laden and, because of its truths, the most disturbing of all the many pages of print she had taken into her eyes between birth and now—? To be fallen upon, out of the sky, so finally? Was it safe to say this? Could anything connected with this overwhelming book be regarded as "safe"? Was there any such thing as safety in any of these burning pages, the more overwhelming and burning because they were so few?

Warten auf Gott. She had bought, almost at the last minute, the Munich bookshop's last copy. Left behind on that shelf had been *En Attendant Dieu* and *Waiting for God*. Like mantras, now, these word-triads. Not Simone's choosing—others had chosen the title, she now knew, chosen it after Simone's death. After the falcon had flown away. But she wouldn't have objected. It was a falcon-title, surely.

No, Simone had had more urgent concerns. *"I have made a practice of saying Our Father once each morning with absolute attention. If during the recitation my attention wanders in the minutest degree, I begin again until I have succeeded in going through it with absolutely pure attention. The effect of this practice is extraordinary and surprises me every time, for, although I experience it each day, it exceeds my expectation at each repetition. At times the very first words, in their purity, tear my thoughts from my body . . ."*

Of course he had been right about words like these. There was truly nothing "reasonable" about them. And nothing in them that she would ever be able to explain, let alone justify, when she met him. That meeting that was now only minutes away. How easy, easy and awful, to picture herself trying to recapture for him what it was about these words that had so gripped her! She saw herself leafing Simone's pages from one underlined passage to the next, losing her place certainly, apologizing for reading aloud a sentence which she would probably judge, while reading it, to be just as thin and naive and sentimental as he would surely be explaining it to be—she, meantime, wondering what it was that had moved her so overpoweringly about pages which now, now that he was here, seemed so transparently . . . well, what?

Immature, probably.

Not unoriginal, however. No matter what anyone said.

Simone's voice came close again, even through the clacking of the train's wheels. *"For other people, in a sense I do not exist. I am the colour of dead leaves. But perhaps God likes to use castaway objects . . ."*

The busy mindless wheels of the train rose clacking, clacking, clacking up again from wherever they had receded to. Why did she shake her head? If he were here, he would ask her why she had shaken her head, and she would have to think of a reason.

Submitted, in part,
to workshop of February 3.
(Only the first part was read)
s.f.

Sherin has left the practice. Such an *aardige vent!** I'll miss him. He's not leaving as a direct result of the threatened Salvioni suit, which was an obvious non-starter, but indirectly, yes, there's a connection. He's just had enough. He's had enough, he told me, of colleagues he's had enough of. He had behaved with a decent professionalism in the Salvioni matter and no fingers had been pointed, but there'd been no support either, notably none from the clinic's longest-serving partners. Those three good friends had lost no time in putting a note on the staff board to the effect that they—speaking, they hoped, for us all—"choose not to stand in the way of our colleague's expressed desire to accept an appointment elsewhere."

Nice one.

* what a good guy (This is how I felt about him at the time . . .)

This leaves me as the clinic's only heart man.

They don't understand.

I'm the one walking out of the field, not into it.

Here's my plan. I will invite Rollo, or Walter, whichever of those names is current, to meet me somewhere. Not at the clinic, not at home, somewhere else. The pretext TBA. To be announced. Meaning that so far I haven't a clue what I'll say.

No, that's not true. I'll say I wish to consult him as follows. The workshop wants, I will say—*requires*—feedback from members' spouses/partners, viz., how do such persons feel about the potentially intrusive role of art, of the practice of fiction writing, on a relationship?

Threatened? Enlivened? Other? And since we want a broad spectrum of answers, and since he is the only spouse/partner with an advanced degree—

On the basis of our earlier phone conversation, I had him down as nuance-insensitive. If that was right, I could probably get away with this. What "this" was wasn't as obvious.

Perhaps, I thought, I wanted him to convince me that he was what I increasingly believed him to be.

And this was, as far as "guilt" goes—doubt-obliterating, nailed-down, beyond-argument guilt—well, I hadn't got quite that far yet. Not quite or not yet. One of those two.

But I was in no doubt where innocence was in all this. Innocence was far off. Innocence had stopped talking altogether, it had lost interest, it had turned its back a long while ago.

So I phoned. And what answered was a voice so calm, so grave, so . . . noble . . . that I found speech difficult. How could any other voice, mine or anybody's, be permitted to intrude here? Who could even want to infect with his own uneven verbal swoops and lunges a telephone line which this lambent voice was even now cleansing of all impurity?

Rhetorical question, ignore it.

In fact I did not speak. Not because of the impurities with which I'd have flooded the line, just that I couldn't. It was not merely that my hearing was filling up with this voice, it was that the entire rounded inner surface of my skull had gone ultra vires, ultra anything it had shown any talent for until this minute, ultramontane—why not, over the mountains—and was now, *right now*, memorizing this voice, printing it, hand-lettering it, in fact, and planting its small lucent letter-pennons wherever a clear space offered itself in there.

Up there.

Perfectly natural consequence of what I was hearing, this seemed. I wanted this voice and its posted afterimages to direct my motions for a good while. Whatever sort of tenure it had in mind would be fine.

Then I asked what I'd intended to ask and Sophie said her husband would be in soon. She probably waited a bit. As I did. One of us then hung up. Perhaps it was she.

Oh. In case you're worrying, nothing here involves the smallest readjustment of my regard for Marianne. By this time I was so committed to Marianne that—well, "love" is a word which for the rest of my life I would rather look at only through an electrified fence, so I'll take a pass on that one. But every day that I saw Marianne, and I was seeing her most days now, I was more conscious of my prodigious, my very good, luck. I was still finding it hard to count on it, to feel confident that it would still be there in the morning. But I was improving in this regard. And Marianne was helping me to improve. She was doing this by often being there in the morning.

Enough slobbering.

No, Sophie was a dream. Insofar as I could plumb my own secret and intricate designs, I had no plans for glimpsing myself inside the dream. I wanted it to go on, however, to continue to be itself, a dream. I didn't want it to veer into that other thing.

Yes, of course I mean *that* other thing.

My turn to read. I brought two MSS with me. One was what I would read if Sophie, for whatever reason, didn't show. The other, a shorter piece, if she did.

She did.

But I was not the first reader. A retired school principal who signed his work "Mac" *tout court* started us off with the first canto of an epic poem he'd been working on ever since his retirement, a poem based on the battle of the Long Sault. This was a skirmish which all Canadian schoolchildren, "in simpler times," he said meaningfully, staring here and there as he said it, grew up hearing about. I'm not sure if he had Wewak or Sophie or me or all three of us in mind when he mentioned those "simpler times," but he might have. If he did, though, he did, and if his engagement with what he saw as a lost golden world had led him to notice how few people in that golden world had owned up to names like Wewak, Führ and Bloom, so be it. "The Battle of the Long Sault," which was the title of his poem, was about a lot of Iroquois versus not very many French, the latter defending the entire colony. Wewak and Sophie and I were anxious to be told the result. Details would come in due course, Mac said. Relenting, he then told us that Dollard and the rest of the French were very brave and won the battle but were all killed. This seemed to us sad. The others seemed indifferent, however. Mac was right, they had always known about it.

There was one PS, a query from Wewak. It was, "Scalps?"

The ex–school principal shrugged.

Wewak's face revealed nothing.

Then it was my turn. I had not brought a story or a poem, I said, but something else, a substitute: a précis of the story or novel which I would someday write. "Here's the plot. There's a young woman, a musician, I think she'll be a singer, maybe a soprano. No, contralto. Right. She has a good contralto voice. She's full of hope and promise. But she has attracted the attention of an older man, more experienced, and the young woman—I'm not sure of her name yet, if anybody has an idea . . . tell me later. Anyhow, she, whatever her name is, decides, against her friends' advice, to marry this man. She does so, he takes her to another country where she finds her life more and more circumscribed. She devotes herself to, let's say, domestic tasks, she's no longer keeping up her voice classes, there may even be a question regarding some form of maltreatment . . . and basically that's it."

I put my single-page non-story face down beside me on the table.

Giorgio said, "And—?"

"And what?"

"So how does your story end, Nik?"

"Like that."

"You're shitting us, Nik."

Larry said, "Keep it clean, big guy."

"Nik . . . come on. What are you saying? She stays home all day, vacuums, all that shit, sorry, Larry—"

"Well . . ." I said. "Anybody else?"

Wewak came through. "Bad end," he said.

"I know," I said. "She could have been a contralto."

A man called Dirksen, sensible bearded fellow, said, "I wish she'd just stood up and got the hell out of there. Personally. Just my personal opinion, OK? Into the car, gun the engine, *hasta la vista*, asshole."

Ragged applause followed Dirksen's contribution.

I said, "Maybe she'll do that. Why not. Nothing easier than for me to . . ."

My words died away because the whole room had started to shake. For me, if not for anybody else. Which was strange, because the voice that was now speaking was quiet. "It may be difficult for her. To go." Silence. "It may not be a physical difficulty. She could leave if she chose to." Still nobody spoke. "She has a belief. She believes that there are circumstances which, although they may not appear happy, are a part of the deeper life. They are a part of the deep flow of life. It would be a mistake, she thinks, to leave these circumstances. Even if they are not what she once expected. She must stay where she is. In the end, this will show itself to have been right."

This time the silence hung on, it endured. It would have continued until the go-home buzzer sounded if it were not for, first, Giorgio and, second, Larry.

"Yeah, eh? I get it. I think I get it, Sophie. You accept life's burdens and learn from them, right? It's like, you know, karma. In India, they—Dr. Kilachand puts it like this—"

"Fuck Dr. Kilachand in six elaborate ways. Sophie, if I may so address you—you know what? That's balls. Entire balls. Somebody's been messing with your common sense. You know?"

There was a surprise here. The language was crude, but the voice was gentle. *Larry's* voice?

"It's all right," she said, "Mr. Logan."

Larry was looking at her.

"It's all right," Sophie said again. She extended her left hand, which was closer to Larry's end of the table, towards him. Only an inch or two, and it was at once lowered to the table's surface again. It had had an idea which had been countermanded.

I was staring at Larry. We all stared at both of them. This went on for three or four seconds. Then Sophie began wrapping a long knitted scarf around her neck. She did it slowly but as if she had often done it this way. Nobody else moved for a bit and then they all started pushing back chairs and standing up and putting their coats and scarves on.

Then everybody went home.

Dec. 5. St. Nicolaas Day. Back in Holland not only is it an exciting day if you happen to be a child (gifts if you've been good, but *Zwarte Piet*, Black Peter, scarily at the door if you've misbehaved), but doubly so for anybody whose name day it is. So, yes, even after all these years away, Cambridge and now here, I always notice the date. And I think of the people, four, to be exact, two doctors, one nurse, one orderly, with whom if I were still in Amsterdam I'd certainly be in a bar that was very well known to me, and I almost as well known in it, after we'd all left work. Centuries-old wooden beams in that bar, black with still-permitted smoke. I'd be being toasted, often. And I'd be buying drinks, and none of us would be in any hurry. And then a taxi home, little nap, and a very late dinner with Saskia in an Indonesian place with a marvellous *rijsttafel* near the Nieuw Markt.

Well, no, not dinner with Saskia. Not now, not if I were in Amsterdam now. Not with Saskia, there or anywhere.

Saskia was nowhere. Fragments of her lovely body were still making their slow way through the processes of dissolution under the new grass of a quite pretty cemetery in Breda, which is where her mother had decreed the body should go. I shouldn't say "decreed." It wasn't that woman's call, it was mine. But since she'd wanted it that way, fine. It must have been the only thing I ever did that pleased her. And I lost nothing by it. I knew I'd not need an incised piece of marble planted at some, any, unvarying place on the planet to induce Saskia-thoughts.

But here in T.O. on my name day I was feeling sorry for several things.

Among which, myself.

It helped, though, that Marianne finally did what I'd guessed some time ago she was half wanting, half not-at-all-wanting to do. That she now had gone ahead with it was a good sign. What this was, it was bringing her two ex-children to the house for a meal. "Ex" because

Clarissa was sixteen and Martin fourteen and both insisted on the "ex." Still hers, they acknowledged, but no longer children.

She and I did the meal together. Each with a circumscribed skill or two: a risotto, a plenteous salad, a "Farmer's" apple and cinammon pie served warm with Decadent vanilla ice cream. Not bad, the ex-children said. Cool house, Martin said. Where's the computer, he said. They both went upstairs.

Marianne stretched her arms out wide and gave me a smile that wasn't quite up to the smiles I was used to from her. Hard to say, at first, why not. Then, *lieve Heer,* I thought—can this be? An uncertain smile, an insecure smile? From *this* lady? Because of—yes, has to be, because of Clarissa and Martin. Because they're here. Because she isn't sure how a certain person might be feeling about them.

I was stricken.

To have reached the status of someone who could make this woman uncertain of anything at all . . . No, I didn't want that status. Keep it off.

"Oh, Marianne," I said, "I do love you."

I know, I know. It's only minutes since I mentioned having a different attitude to that word. Electrified fence, and all.

Can't be helped, though. It's in the culture, the damn word.

Marianne got up from her chair and stood there. Her arms were now not stretched out but looked willing to be so. I was there quite soon. It took only a very short while, but it seemed longer, for that tense body to begin reassembling itself into the clever places-of-contact I was so devoted to.

Jonge, jonge.* How we both wished, here's the thing, that the ex-kids weren't in the house. But they were. When they came down, which was after a while, Clarissa said, "I agree with Martin, you know. It's a cool house." Then she said, "Almost as nice as Daddy's."

Fine.

I did, though, see Walter Maggione, Rollo Maggione, one of the two, not long after. I had had an unsatisfactory session that day with a patient who was an obvious candidate for a cardioversion; he'd been in atrial fibrillation several times before, and his arrhythmia had now recurred. This fellow, an otherwise fit seventy-year-old lapsed Christian Scientist, had retained the distrust of medical procedures which his erstwhile faith had indoctrinated him with, and was now insisting on "hanging in," as he said, with the medication I'd had him on for almost two years.

"You can always slit me up if things turn really sour, Doc," he said placatingly. No slitting at all, I'd already explained, the cardioversion is two electronic bumps with a few seconds' drowse in between, period, but he relished the image. So I agreed he could stay with the medication, called Tambocor, for a month and we'd see if his heart would flop back into sinus rhythm that way. Allowing a patient this sort of prescriptive self-diagnosis was the sort of thing I'd once have had no patience with, so why, I asked myself, as the old boy went off with a chuckle and a still-giddy heart, this change? Bad stuff, Bloom. I was not impressed.

* Boy oh boy.

Nobody in the waiting room and no remaining appointments in the book, so I took the Yonge line north, speed-walked east to Mount Pleasant and home, and went in to change. A run in the ravine might restore a bit of *amour-propre*. Well, no, it was unlikely to do that, but it might blow a fresher wind through me in a way that would allow me to glimpse again, for a minute or two, my less-damaged younger self. I'd inhabited that better self once, of course I had, but how far off it seemed now, and how little use I had made of it! "The waste even in a fortunate life cannot but be felt deeply." I did a circle-walk in my kitchen trying to think who had written that. Nothing came. Then I was outside, a place I really had no business being, not even if I'd been appropriately dressed, which I was not. It was minus ten degrees and a wind chill of a thousand, I was crazy to be here, all by myself in my seldom-admired baggy grey cotton running outfit. Same old ravine, leaves now buried under December's horizon-to-horizon white carpet. It felt like minus twenty. Not a person in sight, everybody had sussed out the day and stayed indoors. This lasted until I was running under the viaduct, where a young man, perhaps twenty-two years old, dressed head to foot in Ralph Lauren, that epicene smirker, came round a pillar and almost ran me down. I stumbled but recovered unnaturally quickly, as middle-aged men in the presence of younger men make a point of doing.

"Holy——!" he said, dodging sideways but then stopping. "You OK?"

"Sure. Fine."

"Sure?"

"I'm perfect."

"Weather like this, you know, a person should run with a partner. Like swimming in the ocean. Like walking into the forest. I mean it. Any darn thing could happen, and who's going to know? Eh? Eh?"

He was right, I said. No question. Although I hadn't noticed *his* partner. But, ah well, better be off home, I said.

"I'd like to make sure that you—you know—get there."

That dumb remark about being on my way home combined with his insistence on seeing me to my door meant I now had to turn right around and head back where I'd just come from. If, to save face, I'd kept going south, maintaining the fiction that south meant home, we'd have had to run for God knew how far, me looking desperately about for some house that had a deep enough porch that I could disappear into it and there, without my inability to get the door open being observed, wait for my self-appointed guardian down below to bugger off.

This was why I got home long before I would have done had the Boy Scout and I not almost collided. And why I found an unknown man just walking away from my front door.

Briefest of descriptions, since we'll have other chances later. Middling height, wearing a belted overcoat. Solid impression generally. Sporting a sort of sea captain's cap. I hadn't seen one of those for a while, though I recalled it as a popular fashion in German-speaking Europe twenty years ago. The *Bundesrepublik's* chancellor Helmut Schmidt had shown up for some big occasion wearing one and millions had sold in minutes, you'd have thought he was Michael Schumacher.

The door the man had been walking away from was one at which, he now told me, he had been "vainly ringing." And he said, "Dr. Bloom?"

I nodded. I had an inkling.

"I am delighted to meet you."

He was the right size. Stocky, solid. "And you are——?"

"Dr. Maggione. Of course you do not recognize me, how should you? We have not met. We see each other for the first time. But we spoke on the telephone not long ago. Your telephone voice is memorable. You asked to speak to my wife, who was unavailable." Conspiratorial smile—"Perhaps she was writing. Off somewhere creatively writing."

OK, maybe he was right. Maybe she *was* off somewhere writing and maybe I *hadn't* ever seen him before. On the other hand—

"But you will have taken advantage of your Thursday evening class to speak to my wife, will you not."

It was not a question, but he was expecting a reply. Following a private trail, I said, "I don't see a car, Dr. Maggione. How did you come?"

"I drive into town as seldom as possible. I take the *S-Bahn*. The subway. When one calculates the cost of parking, the petty annoyances of the traffic, the ignorant behaviour of one's fellow motorists—"

It was odd, but he was, even while speaking, unmistakably edging towards my front door. He seemed to have decided we should continue this conversation indoors. It was a natural choice in the startling cold, but it wasn't going to happen. In my frequently careless dealings with myself, unbuttoned self with buttoned-up self, I have only a few absolutes, but one of them is that I must not invite into any home of mine someone I would prefer to punch in the mouth. Or even *might*, pending further investigation, prefer to punch in the mouth. I have not punched anyone in the mouth ever, so far as I can remember, so really, the reference's inane. But it's a long story. Even in my youngest years in Amsterdam, when I was en route from my parents' narrow house on the Leidsegracht to the boys' school at the corner of the next *gracht*, even when I had to encounter every morning for one entire school year my own very special selected-by-the-Furies moronic bully— even then I did not punch anyone in the mouth. Although I would have loved to. All that held me back was a vivid awareness of the thumping I would get in return. Claes Duikhuis, come back, almost a half-century later come back and let me punch you in the mouth. I am all grown up and will certainly feel differently about you now than I did then. Back then you were two years older and bigger and stronger, but those same two extra years must mean that you are now senile and shrunken and doddery. If you are any two of those things, Claes Duikhuis, come back. Step suddenly, one more time, from behind a parked truck at the corner of Leidsegracht and Kerkstraede, with that imbecilic grin on your face and your fist raised—

"I'm sorry. I can't invite you in. If you could tell me what it is that brings you out into such a freezing day—"

"But of course, Dr. Bloom. When we spoke that day— I hardly know, but I am bound to think you charmed me. Put a charm on me. *Sie haben mich bezaubert.* You understand, I am sure, German?"

"Only when it resembles Dutch."

"Ah. Nevertheless, we Europeans understand each other. I guessed from your accent, that day, you were German of the south. Or even Swiss, as I am. But my wife said no, he is Dutch. I was not sure this was correct. My wife, well instructed in many respects as she is, is not always correct in such things."

I said nothing.

"Though I love her dearly."

"You have not told me why you are here."

"You are not one for the little talk, Dr. Bloom. For the small talk. That is good, that is correct. This is a long story. It is a medical matter, you must be patient. You are sure we could not——?" He took a step towards my front door again.

I had the sort of moment in which unreality, in a blinding image-flash, obliterates and replaces the prosaic scene before you. I had experienced such a thing only once or twice before, most memorably as a youth in a coffee house in Amsterdam ten minutes after someone had offered me, and I had begun puffing at, a *hasjies*, joint. Unknown to me, the joint must have been saturated in one of the hallucinogenic substances so readily available in those years (and still, by the way, not hard to find in that *Geboorteplaats* of mine). The phantas-magoric scene that I so graphically saw then I still, to my very great regret, remember, but will not now describe. I say this in the hope that if I can stave off any specific picturing of that scene for another few years, it may fade from my memory entirely. But what I seemed to be looking at now was almost as bad. Walter Rollo Maggione was lying on the floor in a room I'd never seen before (though I later guessed it could have imprinted itself on my breeched young mind all those years ago in that *hasjies*-infected Amsterdam coffee-house) with the back of his skull missing, and inside the hole which that rounded bone-piece had been protecting was a wounded but still pulsing grey spongey mouse-like creature. I couldn't turn away from it fast enough to avoid hearing the small dam-aged noises it was making. I think I staggered back against the porch railing. When reality returned I was slumped against the railing and Maggione, his eyes temporarily at the same level as mine, was staring at me and looking either puzzled or shocked, I'd no time to decide which.

"Herr Doktor! Tell me what is—are you unwell?"

I was still stunned by what was only now beginning to fade and knew I had to end this. "I'm sorry," I said, "I cannot . . ." I stumbled into the house. When I'd shut the door behind me I leaned against it for a few seconds and then went into the kitchen. There was some room-temperature coffee in the carafe and I half-filled a mug and drank it all and stood there considering myself. I was going to be OK. I rinsed out the mug and stayed in the kitchen for a minute or so just checking on things, their palpability, and then went into the livingroom and over to one of the front windows. My visitor hadn't gone. He was still on the porch, but seated now, in a white plastic chair, one I'd kept forgetting to bring in. Odd sight, with the snow all round. A little snow was falling now. Very still it all looked, and the man in the chair motionless, it could have been a painting, it could have been an Alex Colville, back a couple of centuries it could have been by Caspar David Friedrich and had a title like *I Have Turned Away from Worldly Striving*. Which shows how misleading art can be. A few seconds more and Maggione got up and walked slowly down the porch steps. Preceding, in the new snow, his footprints. Well, of course.

Watching him track off into the falling snow, picking up the pace as he went, I remembered what the question I'd meant to ask him was. What colour of car did he drive, it would have been.

———

She missed the workshop again. How to describe my feelings when, ten minutes into the hour, it was obvious she was not merely late but wasn't coming? I knew very well that the set of emotions starting their slow crackle inside—dread, uncertainty, anger—could all fit under the "obsessive" label. I knew, also, that absenteeism didn't prove there was a victim anywhere near. And finally, it was faintly possible, and I knew this too, that the real villain—because there *was* one of those, not *all* of this was my imagination—might even now be having a really good time quietly hurting somebody I had glimpsed only once and would never be able to help. In which case the man now in my sights deserved better thoughts. But I remembered a Diagnostics course in my student days and what the lecturer had told us. The lecture had been about probabilities. Med students the world over, no matter what language their studies are conducted in, listen to a lecture like that one—they learn that when diagnosing a patient's case you must, you absolutely *must*, at least initially, go for the probable, the usual, not the improbable or the unusual. The likely is far likelier to be right than the unlikely, they are told. The invariable example being, "If you hear hooves, think horses, not zebras."

Which is what I was now doing with that bad scene in the park. And thinking about that scene, and looking out from my thoughts, I couldn't see a zebra for miles. For entire Serengetis.

After class Larry and I walked off together and up Yonge Street all the way to Bloor, where the icy air defeated us and we headed down into the subway. I didn't mention my private seething to Larry and he seemed indifferent to both it and its source. He did, though, have something on his mind. En route up Yonge he hadn't said a word, we were both too busy trying to breathe into our scarves and then rebreathe that saved breath, but I'd noticed the covert glances from the side. In the subway he was still taciturn.

Walking east from Mount Pleasant along our short street, we always came to my house before his. I asked if he would take a schnapps.

"Yes," he said.

Yes?

In he came and out the schnapps came. And down it went. Down both of them went.

We had another.

During one of these, holding one of my stubby Steuben liqueur glasses between thumb and forefinger, rotating it almost imperceptibly and contemplating these rotations in the indolent manner of, who knows who he was being in that moment, not Zbigniew Cybulski now but some staggeringly urbane contributor to *The Yellow Book*, Larry evidently concluded that the time was right.

"So, Nikki. What's it like, then?"

"What's what like?"

"It. My kids gave me the big news. It, man. Nooky with Nikki. With her, booby. With who else? Fuck's sake, Nik. Annie. My wife."

Hardly necessary to say that I'd thought about this before, but never, I admit, urgently. They were, after all, separated. Divorce loomed. Larry had been in Antigua with Terry and probably in one or two other islands, metaphorical or otherwise, since he and Marianne separated. Conceivably before that.

"I'm fond of her, Larry. Maybe more fond than I've ever been. Since I grew up, you know? Since I reached man's estate."

This seemed to slow things down. He looked at me, I supposed he was checking options. Rage, irony, some pencilled-in third thing.

"Since you grew up."

"Uh-huh."

"Well," he said, saying it without a lot of energy, "you're grown up, all right." And as an afterthought, "So's she."

Forty-year-old big-mouthed broad.

I said, "We're about done here, I think." But I poured him another schnapps, which he took and downed. He then placed my stubby glass on a table by the door and started out. On the porch, I hadn't shut the door on him yet, he paused, wheeled about and came back. He stood close, looked me somewhere near the eye, shrugged, and turned and walked down my four steps. A little one-hand wave without looking back.

Not bad, Larry. That wave.

Way better than *The Yellow Book*. A dead heat, if I'm umpiring here, with Zbigniew Cybulski.

I guessed Maggione would be back. The hallucinatory minute had scared him off once, but it wouldn't last. I told our receptionist that if the Swiss doctor called, she should put him off, tell him anything, just keep him out of my appointment book. Keep him far hence, was the point. "Shall I suggest he see Dr. Kyte?" Mrs. Peterkin asked. "Dr. Kyte's schedule for both this week and next is quite, quite open, I see." But I didn't want that either. Even though Mrs. P.'s twice-given "quite" made her sympathies obvious, and even though in the usual run of things I was entirely willing to help out a new colleague who was short of patients, apparently I was not willing to do it in this case.

Why not?

I was mostly in the dark on that, although there were a couple of moving smallish lights out on the dark's periphery, like people who were lost but hadn't quite given up. They were maybe talking it over, gesturing, their flashlights moving up and down as they talked.

Christmas. Marianne spent the morning with Clarissa and Martin and had a "comprehensive," she said, mid-afternoon dinner with both those at her mother's place. After Larry showed up to claim his children for the rest of the day, she came to me. This sequence of events meant I didn't have to cook.

Sometimes everybody wins.

What did I do during all that time? I got up late and put a treacle pudding in the microwave and ate half of it.

So when Marianne arrived, we opened our gifts to each other. Hers to me was a Waterman pen in a sky-blue box marked "Paris" with a nib that actually flowed and moved balletically wherever I directed it. Such a triumph of engineering had never before come into my writing hand. "Tool for the trade," Marianne said. She knew what I was up to. From me Marianne got things to wear that nobody but the two of us, my intention was, would ever see. This was transparently, if I can put it so, a *lumpen* choice, but it's a side of Bloom that surfaces now and then and can't be remedied. Luckily Marianne claimed to be "entranced." I had saved up several bottles of a South Australian Shiraz,

St. Hallett's (1999), my that-season's good guess; I don't see the point of either high- or low-enders when it comes to wine, and we worked on these and listened to, by great luck, an FM station sending into the night Kodály's *Háry János Suite*, the intermezzo of which I hope will be soaring into its own pure heights even as I climb into my final heavenly berth. Otherwise it was entirely up to me, it being my house, which meant a CD of famously maudlin Dutch songs of enduring love, the titles of which it's only sensible to spare you (if I say that roses and little houses are prominently featured, you will know all you need to know), followed by Vera Lynn still promising better days and Barbara Cook doing "Sing a Song with Me" and other tripey violin-swamped things which are to my taste. I had tested my Waterman fountain pen as soon as I'd opened the sky-blue box. Partway through the evening Marianne tested her gifts too. Some while after that I began thinking about my wordless front-porch encounter with Larry a week earlier. This led me to want to know how his wife felt he was dealing with things.

"Things?"

"Us. You and me."

"I don't know that he's dealing with it at all. Darling Nik, do we care?"

"Just wondering how he is. How you think he is."

"He's being himself. Capering adolescently one minute, nostalgic and sentimental the next. When the black dog barks, he's caustic and offensive, as you know. Since you mention us, the other day he asked me . . . never mind. He's treading water, is the gist of it. Not writing much. But that's how he's always been, these great looping mood swings. He'll be OK. That's a shallow summing-up, I suppose."

"What did you say he asked you the other day?"

"Didn't say nothin', *mijn lieve.*"*

"You were about to say."

"Decided against. Sorry."

"Oh-oh." Moment of deliberation. "There's a word for what I'm feeling now, and, um . . . you know what that word is. I mean, I don't as a rule worry over things that might or might not have been said about me, but—"

"Nik. Darling. *Liefste.*† Can we skip it? It was a dumb remark of Larry's and a dumber mentioning on my part."

We skipped it. Not hard to guess what it had been. I'm twenty years older, almost, than either Larry or Marianne. A guess wasn't out of reach.

But skipping it was fine too.

That night was the longest uninterrupted time we had had together. We talked off and on for six hours, contents indistinct in memory now. But I do know that at one point Marianne, addressing my left nipple from half an inch away, don't ask me why anyone would voluntarily do that, said that any time I felt up for it, she would be very willing to hear more than she had heard so far about my "late," as they absurdly say, wife. (Marianne didn't say "as they absurdly say," that's me.)

I said she should ask whatever she wanted to ask. Marianne said, well, on second thought maybe she would save that for some other time. When it wasn't Christmas. When we were at least a little unhappy together. Which we were not now, she said.

It might come more naturally then, she said.

* my love
† lovedest; most loved

Saskia drifted away from us. I'd like to think that's how she would have preferred it.

O'Blomski at an ice hockey game with three-quarters of the Logan family?

Boggles the mind.

Nevertheless, yes.

Brief explanation:

I have spent hundreds, I hope not thousands, of hours watching Ajax football from the stands in Amsterdam or on the telly from somewhere else in Holland or the U. K. For ten years I was an obsessed admirer of the world's first and greatest *libero*, Johan Cruijff. I admired him even after he abandoned Ajax and danced his static dances—those dances that led inevitably (just as the defender was deciding he could permit himself to glance over at the rest of the field for one split second) to one of his miraculous ball-nursings towards goal—in front of hundreds of thousands of Spaniards instead of us, his adoring nation. When I watched his retirement ceremony and saw him leave the field, glistening-eyed as I myself was in front of my set, I watched one-tenth of my life leaving me forever. If one-tenth does not seem much, I want to say that I am calculating the amount soberly. It's a serious fraction.

I mention that by way of anticipating, when I now confess to caring not much at all about ice hockey (I know, I know—"hockey," no modifiers), the odd raspberry from the cheap seats at the Air Canada Centre. From the purples. I will understand that raspberry if it comes. People hereabouts feel about the Leafs as I still feel for Ajax, so, fine by me. But I can't be moved by what I don't know, and I miss what I do know, is all. In hockey you never see a developing eight- or nine-pass pattern at midfield leading to a perfectly flighted ball dropping into the goalmouth and then, sometimes, a blur as it's headed past the keeper. Hockey's too fast and the ball's too small. I *know* it's not a ball. Since nobody can get tickets for a game here in Toronto anyway, I feel that my attitude is only sensible. On Leaf nights I stay home with a book or lie in bed staring at the ceiling and reviewing, with outward sang-froid, the more plangent episodes of my life. While everybody else is at the game or at home, glued.

To repeat. Fine by me.

I needed to say all that because here I was going to a game with Larry Logan and his son Martin and his daughter Clarissa when I could have had an entirely guilt-free Saturday night with Larry Logan's wife, Marianne, her place or mine. Marianne, who had seen almost too much of her children the last while, had neglected to tell me she'd be totally free for all of this weekend. And Larry had made sure I would not find out from anyone else—not until after I had accepted his invitation to sit in one of the four purples he'd got from an ex-student. Point here is not that Larry was seriously begrudging either his wife or me anything. In fact, Marianne and I had separately come to the conclusion that the very fact that "we" so blatantly existed made life easier for Larry in a dozen ways, not least in his children's eyes. Innocence regained, up to a point. The parallel failings of others which make one neo-blameless. So the only goat, and the only one who was in a really, really bad humour as the evening began, was me. Was I. It was up to me to disguise that state of mind. "For the children's sake, Nik," Larry had solemnly intoned.

Wat een hufter. *He was enjoying this a lot.

The seating sequence went me, then Martin, then Larry, then Clarissa. Lots of electronic music. Lots, also, of electronic cheering from long-dead crowds, their recorded cries now touchingly louder than ever. The two North American anthems were sung by someone standing on a carpet unrolled for her benefit on the ice surface. Then we all sat down again and the puck was dropped.

Sudden arrivals at and departures from either end of the rink. The skaters would cluster and jostle and then some of them, often the latest to arrive, would, clearly disappointed, skate backwards again. This went on for half an hour. At about that time Martin dug an elbow into my ribs and screamed at some length. A red light had just gone on. "How about that, Marty!" Larry shouted, and punched him on the arm. Martin was delighted. One-nothing for us, he told me. There was no need, I knew that.

On the other side of Larry, Clarissa was much more dignified, which I think was why Martin said, during an intermission, "Don't bring her again, eh Dad?" I'd no wish to be brought again either, nevertheless I try to pre-empt offensive remarks being said about me in any context, so in the second section of the game I thought I would chip in with the shouting. "Go Leafs!" I cried. There happened to be a silence just then, so I was worried I'd broken some generally understood taboo. But although Larry and Martin and, from beyond Larry, Clarissa too turned their heads to look, nothing came of it.

On our way home, driving north on Bay, I saw a familiar figure hastening in the same direction. The sidewalk

* What a smartass.

was crowded with people showing lots of blue and white but I still might not have picked him out had not his hurried gait (together with what looked to be, just as we drove by, a sudden spurt to get past a couple who were strolling too slowly for him) been so out of sync with the general rhythm. But the general rhythm may have been something Sophie Führ's husband never gave much thought to.

Funny how an image will work towards its own clarification in your mind just by hanging around. Proximity's often underrated. An hour after getting home that night I knew what that glimpse on Bay Street reminded me of. It reminded me of a word that had come to mind when I saw Maggione sitting in the white plastic chair on my snowy porch. *Sitzriese.* It's an untranslatable German noun describing a medium-sized man who, when he's sitting down, looks a giant. "Seated giant" is close, but that's two words instead of one. Big upper body, largish head is what's requisite.

Sitzriese. I've always found the word impressive. Not heartwarming, necessarily, but it makes a point.

The advantage of a language that crams images together like that.

Marianne was gingerly sipping a too-hot coffee before leaving for the office when I handed her my copies of Sophie Führ's two workshop submissions. Not good timing on my part, but I wanted a learned opinion. After a quick browse Marianne said that a quick browse wasn't on, could she have a longer look later on? So that night in Grano's, back into the coffee after dinner, I watched her bring her scholarly, deciphering-incunabula face to that story of a Swiss couple en route to a day at the lake, plus that fragment of another and longer story—the woman on a train from Basel to Munich, thinking. And what, between caffeine hits, the Professor of Psychoanalytic Psychotherapy said was this. First, that whatever she might say right now, she would later, if needs must, deny on oath having said, "Since all I've been given so far is hearsay plus an exercise in creative writing, right?" It was a fact, however, she said, that although she had spent many, many hours of her working life contemplating letters or journals or taped conversations or interviews which had emerged from the psyches of persons loping erratically about on the hills and in the dales of some quite startling interior journeys, this present business was, "Well, let me say . . . it holds its own. In a largish, really motley company, it stands up well.

"As long as it's understood that 'well' here is not a positive," Marianne said.

Take the account of that day trip to Lucerne, she said. "Ruminations of an insecure female narrator trying to please a man who himself is untainted by even a hint of self-doubt. It's a kind of black pastoral, isn't it. In the, you know, straight-up outdoorsy aspect of pastoral. But it's also unpleasant."

Syndromes like this were "easy to rant on about," my firm-voiced ranter said. Adding, "I obviously don't know nearly enough about this, though. See, I've never cohabited with anybody who I thought was an über-being. I'm entirely open to spending a lot of time with an *admirable* being, nothing against an *adorable* being, come to that. You take my drift. But the über-stuff . . . no, doesn't do it for me. Whereas this kid's—sorry, this woman's deference here, her en-route thoughts, the running like hell for a bus simply because the guy she's with has a big need to always be first . . ."

As for the other piece, the fragment that "kind of swims in holiness," Marianne said, "it's a story, yes? It's fiction. It's not autobiography?"

Story, I thought. Although, I added, adding this entirely needlessly, there was always this thin line. The one between fiction and undisguised self-revelation. "The writer'll know where specific details come from, but he won't be too sure about the, you know, background colours. The source of the attitudes. The underpainting."

"What I was thinking. Because this whole thing has the ring of—I think— Tell me, Nik, among the rustling words here, would you say there's some sense of knots to be untangled? Somebody with a secret? Among the words' little rustling sounds, a secret?

"The more I think about it"—we were standing up now and about to move off into the Yonge Street night— "the more I ask myself what you and Larry are doing about this woman."

The answer to this seemed to be, though it was late enough in the evening that I didn't need to say it, *Nothing.*

For years I've had trouble knowing how to feel about antonyms like "famous" and "unknown." For instance, my alter ego wrote in a letter that "the truly gifted are always in the shadows." Now that's the sort of statement that appeals to me. Uncounted times it has caused me to recoil from basking in some minor accomplishment of my own, which could be nothing more than, e.g., the excessive gratitude of a patient, or, for another instance, my tachycardia paper, read by twenty-seven people, shredded by twenty-five and improved and hence made obsolete by the remaining two. And it has, from another point of view, upped by a lot whatever contempt I might already have been feeling for one or another overpraised contemporary. This is how I feel even though nothing is clearer to me than that Chekhov's claim is one hundred percent wrong.

I mean, "truly gifted . . . in the shadows"? *Always?* Come on, St. Anton. Most of such people won't hang about in the shadows long. Even if they live like that other and certified saint, Francis, humbly and away from the limelight, they're still going to be noticed. As Francis was. The shadows can't wait to run, like rainwater, off such people, leaving them glossier than ever. Come on.

Which doesn't mean that those shadows do not, often, look very good to a thinking person. Since the people in the light continually disappoint—the closer you get to them, the more you notice their vanity and their offstage mediocrity—it's easy to find yourself looking into the shadows instead, in the expectation that a different order of being lurks there. An order of being that's *truly* original, but is spendthrift with its gifts and careless whether you'll ever notice them.

I know now that it was this sort of thing that the young woman called Sophie Führ, whom I really knew only through Larry's workshop, came to mean to me at that particular stage of that year. Aside from a few paragraphs which she had read aloud to us, I'd had practically no words from or with her. So there'd been nothing limiting, nothing disappointing, to associate with her. Only the awareness of this passion, this almost Passion, of hers, and of this odds-on unpleasant relationship she was in. And the pall, the hush over both these. While nothing really stopped.

I woke with a dream still sounding in my ears. A hunting horn was blowing in a forest, and as I listened, both in and on my way out of my dream, I knew that it signalled something very sad. The more I awoke, the farther off the horn sounded, but this only made it worse. I felt I ought to be there, I shouldn't be missing all this sadness.

Turned out it wasn't a hunting horn, it was my doorbell. And at the door, smiling as if he knew that this time there'd be no way I could keep him from entering, was Walter Rollo Maggione. He was right, I couldn't, in he came.

"What time is it?" I was not at my best, I was still a little worried about that hunting horn. What a forlorn calling that had been. Calling for me? I worry about it now, writing this down.

"Doctor, a thousand apologies. This is an inconvenient hour?"

Shaking my head—"Come in, come. Find a chair. I'll be down in a minute."

It took me more than a minute, though. I didn't exactly dawdle but I was trying, still half awake, to understand why I had allowed him to come in. The hunting horn, of course. Its faery sound had trivialized even this, even him. I then tried to formulate the several clipped sentences I would need to rid my house of him. Eventually, minus any ready-to-go sentences, I was back in my living room. He was admiring an acrylic on a side wall. It was a portrait of a fair-haired woman, thirty-nine years old at the time, in a dark glowing gown.

God, how beautiful.

"Someone known to you, *Herr Doktor*?"

"My wife."

"Ah. I did not know you were married. My wife did not say so."

"Why should she?" Watch it, Bloom. "There was no reason. My wife died years ago."

He seemed not to have taken offence. "Indeed, why should she. Except that she tells me so much about your— this group. And she is so attached to you."

"Herr Maggione—"

"Excuse me, Dr. Bloom. I too have my doctorate. From the University of Zürich. The studies I am pursuing here aim at a second such degree. Again, I regret that my wife has not mentioned this to you."

"Such a disappointing wife." Thinking that was one thing, but I hadn't meant to say it.

"*Wie bitte?*"*

"No. Never mind."

"Please. Disappointing, what is this you are saying?"

"Only that this is the second time in a minute she has disappointed you."

His stare became, though not instantly, a smile. "You are quite mistaken. My wife suits me in every particular. To a—a T." A more secure smile now. He liked that T.

"You say she is attached to me. I should tell you I hardly know her. I scarcely know her name, and since neither of us have used it here—"

* "I beg your pardon?"

"You are perceptive. Perhaps I should speak her name more frequently. It is Sophia. To the Greeks, wisdom. A small paradox there, perhaps." The smile had established itself, he had decided to keep it.

It had been, since long before Ms. Führ crossed my path, my favourite name in all the world. I had at some early stage awarded a face to it, to the unknown bearer of such a *clair de lune* name. It was a face I was resigned to never seeing, but which I could have picked out in any crowd. Black hair worn close to the head. The palest of skins. Very dark blue eyes. Heartbreakingly intelligent profile. Rosebud mouth. A Circassian face, I used to think. I who had never met a Circassian.

No idea why the rosebud's there. Unasked, the antique word just always appears.

And no, it didn't describe Ms. Führ. Dark hair worn close, obviously. Pale skin, yes. Blue eyes, unsure, always too far off. Circassian? I'll go on liking the word anyway.

But right now I shouldn't be thinking of her. I should think instead of a man I didn't want in my house.

"You are wondering why I am here, Dr. Bloom."

"My mind was straying."

"*Sehen sie**, I am normally in excellent health. During my year in Toronto I have had no occasion, until now, to consult a doctor. Indeed, I know no doctor in this city— except for you. And I am presumptuous in implying that I 'know' you, yes?" Now the smile was eroding. Noticeably regular and white teeth. Aside from the teeth: dark hair in tidy retreat from or off a broad forehead.

---

* You see

A generally fit-looking man of, you'd have guessed, forty-five. Wrong guess.

"Dr. Maggione, I can save us both time. I do not, cannot accept new patients. I have greatly reduced my practice. Until a few years ago I was not in general practice at all but was, and am still in terms of my professional qualifications, a cardiologist. I can, however, recommend to you a colleague, several possible names, and if you were to call the clinic today before five—"

"Dr. Bloom, Dr. Bloom—please, please. Allow me to explain."

"There is really nothing that you—"

"*Aber ja, ich muss*—pardon me, but I must, you see, the background, this is essential. Then you will understand."

He had, he told me, speaking rapidly—he must have noticed my unsubtle interrupting motions—been brought up in the neighbourhood of Lugano. "On the Swiss-Italian border, yes?" Italian father, Swiss-German mother. These two, *"schon lange tot,"** had owned a small hotel. They had been "without ambition," he said. And he said, "I was not."

As for his wife, "My Sophia," he said—a complicit smile accompanied the name—"is from a quite different culture. *Zürich hoch-intellektual, wissen Sie.†* Bookish. Although her father's pretensions to the professoriate were never fulfilled. At some stage he failed, who knows why. How he must have disappointed them, his family! The celebrated Führs. Curious. Is it not curious? He contented himself with the publishing of travel essays, likeable little collections, one must

* already dead a long time
† Zürich top-intellectual, you know.

say. Perhaps you have heard of these. No? Nor of him? Bernhard Führ? He and Sophia's mother were killed in an accident on the autobahn some years ago. On their way home from Genf. Geneva, I should say. Evidently he saw too late an exit sign. He was an old man, he should not have been driving. Between us, Doctor, it was a matter of some, I do not say scandal, but folly, yes, precisely, that his family permitted him to take the wheel of a car. But that is how they are, all of them. Permissive. Careless. Her brother—ah, well. Such tales I could tell you! Had I been a member of the family at the time, I should certainly have insisted—

"But too much of this. What I wished to say—"

"Dr. Maggione, I have something to say to you. This is a sacred hour for me. At half past ten I invariably run in the ravine."

This was loosely calculated. My invariable time was (a) not before eleven and (b) not invariable.

"A thousand apologies." He shrugged, he forgave himself. "Let me speak frankly. No, no, I shall be brief. I have several times lately awakened during the night with a sensation in my chest. How to describe this? I have never had trouble of this sort, the area of my heart, it is important that you understand this. This is why I wanted you to—to know my background, you see. In Lugano in 1968 I won an award. It was for fitness and strength, I was named *Uomo piu forte delle Regione di Garda e di Lugano*—the strongest man in the regions of Garda and Lugano. A grand title for a small matter, to be sure. Nonetheless—it cannot be the heart. Something else. Something is—was—irregular. A lurching."

I must have nodded, a great concession. It encouraged him. He leaned forward.

"You cannot decline my request, is this not so? You have forgotten this? When a physician is asked for assistance, he must, unless I am in error—you have this oath, it is named from Hippocrates—"

All at once I had overwhelmingly had enough. I had almost forgotten in what kind of drama we were acting. This man, he must be the one (I was hearing the drumming of hooves, and yes, these were horses, not zebras . . . although, what was this, incongruously running just behind them?—a soundless, bounding flight of antelopes), had punched his weeping wife with what had looked like a well-rehearsed efficiency.

While I watched.

I scribbled our clinic's number on the notepad on my hall table. "Call this. They'll find someone for you." I tore off the page and held it out to him. I moved my head to show him the direction to the door. I'm not sure what would have happened if he had not turned, slowly, he was still thinking about this, and gone.

There isn't much ravine running in February. Lowering clouds in the mornings, temperature in the minus tens or worse, and a wind which typically is bearable for the first ten minutes so that if you don't know any better you can easily be misled and set off running thinking, *This is not so bad, why all the fuss?* Very soon after that your face begins sending you messages like *Terrible news from me to you unless we get home fast.* Experiencing this uncomplicated sequence of events twice was all I needed to get the point, and in fact why twice? The daily run with Marianne was put on hold.

I was still seeing her, indeed with every passing day I was becoming more convinced that I ought to do this, possibly on a contractual basis, for the rest of my life, but the news exchanges between us that normally took place along the familiar paths or during the bench-breaks or while breathing those aromas out of the Styrofoam cups at the Central Don—in this weather, no exchanges, no news. So I wasn't told about what comes next until a day after it took place. Which was a halfway bearable morning in the last week of the month, a morning in which Marianne phoned and said, "This is your mole reporting in" and followed that with, "Meet you down below your place in ten minutes?"

What a nice start to a grey day. As noted above, meeting Marianne hadn't been routine lately, but when it happened it was nice. There's something to be said for having your first look at your favourite person only after you've been up and about for, minimum, a few minutes. An hour is OK too. Half a day is also fine. That tiny minority of couples who, to keep their senses, visual, olfactory and tactile, alert, keep separate addresses—I'd begun noticing how they were getting along. The ones who admitted doing it, that is. Mostly they seemed to be doing fine. Seemingly much better, the ones I'd been spying on, than the national average.

Although nothing's perfect. In order to keep that first-sight-of-the-morning unjaded, you must awaken alone.

But you've been doing that for years, Bloom.

Very kind.

Anyway, off we went. The black-and-white outfit with the rhythmically flouncing bandana again. My favourite, as Marianne knew. Marianne had several such costumes, including one the colours of the Swedish flag, colours

I loved, an unusable love which, although it is unusable, I will retain forever. But this one kept edging it out.

In the interim I'd got myself something more presentable too. I draw the line at describing it.

When we took our first break, sitting on a bench from where we could look east up the wooded hill towards Leslie, Marianne started the reporting-in. First three words: she'd met Sophie. She was looking up at the wooded hill as she spoke and she seemed a little, I didn't know what—muted? She hadn't felt able to wait, she said, saying this almost apologetically, for "my two well-intentioned guys" to do something. "I just . . . well, you'll hear." So she had worked out her own battle plan. The challenge being how to get to talk with a woman she'd heard much of, felt a complex of emotions about and had never met.

She was still talking in this curious manner—the effect of our longish run, I'd decided—and then from one minute to the next I knew that this wasn't it, and knew, also, what it was. Rehearsed is what it was. What a relief, because the monotony of her tone, the single-note trudge of it, hadn't been easy to ignore. So she'd tested this out. OK. Something was up.

Meanwhile Marianne was too intent on what she was saying to notice all this lucidity flying around. She'd found Sophie's address on my telephone table, she said, and had driven to Bernard Avenue sometime after 9 a.m. There she had parked in front of the next-door house, and waited until somebody—"bodybuilder type"—had come out. The bodybuilder had driven off in a small red car. There were two bells to choose from, one with two hand-printed names on the narrow card, one with only one. The single-name card bore Sophie's husband's name.

"And then there she was, observant Nik, just as you'd described her. She'd obviously come pretty quickly down a longish staircase. Tall, skinny, leggy. I don't think you'd mentioned the legs but it's not an issue. Some girls have 'em. Had to be her. She. Wearing a nightdress and a sort of linen wrap. Before I'd said anything—I imagine I was showing a nervous smile instead of saying anything—she retreated a step. It was as if, gosh, as if I now had the right to walk in. As if it was up to me whether I came in or not. I said I was the wife of Larry Logan. Oh yes, she said. I think, to be accurate, she said oh *ja*. Could I come in for a very short while, I asked."

Marianne stared in front of her for a couple of beats. Then looked at me. "I don't know, maybe we better start the tape again, OK?" I was pretty sure she didn't want any comment from me, so I made none. Small sigh from her. "You know, I don't normally run messages for people. Neither do I go off collecting intimate secrets from unhappy wives and then spilling them forth just to make myself interesting." She looked back up the hill towards Bayview. "I don't know," she said, "if I should go on . . ." She turned her face towards me, a face full of uncertainty.

And then it came. What she'd half wanted and half forbidden herself to speak of.

Which was everything we had guessed, and more than we had known.

"I'd already decided that if I was going to have to invent complicated reasons for being there, I'd do that. Lie to her, I mean. Why? Well, because she was such a—from what you'd said, plus those two sketches she'd written and I had read, she seemed so zipped up. So hard to make serious contact with. And in the first one minute or so there, I still didn't know. I mean, who was I? To be let in like that and all? Shouldn't have happened. Bugger off, wife of Larry Logan, is what she had every right to say to me. But as soon as I sat down with her—same sofa, different ends of it—I got a clear message not to. Not to lie, I mean. Not to be devious. No verbal message to this effect, it just seemed very clear. I understood that I—I realized that I had an unusually strong desire to be as simple and truthful as I could be. As, perhaps, I once was. As I hope I once was. Let me reconfigure that just one more time. *As I learned while I sat there that I was longing to have been, once.* She was looking straight at me. No fluttering about, no restive things. We were just there, looking at each other. And so I told her that Mr. Logan—Larry, my husband, I said—had been worrying about her. He liked her work, I said, really liked her work—I don't know if that's true, Nik, is it?"

"Don't know either," I said.

"So I was lying already, see? Anyhow. My husband had been puzzled, I said, by—by a couple of things. Her absences. He thought she was the kind of person who'd have phoned, or something, if she wasn't going to be able to make it, especially, for instance, on the nights she was scheduled to read. Which, twice, I said—I asked Larry about this and that's what he guessed—she hadn't done. Just hadn't shown up, no phoning to explain. And when she had come and he had tried to talk this over with her after class, to iron this out, some man was always there, Larry'd said. Waiting for her. Husband, my husband had decided. And there'd been something about all this that hadn't felt right to him.

"That was just for openers, Nik."

"Hard to improve on that, Marianne," I said, "for openers." Stroking her hand, meaning, *Ignore me, just go on.* There might be some tension here, I was thinking.

"Well, that was the last time in those two hours that I hid behind Larry. Or behind anybody else. I'd already been cleared to call her Sophie. So now I said, 'Sophie, I'm a woman. Larry's a man. Men are often big on worries and plans and sometimes these even work out, but some other times there's, you know, such a lot of horsing around first'—right away I realized that *horsing around* wasn't getting through, she'd never heard the phrase, it'd been a dumb use of—well, anyway, so I blathered on for a bit and then—

"And then I just said, 'Well, right now it's just you and me. I hope that's OK.' And I said, 'Is this being OK?'

"She may have smiled there, Nik. Not sure. I think she did.

"Then I said to her, 'I don't know how to say this mildly, and I'm sorry that I don't. I have to ask. I'm a sort of doctor, so I'm used to asking rude questions. And I'm not going to be shocked by any answer, not *any*. My question is: is there somebody—is—is somebody mistreating you? Your partner, husband, if that's who he is? Please, please, tell me.' That's how I thought we had to start—"

I was nodding, this seemed a perfectly good place to start, I was inwardly settling back——-

"Oh, Nik—Nik—" Marianne was untying her bandana, it barely came loose before she'd angrily pulled it free of those dark curls and thrown it down on the bench. At this point she began crying loudly.

"Jesus, Marianne—" I was beside myself. I'm never sure how that looks, really—beside myself, what am I,

twins? How is that supposed to convey what I was feeling?
"Dear one—"

Great wrenching sobs. Christ!—what to do? I was holding Marianne's two small shoulders and putting my face
close to hers, and the sobs were terrible, she was having trouble breathing, I could hardly keep her shoulders from bending down below the bench. "Dearest Marianne, Marianne,
stop, please stop, please, Marianne, *liefste , liefste*—"

There was no reason why she should stop, really. If she
wanted to sob, it was clear she could sob. Just, I don't know,
tell me what, why, tell me anything, or something.
"Marianne, love—"

The sobbing went on, and on, until finally, oh, thank
somebody, it was diminishing a little. I was still holding her
small shaking body, it was almost entirely inside my two
arms, but not quite as tightly inside as a minute before.
There were some huge breaths and then a pause, and one
more big breathing-in, and then quiet. Marianne looked
around, looked about her in a half-normal way. I could see
her lips moving in a pattern that meant "bandana," no
sound though, and then she saw the bandana, which was
lying on the snow under the bench, and she picked it up and
began wiping her drenched face with it. We sat there, me
with my arms around her, she with her whole body slack.

Good that nobody came by. Well, I don't know. Who
would have cared if anybody'd come by?

Not me. And Marianne wasn't budging.

Her breathing, though, was almost normal.

I said, "We can walk back home, all right? Back to my
place. Walk now, talk later. You OK with that?"

She shook her head. Wasn't OK with that. Fine. Not
fine but all right. We sat there some more. Her breathing

was quiet. She was hoping to make it totally back to normal before speaking again, no prizes for guessing that.

"You know," Marianne said, "you know what she did? What she said?"

No.

"What she said was that nobody was mistreating her. Nobody at all, she said. Whatever was done was done for good reason, she was sure about that. No matter how things looked. Unfortunately, though, or fortunately—Nik, I may be losing the ability to judge of these matters—fortunately, I suppose, she stumbled when she got up, I think she was getting up as a sign that it was time for me to go . . . stumbled, anyhow, and the wrap she was wearing, or holding, it was kind of loosely over one shoulder, it slid south. Just slid down. Off. I suppose it *is* called a wrap, that sort of thing. Whatever it's called, Nik, I—" A big breath. Marianne sat up very straight. A loud sob went out from where we were sitting on a bench among the bare trees and continued on over the white carpet of snow towards the slope up in the direction of Leslie. *Lieve Heer*, I just had time to think, and then Marianne got control again. "She was wearing a—cotton, I guess, nightdress, pretty thin. It didn't hide enough of her. Of the discoloured parts. These parts were, I'll just say—they were below the collarbone area, and in the front, you know? Very concentrated there. Although she's not big there at all." Another huge intake of breath. "Goddamn," she ordered herself, "stop it. Nik, the sonofabitch, the—"—sigh—"the sonofabitch knows two things exactly. He knows what doesn't show when she's dressed, and he knows where a woman hurts most. He—I—"

I'm stopping this scene right here. For three reasons. One, why should you have to endure any more of this, supposing it matters to you? And two, if it doesn't matter to you, just screw off.

And three, at this stage I began worrying about making some unusual sounds myself.

In fact I didn't make any of those sounds. And the worry that I might lasted no longer than ten seconds. We had to get home, didn't we.

Sometimes when a death or some other awfulness has happened, it seems nothing can be said about it at all. You're in an airless closet where everything's impossible. Occasionally, though, not often but occasionally, art can alter "impossible" to merely "difficult." This is a risky business to generalize about, however. Because sometimes it's clearly neither impossible nor difficult surviving this sort of event. Sometimes somebody dies and the surviving beloved is out there with a sixty-page elegy in wonderful time for Christmas. This is not what I mean.

In the days after our (you would think I ought to say "Marianne's," but it soon became, as you'll see, "our") closing in on the hard facts about Sophie's marriage, we went around saying very little to each other. *Stunned* would be a fair description. Turned out we were both doing a lot of brooding, but that's it. Marianne stayed home with Clarissa and Martin the first forty-eight hours and didn't telephone. This worried me some, but I got over it. I got over it when Marianne gave me to understand that although I undoubtedly was male, as Maggione was, and lived in Toronto, as he did, and although he and I were *circa* the same age, and although it was possible, she confessed, that an involuntary comparison-thought or two had floated past her, I had emerged unscathed.

Better than unscathed, Marianne said. But God, she said, how difficult things can be. And how unfair it is that when certain images, unsettling and disturbing, or even foul and monstrous images, make it out into the public air, they can drift close to a good human being and make him look, even fleetingly, like a bad one.

The word Marianne actually used in describing this hard-done-by person wasn't, to be exact, *good*. It was a more sought-out word than that, and one I'm keeping to myself. This is because a word like this, if it's kept quiet and unused, if you don't crease it up with imprecisions or embellishments, such a word might be a nice thing to have around later on. It might hearten you with a vivid thought about yourself, when you're old and alone and things have been grey for a while.

Deep winter faltered towards late March. The workshop was faltering too. Larry's mild treatment of contributions he'd have flayed alive in the fall meant that even Giorgio was listless. Sophie missed class from the middle of Feb. to the middle of March.

She and Marianne, though, met several times during those weeks. Sophie had phoned Marianne a few days after that strange first meeting of theirs, to say she'd like to see her again. No explanation why. Marianne speculated that it was because no one but she had been inside the door of that upstairs Bernard Avenue apartment since its Züricher tenants' arrival, and that this made her the closest thing to a friend Sophie had. In any case, meetings began. Sophie would phone unpredictably and Marianne would, if she could, clear her appointment book and head off. Sophie wasn't a patient, which meant that Marianne didn't feel bound to her professional role; if indignation was what, listening, she felt, she could show it. And if she felt like discussing with me whatever had come up, she could do that too.

What came up? Talks about Küsnacht and childhood. Also about Maggione and the university job he would soon surely be offered in Zürich. About the extraordinary dedication he had brought to his preparation for this. Striving Maggione, virtuous Maggione.

And about the year of their marriage. Five years ago. She had been twenty-eight, he fifty-three.

Marianne (to me): "I was surprised she didn't refer to it as 'Walter's marriage.' Everything else is Walter's. But in this case she went for the conventional 'our.'"

Marianne (to Sophie): "Your husband was the same age as your parents."

Sophie: "Yes. What an exciting year that was for them. I am—I was their only daughter, and Klaus, that's my brother, was not married. So we both had always lived with them. He is forty years old now and is still not married, Marianne. Everybody always thought he would marry and I would not. So, that was one of the two unknow—unexpected events for my parents that year. The other was, my father won his prize."

Prize? Well, yes, said Sophie. That was the year he won the *Preis für Ausserordentliche Leistungen in den Humanitäten.*

Marianne: "Sounds very grand."

Sophie (laughter): "You mean boring, don't you, Marianne? 'Prize for Outstanding Achievements in the Humanities.' The texts he'd edited for high schools. But I think it was mostly for his translations. He translated, English to German, Victorian works on schooling, on educational reform, things like that. English was his great passion. We used to have to speak it at dinner, all of us, when Klaus and I were small. How we hated it! He was always taking on more translation assignments than he should, and when he got really behind, I might be asked to help. He would give me a chapter to do. I remember saying, that first time, No, I cannot, let me just do the index, but he said he was tired of reading male authors' thank yous to their wives or daughters for their indexes and their patience, he didn't know which was worse, indexes or patiences. Probably patiences, he thought. *Did we name you Griselda?* he asked. And he said, My dear child, do this chapter for my sake. So I did. I think nobody noticed the difference.

"He always wanted to write a novel, but he kept postponing this for his retirement. So of course it never happened." She shook her head wonderingly. "Marianne, he loved literature as your friend does. Your friend who is in the workshop."

Well, there was just one more thing, Sophie said. Just a month prior to a bus's skidding on black ice into an old Citroën in which Bernhard and Ulrike Führ were passengers, a small monograph had appeared in chapbook format from a Lausanne publisher. It detailed a special friendship Bernhard's parents had had in the early 1920s. With James and Nora Joyce.

"But your command of English, Sophie—your father must have been so pleased. It's wonderful."

"Thank you."

"What a help you must be to your husband."

"To Walter?"

"In his studies."

"Oh . . . Perhaps."

"Well, I just thought . . . doesn't he—aren't there times when his understanding of the language doesn't quite, you know, do it? And you can help with that?"

"Oh, yes. Yes, there are times like that."

"It's terrible, Nik. I keep wanting to shout at her, How are the bruises today, Sophie? And she keeps on smiling at me from just above the roll-up collar of her bruise-obliterating turtleneck, and calling me 'dear Marianne,' and asking if I have time to listen to this, and then she'll bring out a CD, could be arias, could be lieder, Fischer-Dieskau's 'Sei mir gegrüsst' or 'Der Erlkönig.' She loves all the stuff I love. I'm not saying that's uncanny or anything, but I've never been more pleased with my taste in my life. Last week it was Jussi Björling, whom I also happen to love and to still lament. *When I by myself through the dark woods walk.* He wasn't as old as you are, Nik, when he died. Drank a lot more beer with akvavit dumped through the foam, though, I bet. I bet you haven't tried that. Sophie heard his son sing once, in Zürich. In a park, she said. Once was enough, I got the impression. Have we ever—no, we haven't—let's talk about Björling senior sometime, Nik."

———

"I was thinking about what you said. About me helping Walter in his work. Do you really think—were you just saying that to, you know, make me feel—"

"For God's sake, Sophie. No."

"Only I was wondering."

I've just got something straight that was not nearly so straight before. It's this: Rollo/Walter is going to be *my* business. I could have been luckier. I could have drawn Sophie.

No, better like this.

Who else who could have taken this on has the resources I seem to have for it? You could say I've been pointed towards this all my life.

And all his.

When, that day, he called at the house, asking me to accept him as a patient—and then informing me that I was "required" to do this—I was as curt as I knew how to be. When he afterwards phoned apologizing for that "untimely" house call, and *asking*, now, for an office-hours appointment, I was brusqueness itself. No, no and no.

I'd given him the general clinic number, I said. And I said, Use it.

No way it should have led him to me.

Nevertheless a week later there he was in our waiting room when, once again due to the weather, I made one of my rare entries through our front door. He looked up as I came through and nodded, an approving nod. I had done well to come, the nod said.

Mrs. Peterkin, the receptionist who had been with the clinic much longer than I, and who, when I checked the book, was the one who had registered his appointment, explained. "But Dr. Bloom, Dr. Maggione assured me he had your permission. You would be more than willing to see him, he said. And he said his visit need not be a long one."

I kept him waiting nonetheless. When he finally came in, I realized that the delay had annoyed me more than him. I'd been thinking about why he was coming and had asked myself what, if I had a free choice, I would prescribe for him. Easy answer. *Patient is to be hanged, drawn and quartered* the prescription would have read, and off he'd have had to go to his appointment with the folks who were good at those things. *Good*, in this case, meaning inefficient and slow. And I, watching him go and realizing that I'd never been clear as to which of those three treatments would come first, which second and which third, would finally decide that since I couldn't at all picture the hanging or drawing of one-quarter of anything, the quartering must come last.

Whichever. As long as none were omitted.

And now here he was. "So kind," he said, extending his hand. As hands go, his was suspect, and I managed to be already turning away before the hand got too near. "Your receptionist," he smiled, a collegial smile as he withdrew that hand, "I believe she has a great respect for titles. Without my Doctor-title I fear she would not have allowed me to be here."

Asking him what was wrong with him was a mistake.

"Ah. This is my problem, Doctor. *Sehen sie,* I have no fever. I do not shake, I eat normally. My good wife contents me in"—a pause—"every way. And yet, what can I say? I feel unwell. As I told you."

We were both standing. His eyes glittered up at me. The glitter was for *contents me in every way*.

"I've explained how things are. I'm simply not free to—"

He may have been listening, but he wasn't looking. He glanced about him, took two steps, sat down. "And yet here I am," he said, "in your consulting room. What is to be done about this? How can we deal with this, *Herr Doktor?*"

I began again with my disregarded refusals. Even as I did so, I was aware of a curious powerlessness, a wish to fail in what I was saying. There was something about this man, this *Sitzriese* and his young wife, this Grimm Brothers fable, something that felt as dark and festering and secretive as those fables have always been. *If I now drive him away I will never know how the fable ends.*

He interrupted me. "I have made enquiries, Dr. Bloom. Years ago you published certain papers in the highest-standard European journals. You have worked in Europe, which of course is your native habitat and mine, longer than you have here. Your reputation in your birth-country as in mine is unblemished. At Addenbrooke's in Cambridge they speak with admiration of your work. You see, I have made my enquiries. Do not be modest. I wish to be your patient. Oblige me. *Bitte.* My wife adds her pleas to mine."

I was trying to think what Larry would do in my place. Faced with this Old World snobbery he would probably adopt his super-rural persona and gnaw the end of a tongue depressor in lieu of a straw. A few expletives would be untethered to aggressively circle the room. But that was Larry.

I admit I was impressed by the research, the papers, the Addenbrooke's reference.

"In what way have you felt unwell?"

"If I knew! A *malaise*. Inability to sleep. Normally I have ways to deal with this, they fail me now. Normally I find it is quite enough to be ministered to by my—well, well. But lately, the worry I have mentioned to you. My heart."

"Yes?"

"Several times I have felt this. This inner commotion. Once it was more bad than that. But it was not over the heart, it was"—pointing—"here, the middle, so I dismissed it. But then I read an article in my Züricher *Zeitschrift*—"

"When was it worse?"

"One week ago. Exactly."

"I mean, what caused it to be worse?"

"I don't think I—"

"Unless you tell me, it will be difficult for me to advise you."

"It is indelicate. You understand? You are a man of the world, Dr. Bloom. *Homme moyen sensuel*, I am sure you know that phrase. It takes the 'worldly man' of the English phrase a little further towards—no, into—the more common side, the steamier—"

"I think I understand. You are involved with someone else. Sexually. Woman or man?"

He had been quite comfortable through all this, he had been allowing his eyes to range over my desk, my papers, the prints on the wall, he was all ease.

No longer. The eyes burned.

"What—? You dare to suggest—!"

I haven't mentioned that by this time I too had seated myself. He rose and took a step towards me. His face had gone instant pink.

There he stood, stood very still for a few seconds, looking down at me. Face blotchy by now, small tremors about the mouth. He stared down at me for, oh, five or six seconds, not a sound except his breathing. Then came a longer breath, a sort of sigh, really. And he shuffled his feet and looked off to one side. He took two steps off towards that side, and looked down, and then glanced back towards me.

"I think," he said, "we must discontinue this. I regret . . ." He passed his hand over his face, wiping his face roughly with his hand. "You see, Doctor, you have upset me. Yes. If I wish another appointment I will phone your reception woman." He seemed unsure what to do next. I felt certain he was thinking should he leave now, or not? How would it look? Childish? Correct? *Bürgerlich?*

He took the risk. He went. I thought I'd never see him again.

But two minutes later Mrs. Peterkin buzzed through on the intercom to tell me he had not left the building. He was standing, she said, at her counter, where he had just requested a re-appointment. Whenever I had a minute, he had said. He had failed to apprise me of the most critical aspect of his condition, he had told her, and he was certain that when I learned of it I would surely be glad I had seen him.

I doubt that, I said. very much.

Oh Doctor, she said. I don't think he'll leave. She was whispering.

I said OK.

A chill came with him. *Sans* any greeting he said that he realized he must "put aside" his justified resentment at my imputation of "an abominable sexual preference." I would be unable to diagnose or prescribe for him, he acknowledged, unless he co-operated. He barely took breath between these utterances. Plainly he'd determined to say what must be said, listen to what I'd say in return, and depart, all in quickstep. An unpleasant but necessary episode.

"What I must tell you is confidential, yes?" He went on without pausing. "You asked what I was doing that evening. Now I will say. There is an address I visit, an apartment. It is—let me first tell you something, Doctor— Doctor—?—yes, Bloom. Excuse me, I had forgotten your name. In Zürich, Dr. Bloom—"

My thoughts were: What is this? *What is this?*

"—in the old quarter, across the Limmat from the Bahnhofstrasse, there are a number of addresses known to men of a certain social class where one may—where a man may find—may find comfort. May find whatever he wishes to find. A range of services. You understand? This is considered by all reasonable people—it is considered to be—" He shrugged.

"Yes, yes."

"You understand. *Schön.** I felt sure you would understand. Here in Toronto these addresses also exist, although the awareness—the acceptance that this is a normal convenience for a man—this is lacking. Such hypocrisy, Doctor! And the result of this hypocrisy—well, well." Pause, a resigned shake of the head. "If it were not for my doubts concerning my health, I would speak no further of this. On the evening of this pain in my chest I had visited a woman in her apartment downtown. She is a person known to me for some months now. I stayed with her for a time, I was served by her, I then began to walk home. It was a

---

* Fine.

warm night and I thought this would allow me to—walking home would allow me to cleanse myself, you understand. To have new thoughts. As a man of the world you will appreciate how this—"

I nodded twice. The two nods signified, *Go. Go. Get it said and go.*

"*Ja, ja.* I will say what I have to say. There were crowds on the sidewalk, I realized I had chosen the wrong street. What was the street?—Bay—not usually a crowded street, this is not a bad or crowded area—and the woman's apartment, we are not speaking here of a brothel, you understand—the woman's apartment is in a good area, very clean, very nice, very clean and nice inside always. But I was jostled, I became—I became a little angry. It was disturbing and vulgar. Such crowds, all walking northwards. I tried to leave them behind, I was forced at times to walk on the roadway to avoid the jostling—"

He had arrived home feeling, he must confess this, disturbed. Perhaps "disturbed" was not the right word. Not at ease, he said. "Quite unwell." There had followed a disagreement with his wife, he absolutely did not intend to speak of this. At eleven o'clock that evening he had felt "a great hand gripping my chest. I was preparing for bed, I was a little tired"—and now again it was difficult to find the right words, perhaps I could help him?

I didn't think so—

"My wife, you see—"

I saw, and my mind was hard at work. My share in a dialogue which this man and I would never have went like this: *You were not pleased with yourself because of the woman who had allowed you to do certain things of your choice in her apartment. Or because you had gone there and felt you*

should not have. Therefore you began doing these things to
your wife which you do when you are not pleased with your-
self. Or for other reasons. And since you were already tired,
this second series of things that you regularly do was exhaust-
ing and . . .

"—by now she was lying in our bed, with her face turned away from me. I asked her to turn back and she did not. I was forced to ask her again to at least turn her head. So that she could, you understand, so that she could hear what I had to say. This was only reasonable. I wished to speak to her, I said, of our return to Zürich, which for both of us, I was sure, could not be too soon. I was quite certain she would agree to this at once. But I was—I was taken back, you see, when— no, I think that was incorrect, yes? taken back?"

"I understand what you're saying."

"I was astonished, truly astonished to hear her reply that she would prefer to remain here, in Toronto, until the end of the academic year. I thought at first I had heard wrongly. I had to again ask her to turn towards me, she had turned partially away, you see, and her voice as she now spoke to me was directed into her cushion. Pillow. But this idea of remaining here was nonsensical! You can under- stand that when my thesis defence is completed, there is then no need for us to wait longer before returning to Switzerland. None. We will be free to go."

"Except that Sophie—except that your wife prefers, as you were saying, to complete her course here."

His strained, complicit smile was back. "Yes," he said. "Except for that."

"That's nothing?"

Scorn lifted his voice. "What is this, Doctor, this mad idea of hers? This *soi-disant* workshop? One indulges one's fantasy—one has written nothing of any value at all, nevertheless one imagines one is a great writer—and one's sole reason for imagining this is because a number of one's fellow fantasists, all of whom meet regularly in a very small group, keep assuring one that this is so. And this they do because one continually assures them of the same thing."

There was some truth in this. But, "I don't think anyone in our workshop imagines he is a great writer. Or she. Not even the instructor thinks that highly of himself."

"And should not, either. He is scum, your instructor."

"You have read his books?"

"Read? You imagine I would read a book by this—this carrion? Whose behaviour is—"

"You know," I said, "I am really badly behind schedule. With my other appointments."

"Yes, yes. You lack patience. That is regrettable. Nevertheless I will finish. We were arguing, my wife and I. This is the origin, as you call it. My wife had the—my wife so far forgot herself as to reject, well, of course that is incorrect—she wished me to alter, to—alter—my plans for our return home. 'Reject' is of course too strong. Sophia would not do this." He attempted a chuckle. "Yes, Doctor. Now you have it. A domestic quarrel. As banal as that."

"But your chest? The tightness?"

"A small twinge," he said impatiently. "At first only a small twinge. Just as I turned to my other side in the bed. The rest of it came afterwards. Two hours later. *Furchtbar. Volkommen unausstehlich.* * It made me to—to bend, but also to keep still, to try to not move in my attempt to—to breathe. I called to my wife, she came to my side of the bed

* *Terrible. Absolutely unbearable.*

swiftly, I suppose, in any case she has several times assured me that she came swiftly, but I, I cannot describe—"

"Angina pain has frequently been described. There was nothing else that might have brought this on? Between the bedtime argument and the more severe tightness? Or before the argument?"

Nothing, he said. Only what he had told me.

I had never wanted to be close to him. That glimpse across a park had been a glimpse through a haze of incredulity and anger, more of both of those things than I may ever have felt before. Some of that had changed, in a sense it had settled, as it had to in order for any kind of routine to reassert itself in my humdrum existence. Now, though, the proximity broke unexpectedly back through whatever had "settled," and it was too much. I wrote him out a request for an ECG at our outpatients' lab, told him he should get that done and that if he had, tonight or any time, a repeat of the chest pain, he should phone 911 or go to the nearest hospital's Emergency. He might also, I then added—surprising myself by adding it—see me again. I gave him a page of instructions, what he should bring if and when he came.

He wasn't quite ready to go. "This woman," he said. "The one in the apartment. You judge me for this, Doctor, I think."

I said I did not. I didn't want to relieve him of anything at all, but I remember what I said and that was it.

He seemed to hesitate and then began a sentence he didn't finish. "Sometimes a man has to be—" He looked at me uncertainly. He was plainly about to go on but decided against it. There was a soundless movement of his mouth, a nod, and he went out, shutting the door after him.

After he'd gone, after the rest of my patients that day had gone, I thought of his implied question. The woman. The one in the apartment. *You judge me for this, I think.*

My response had been too quick. Better would have been, *It depends. Depends what you were doing to her.*

Have I mentioned that Saskia was the most beautiful woman I ever saw naked? Even when that first-glance sleekness, bliss of an intern's cubicle, had deferred, over the ensuing ten or eleven years, to the casual plenitude our northern painters seem to prefer—think only of her namesake, Rembrandt's second wife—nobody ever came close. Saskia had perfect skin, the Lowlander's pale blue eyes . . . I could go on annotating her, listing her, a flypast of praising modifiers, but there's no need.

For most of the years I was with her I felt sure that whatever else might trouble her she would never feel less than blessed, or, more mundanely, lucky, to appear in the world's eyes as she did. By right of her looks, the sun and all the other stars would forever shine on her. Nobody, I thought, meeting her, seeing her pass by, could think otherwise.

Well. It wasn't how *she* felt, and there may have been some who guessed it. All of them wiser than I.

Long ago—it was one of our early years in Cambridge, when we were still attempting not only to seem but also to be content, living the typical life of a recently elected fellow and wife, going to parties and college dinners, giving dinner parties ourselves with a college servant or two to assist us as needed—during that year one of the other Queens' Fellows decided he was in love with Saskia. That may not have been quite what he decided—"in love" was, however, the phrase he used. He had never spoken to Saskia before the evening in question, and did not speak to her during it either, but after we returned home from that night out—it was the obligatory college feast marking the end of the Michaelmas term—she found his crested note in her handbag. One of the white-jacketed college servants must have obliged him during dinner. Showing me the note, she asked, "Who is he? What does he teach, this man?" And also, "What did I do? How could he think that I—?" She was filled with contempt, with disgust, and not only for him.

Most of the men I knew in those years were colleagues at Addenbrooke's rather than academics at Queens', and the only Queens' Fellow I ever went out drinking with—this being not quite a necessary badge of friendship, but close—was the Supervisor of Studies in Romance Languages, a man well known in the university community for his fluent, bordering on the histrionic, poetry readings. Him I told about the handbag note. "He probably thought you'd be flattered," was his comment. "Both of you. His pedigree, don'tcha know." And he went on, "There are probably a dozen fellows' wives within lecturing-distance of us right now who've been favoured with the identically worded note. He may even have been in the habit of asking them to return it when the afternoon visits to his rooms began to pall, and was gallant enough to tell them why. *Noblesse oblige.* Come to think of it—was it seriously creased, Saskia's note, or has he perhaps taken to re-inditing it? A crisp new page? A signal honour, my dear Nik."

Much later that evening in the bar of the Garden House Hotel, my companion was reciting poetry at me, all gone from memory now except for one line from, and I'm not likely to be wrong on this, Baudelaire. You'll understand why it's never left me. The poem shows a woman crying out, in the still of the night, *"Que c'est dur que d'etre belle femme!"* The Supervisor of Studies in Romance Languages may have had my story of Saskia's note in mind when he spoke the line, he may have spent most of our Garden House time working towards it, fitting line to occasion, preparing occasion for line, how should I know.

I'll guess not, though. I'll guess he just loved the line.

It would have sped unnoticed past me, as so many lines of poetry that I thought I would never forget have sped past, if it hadn't been for the context, that near exact fit. Within a few minutes of hearing it I walked home through a chill December midnight, not a creature stirring, just the occasional buzz of a sodium lamp in the stillness to keep me company. Along Trumpington and past the Fitzwilliam Museum and then the long stretch of the Botanical Gardens towards Barrow Road and its leafless almond trees. I remember running my ungloved hand along the Botanical Gardens' railings, which were covered in a thin white frost.

The Swiss doctor had called again, Mrs. Peterkin told me, and she had booked him in as the afternoon's first appointment. Why not. In he came, showing his white teeth. No, not baring them, that would be me.

He handed in his bottle, filled out his form, which I glanced at (form, not bottle), blood sample done. Normally, he would now see my medical technologist for his ECG. I'd decided, though, to do that myself. It would be the first time I'd done an ECG since some dusty date or other at Addenbrooke's, but I guessed I could manage it. There may have been a raised eyebrow when I told the technologist, but there were no raised words, or none that I could hear. I had few words about it for myself, either. It simply seemed a good way to proceed. I wired him up and stood watching the pattern declare itself.

He was silent and seemed preoccupied. His eyes flickered towards me a few times but otherwise studied the ceiling. I watched the delicate little stylus record the rhythms of his heart.

Which were not unusual for his age. The occasional extra beat, the whole a touch on the quick side, nothing remarkable. Having told him so, though, I added that on the basis of his description of his severe pain the other night, together with other recorded symptoms, I should see him again. There might be no heart damage at all, but we needed tests to confirm this. This was all I wanted to say for the moment, and because it was so unemphatic I expected it to pass without comment.

I was wrong. Here was a man who had spoken to me of a "lurching" heart and had demanded, and demanded more than once, to be treated—and who now plainly didn't want anything remotely *like* "lurching" allowed into the same room or paragraph with him. He stared up at me in obvious disbelief. "I cannot think—" he began uncertainly, thinly, but his voice was thickening as he spoke, "I will not believe that I—you must know that you speak now to a man who—*einer dessen Vater neunzig Jahre lebte.* You tell me you don't understand German, this is strange, you Dutch are so near! I am a man whose father, this was my phrase of a moment ago, lived to be ninety and who—are you listening?—remarried at seventy, this was my mother—"

"There is no immediate cause for alarm," I said. "There are procedures—"

"He never visited a doctor, never, not once until— until— What are these procedures?"

I told him. "We may never need them," I added. He would be monitored, tested, perhaps I would send him to a colleague (there was no need for this: that this man was angina-prone would have been clear to the most indifferent of passersby in any med clinic's corridor) who was more attentive to the latest developments in the field, after which we would decide. There was no real urgency. The best facilities were all at hand.

He interrupted my explanation. Obviously he felt enough momentary relief that that tense surface of his relaxed, relaxed just a little, and he said, though his words still tumbled and competed, "You have heard of such a case? Such stamina? At such an age? Let me tell you, Doctor—Doctor—what are you called? Again I have forgotten your name!"

He stopped, the blotchy face was back, the breathing noisy. "Perhaps I must go," he said, a whisper. "It doesn't signify," he said. And again, "I supposed that I was well."

Strongest man in the region of Lake Garda and . . . some other lake.

"You may be so. You probably are."

"But you are telling me I have an inferior heart. A damaged heart, this is what you said. Is this what you are still telling me?"

"We need to run further tests, is all. A stress test, for one. Not today. Today doesn't seem the right—no, such a test must be booked in advance. The tests may show that you have the best heart since I don't know who."

(Well, you could try to know who, I admonished myself. So I tried. Best hearts? But aside from Emil Zátopek and the brothers Cheeryble, I came up blank.)

At least he wasn't shouting. "I have told you of certain symptoms I have experienced. I have explained . . . events. There may be additional reasons of which I have not spoken, but what I insist upon is—"

"Additional reasons? If I don't know what the full background is, how can I advise you?"

He was studying me. I had a clairvoyant moment: he was thinking, I knew, that he had an interesting secret to tell. Or not to tell.

In such cases it's hardly ever *not*.

"You see, Dr. Bloom—there, I have remembered your name—I must warn you, what I will tell you now will not be gallant. I consider myself a *galantuomo*, but it is, as you know, not possible always to be so. Much as one may wish it. Do you agree?" He was nodding affirmatively, he had decided that I agreed. "I must tell you," he went on, "that I am something of an authority, a minor one it is true, on the early autobiographical works of my great countryman Carl Jung. A very great man."

Amazing to hear a measured sentence, no matter what its content, from this so recently convulsing mind.

"Your doctoral thesis, yes."

"His is perhaps the greatest humanist mind of this century. What am I saying, the last century, of course. Do you agree?"

I shrugged.

"Of course you do not agree. How could a citizen of such a country as Switzerland, so small, so remote, be a great man? I know what is said about my country. Nevertheless—"

"The pain. Tell me your additional reason."

"Wait, I will tell you. I will tell you. But remember, you are warned. Do not judge me. The additional reason for my discomfort—'discomfort,' yes? It is all right?—is a person, and the person is—is my wife. Yes. She it is I was speaking of. Or *not* speaking of, yes?"

He went on. "Such a very special woman. We met— has she told you? No? You are certain? We met in—yes, in Genf. Geneva, I believe you say. But of course you too will know it as Genf. I was doing research on, it is of no matter, a minor figure in the Jungian pantheon, the Master disowned him, very justly, the fool merited an even more severe—*passons, passons*. My wife was in a retreat, she was a *religieuse*, did you know this? A *religieuse*-in-training. Perhaps she still *is* a *religieuse*." He paused, this was my chance to agree that Sophie was a *religieuse*. "Our meeting was a pure accident. Literally! She had come into Genf with other people from the retreat. Their party had become separated due to a breakdown of a bus, some but not all of them had been picked up by a second bus. Some had begun to walk. She was the first to arrive at the Bonadea Gallery, which was not yet open. I too had arrived early. It was one of my customary working visits. We stood and watched what was to see, we could just see the tip of the famous fountain—I pointed this out to her. I had been there many times, there were works there which Jung comments upon in the journals. It was these which I would be considering, offering a fresh perspective on, if I may claim so much, in my doctoral treatise. We talked of this and that, I was able to give her detailed descriptions of the major paintings she would be seeing. Eventually we noticed we had come on the wrong day. *Fermé le lundi.* Of all people to have failed to notice this! Every Continental gallery is closed on this day. You are sure she has not told you of this meeting of ours? Such a trick of destiny?"

"No."

"Ah. She talks with your friend very much. I thought therefore that you might—what do they talk about, I wonder. I have attempted to discover this from my wife, who claims they speak of women's matters. Do you know what they speak of, Doctor—Doctor—how odd, once again I have forgotten your—"

"Bloom. I do not. Know."

"*Schade.** When we were first married, she would tell me everything. Of course, she was learning so much in those days. When we were first married . . ." His voice slowed, paused. I felt he wanted to repeat those two sentences; mantra-like, they would hang in the air, and neither of them would ever continue on past happiness. "Of course, she was totally inexperienced. But so grateful to learn from me. I believe, Dr. Bloom, I fell in love with her gratitude."

He had remembered my name. I gestured with one hand. I opened it and shut it. This seemed to meet the case.

"Tell me, *Herr Doktor,* have you heard of such a thing?"

"Sorry?"

"Gratitude. To fall in love with gratitude." He was plainly without expectation or interest in that of which I might or might not have heard. "What a joy she was to me. In those days our minds, *wissen Sie,*† were as one. How she would listen! She would—" He turned his head sharply. "What is it you say?"

* Pity.
† you know

"I said nothing."

"Really? . . . Really." His eyes were still looking far off. He then said something I couldn't hear. Obviously he sensed I hadn't heard, because what he next said was surely a repetition.

"Sometimes a man has to be unworthy in order to be able to go on living."

"Unworthy?"

"One commits acts which one . . . regrets. Jung, you know, recognized that he too was capable of unworthy acts. Hence the quotation. It is Jung I was quoting from. A man has to be—" He stopped and looked sharply at me. He was assessing what I might have begun to feel about what he was, just now, deciding not to continue with. "It was a quotation, *sehen Sie*. Merely a quotation. Perhaps it is true."

That was all that passed between us that day. He left without telling me what the ungallant thing was. Or the unworthy act.

From my newest story,
perhaps to be entitled Lena. (still in progress!)
s.f.

Even though the deeper sightings they told of would never be for her, the writings of the blessed ones could always console her. She experienced these not abstractly (she was, as he had several times pointed out to her, not philosophically inclined), but she had learned that one could feel close to things one did not understand, and as long as the book was open and in her hands she could linger in that closeness.

Staying close to things you do not understand may be, she
wrote in her journal, the best way of understanding them.
The enemy was in any case not her failures in understanding, it was simply and always herself. Proofs of this would
arrive without warning. For instance towards the end of a
long day, when it seemed too late for anything to spoil, to
damage that day, even then some self-regarding thought
could disappoint her. It might be a doubt as to how much
this person or that one cared for her, or, which was plainly
no better, whether that same person valued the extent of the
feelings she had for him. The essential thing, though,
always, was to learn from those who had gone before. From
the blessed ones, as she called them. It was a naming, a
phrase, that her father would have smiled at. *Lena, meine
Liebe,* he would have said, or, equally likely, *dear Lena*—
and then a gentle rebuke. Never mind. "Blessed" was just a
word, they both knew there was no harm in it. Whatever
these were to be called, blessed or wisdom-filled or (this
would be quite enough to say!) *good,* they were continually
describing journeys which took them beyond anything she
had known or even guessed at, journeys she would only
ever be able to take, as she knew very well, through their
pages. Hardly bearable descriptions of solitude, for
instance, word-pictures of the barren lands through which
they had roamed, some of them, for years, lost and terrified. Meister Eckhart, in the little blue book she had spent
so many hours with, called such a place *"eine stille Wildnis
in der niemand ʒuhause ist"*—"a still wilderness," she had
translated this, "where no one is at home." And hundreds of
years later, someone else, standing, or so it seemed, in
exactly that same empty and barren space in which Meister
Eckhart had stood, reported on "the great wastes, *die*

grossen Wüsten, that have neither image, form, nor condition." *Grosse Wüsten, stille Wildnis.* How frightening these imageless places would be, she felt, and knew her utter unfitness to be there. "Neither image, form, nor condition"! Be grateful, she had instructed herself, that at least *sometimes* you can see through the small webs of your mind, and listen even through the small cries of your body! *Live without any image of yourself at all,* was the best advice, but it was so hard to do. Yesterday as she stood at an open window, scarcely noticing the faint warmth of the early spring air, an unexpected sound had reached her. It was the clop-clop of hooves on the street. A policeman then came into sight riding a beautifully stepping chestnut horse, the rider gazing up at, she thought (noticing these herself for the first time that day), the delicate pale green leaves which, overnight it seemed, had emerged along the branches of the maple trees. The horse continued at the same even pace, its deliberate clop-clop, the rider gazing upwards at the new leaves, until both passed out of sight—she herself having, luckily, the sense to stand almost without breathing so that she would hear the diminishing sound of the hooves as long as possible. When the sound was gone it took her, how long, several minutes, to return to herself. And as always when she returned from such a pure absence she was intensely aware of how brief that purity had been and how pitiably egotistical her thoughts *still, still, still* continued to be, no matter how high in the realms of gold—or of simple blue sky!—she had supposed they were travelling. Although it was true she was still aware of that horse and its rider and the faint enduring newness. Still grateful for what the clop-clop of the beautiful horse's hooves had so freely made a gift of to the street and which the rider, watching up into the small new leaves so peacefully, his mind so noble in its unselfish contemplation, had been an important part of, she felt herself at least a little readier (though this wouldn't last, doubts always flew swiftly in after it) to continue on in her journey—even if what was next would be a "still wilderness." Even if, the thought now unexpectedly came, she were already there. Even if her present life was already that "great waste."

It was a new thought. What to do with it?

And here came Teresa again, different and yet the same—

Reflect carefully on this, for it is so important that I can hardly lay too much stress on it. Fix your eyes on the Crucified and nothing else will be of much importance to you. Do you know when people really become spiritual? It is when they become the slaves of God.

Read to Mr. L. Logan's workshop on April 12th.
Sorry for taking so long.
(The italicized paragraph above is
from Teresa of Avila, *Interior Castle*,
Image Books, 1961, p. 229.)

Odd, "weird," you may be thinking, that although I've reported at length on the comings and goings of persons I cared nothing, zero, about not many months ago, I've had so little to say concerning my new-found-land. The acres of words I'm right now roaming in. My writing.

Two reasons for this. One, there hasn't been much of it—prolific I will never be. Precedents for the unprolific are, of course, many. Cosimo de' Medici, mentioned earlier, although he was truly one of the world's great bibliophiles, never wrote a book himself, since he "never managed to finish a paragraph that wholly satisfied his exacting taste." *Exacting taste*—two words that say everything. A third of the way through *The Plague*, Albert Camus famously permits his readers to glimpse the opening sentence, the *single* sentence that has been completed (actually, Camus confides, it's *not* completed yet, the sentence is still only a draft), by a character inside that novel who's been working on this first line of his novel for most of his life. And Camus tells us that his character, Grand, will never cease editing this sentence, never be satisfied in his perfecting of it. Here it is: "One fine morning in the month of May an elegant young woman might have been seen riding a handsome sorrel mare along the flowery avenues of the Bois de Boulogne." This reads slightly better in French, but French or English it has too many adjectives. Grand doesn't know this (in spite of having worked so long on it), but Camus (who didn't work nearly as long on it) does. An even more extreme case is the artist in Alberto Moravia's novel *The Empty Canvas*, a painter who decides that the untouched whiteness of the canvas on his stretcher is greatly richer in tension and hope and melancholy and, most obviously, in limitless potential than any finished painting has ever been or ever will be. That is, to *infinitely* aspiring minds any completed thing records a failure. One can of course see what Moravia's painter means, even while running miles away from his position. If you will forgive my own appearance in this paragraph of *exaltés*, let me say that I am far more willing to chance my hand and pen than either Cosimo or Grand were, to say nothing of Moravia's timid admirer of an empty dazzle. But I recognize in all of these my almost-similars. I would always choose their 'exacting' company before that of the Rushdies and the García Márquezes and others of that incontinent persuasion.

Which brings me to the second of my writerly hang-ups. It is my love of reading. If what I am reading is or seems (these are exactly the same thing in this context) closer to my mind's core than that paragraph or page of my own which I have just left on my computer screen, the latter can languish a long time undisturbed and unimproved. Why shouldn't it? You see where we are—we are back at the old conundrum regarding a perfect world. If there *were* such a thing as a perfect world, art would not exist. If one's imagination is *fully enthralled*—that's *fully*, mind—by the world around one, then to turn from that to any kind of *story*, or *picture*, or *piece of sculpture* or *music,* would be to turn to what is lesser, something for which there is no space or niche or embrasure left in the mind.

I've maundered on too long with this. Point is that if your aim is to write abundantly and publish prolifically, it is not a good idea to have your shelves stuffed with the world's best books. How does your own page, this paragraph you have just now dotted the last "i" in, feel, snuggled up close to a conversation about the meaning of life between Pierre Bézuhov and Prince André Bolkonski? How does your own just-described protagonist feel to find himself sauntering along a boulevard in Vienna in the company of Ulrich, that coolest of August 1913 dudes, the one who masquerades as a "man without qualities"? Or drifting among Dorothea Brooke's dreams of a pure commitment or Gwendolen Harleth's spirited failings? Or, *bon Dieu*, existing in the same small ducal town with *Adolphe*, or eyeing the pretty women in the Triestine cafés with Zeno, or warmly tucked in on his chaise longue on a balcony beside Hans Castorp, looking way, way down from way, way up on the *Zauberberg?*

Not to mention that most incandescent of all twentieth-century pages, where my Dublin namesake, after the drunkenness and squalor of his Nighttown spree, sees his long-dead son Rudy, "a fairy boy of eleven," standing against a dark wall holding a book in his hand and reading, and "(*wonderstruck, calls inaudibly*) 'Rudy!'"

All such remembrances of books past are capable of enforcing upon me, no matter what plans I had for a busy day in the mines of Art, a printless page.

The keeping of such demanding company may also, though, once in a long while—during some rare moment of the Muse's inattention—allow some lesser being to haul himself close.

This is what I believe, in any case. And hope. Although if it isn't so, it's all right.

"Could I borrow the book? The saint? Is her name Teresa? When you're finished with it, I mean?"

"I—could you find one for yourself, do you think? I read mine, you see, quite often."

"Oh, sure. Sorry."

"Don't be sorry. I hope you can find it. It's sort of a mustardy colour. In paperback, I mean. Like this."

"Are you finished, Jim? That all you had to say to Sophie?"

"All yours."

"Thanks. The long sentences, Sophie. Do you think they could be broken up a little? They might be even more effective."

"Yes, I'm sure you're right, Ms. Madell. Thank you. I'll try that."

"Call me Irma. I called you Sophie."

"All right. Irma."

"Nice to have you back, by the way. We've missed you."

"Thank you. Irma."

"I very love the part of the horse. Clop-clop. Very good, Ms. Führ."

"Thank you. It was a lovely horse. Strong and peaceful."

And just before the end of that session, after two other readers had read, when talk was becoming general—

"I've been thinking about that paragraph of yours, Sophie, when you're standing by the window and all. I was trying to figure out why it's so great—because it *is* great, trust me, Uncle Giorgio's a great judge of these matters. It's straight out of life, it's what's called *reportage*, is why. Real horse, real cop, nothing invented, am I right? Why invent when the world keeps on handing us these amazing pictures of itself? And you did real well with what it handed you, Soph, I love it. Love it. Totally, OK? And Larry, if you'll allow me to change the topic, although not really changing it—you'll see what I mean in a sec—I was with this acquaintance of mine up in Willowdale recently, we were standing around waiting for, you know, Godot, and if I may be allowed to draw a comparison—"

"Probably not, kiddo. But here's a question for everybody. Since Sophie's piece—don't know what to call it, page, piece—not *reportage*, that's for damn sure—since that's now been mentioned again, what do you people think about what happens to it halfway through? When the cavalry arrives, y'know? Cop on his horse? Bit of a tempo change, isn't there? Did you want the inner stuff, you know, the contemplative stuff to go on longer? Glad to see it end? A bit of candy floss here and there, maybe? Or do those sugary bits actually work? Anybody? . . . Anybody?"

"In a hurry, Nik? I have a thirst."

Cruddy's again. A quick-march six minutes from the Ryerson main entrance.

"Reading week's coming up. Any plans?"

"Haven't thought about it. When's reading week start, then?"

"Christ, old mole. Get into it, we follow the Julian calendar over here, not like jolly old Amsterface. Starts next Monday, meaning the previous Friday for people like me. I don't know about you."

"I'm due some holidays."

"All *right*. Here's what I was thinking. I'm into a good patch, getting about a thousand words a day on this current piece, so I'm not going anywhere that's away from my screen next week if I can help it. I thought—if you like the idea—you might want to have a look at the islands down there. You know, not necessarily Antigua. Lots of beaches."

"This is very thoughtful of you, Larry. I'm moved. Yes, I think I'm moved."

"Just a thought."

"D'you have an errand I could do for you on one of those islands? An unostentatious suitcase someone will hand to me to bring back?"

"Get knotted, Rembrandt van Stiltskin. Hey, Harold!"

Wordlessly sitting until Harold brought another pitcher.

And continuing to sit while he poured himself a very full glass. Larry's an unusually polite fellow in the unremarked niceties of the culture, so when he placed the pitcher near his farthest-from-me elbow, I knew something was bothering him. He sat back, gave himself a broad white upper lip, put the glass down and remained slouched, staring about.

And continued staring about. I looked around too. I was half expecting to see King Kong in a biker's jacket rotating down from his stool.

"OK, Nik. No point in being fractious. Here's the thing. Annie needs a break, seems to me. She's been getting difficult, you know? Finds the kids a bit much, thinks I never see them—which I do, course I do, never less than a couple of nights a week. Fact the motive behind this proposal of mine is that a whole week without Annie, no Annie close enough to run home to, would do the three of us, Clarissa and Martin and me, especially Clarissa with me, a major portion of good. Also, though, I admit to thinking you might welcome the idea of a frolic down there, just the two of you. Eh? Mightn't you? I could help out a bit, you know. Give me your glass, sport."

Handing over my glass, saying, "As long as you haven't broached this with Marianne—"

"Broached? *Broached?* Annie and I don't broach any more, I thought you knew that."

Was it that same evening that Larry, certainly without setting out to do so, allowed me the only look I'd ever had, the only look I've had to this day, at his younger self, his naive self, his—what to call it? The undergraduate's obligatory dallying-with-the-divine self?

Yes, it was that same evening.

But it didn't begin that way. It began right where some of us had been with our thoughts for half the winter, it seemed—

"What a patsy he's got there, Nik. That husband, whatever his name is. You listen to that crap of Sophie's? I mean, it's classic. I once had a wife who would have known all too exactly into which Psych 101 category this would have fit—"

"OK, Larry. We were going to skip the Marianne-bashing. What's so *classic* about this?"

"Slaves of God, for God's sake. Think about it. No, don't think about it. Think instead about the bleedin' awful confusion we find here between the capital-P Patriarch in her sky and the small-p prick in her bed. Scenario's such a cliché it's embarrassing. That this sort of crap still goes on—and on!"

"Always thought that's what makes things clichés. That they go on and on."

"You bet. Only—to see it up close like this. To hear it. 'Consolation in the writings of the blessed ones'—I think

I've got that about verbatim, haven't I? I mean, nothing against the blessed ones, only . . ." He sighed. "Dunno what to say. I mean, blessed ones, holy ones . . ."

As I ran the last of the pitcher into our two glasses, Larry went on. "I . . . OK, why not? Here's a story. I once knew a kind of Sophie. A proto-Sophie. A rudimentary first-draft of Sophie, as it were."

"What's that look like, then?"

"End of my second year at UC there was this girl. I just kept running into her, we were enrolled in the same courses, we browsed the same shelves in the library stacks, stuff like that. Either a nuisance or amazingly serendipitous, depending on the degree of ache in the silhouette. Her silhouette had seemed just average to me all year. But one day just before exam time she handed me a library book, just handed it *at* me, book written by some Spanish nun of whom I had not heard. You guessed it, *Interior Castle*. She said it had four days left on it, would I return it when I was finished. I should tell you that up to this stage of my life I'd been irreducibly chaste, not out of any wish to be so, just, in retrospect, unlucky. But of impure fancies I was having my share. So. I looked at this book in my hand, and then I looked at this girl, I forget her name, and things kind of— for some reason I concluded that this girl might be as delayed in her development as I was. And nearly as anxious to, you know, do something about it. The auguries were excellent. This Spanish saint seemed to be guaranteeing it. I had the bright idea that this girl and I'd be two little instant miracles for each other. Haloes floating over the entire enterprise. So off I went with her library book and a few days later this odd thing happened. We were lying on a blanket, yellow, I still have it, hasn't faded a bit, grossly underused of late, under a tree behind Trinity at three or four in the morning, a really warm night, and no, we hadn't done a thing yet apropos our shameful circumstances, we'd just been talking for quite a while about the rooms, mansions they're called, in this so-called castle, debating what they meant. And now you have to picture us just lying there. Yellow blanket, got it? Quite close but not a police matter. I'll admit that a good bit of the time while we were talking about Teresa I'd been thinking about this other, as I hoped, pending business. It seemed incumbent upon me to, you know, get on with it. That or else for the fifty-third or -fourth time slink off still unacquainted with the dream at the heart of the world. Which, if that's what would happen, the slinking, I foresaw would ruin me forever. It was weird, though. There we were, both of us irradiated with these mantras of saintly abstinence and our other half trembling with you know what. I don't mind telling you that insofar as miracles were concerned, I was on miracle's very brink. If you understand me rightly. Thing is, though—" Larry shook his head. "Thing is, just then a voice called to me out of the leaves right over our heads. Out of the rustling leaves, for God's sake. Called not to her, just to me. *Lar-ry*, the voice called. *Lar-ry*. An oddly remote but crystalline voice. Causing hundreds of tiny shiverings to scurry up and down the back of my neck while I listened. And oh, was I listening! I listened as I'd never listened before and have never, come to think of it, listened since. Voice out of a tree-full of leaves."

I suppressed a crikey.

"Weird, Nik, eh? It was calling me to something—who knows what. Well, of course it wasn't, it was self-induced, I was full of the May night and my body's toppling-over needs and then with all this God talk . . . naturally something was going to fall out of the heavens. Or out of a tree. No problem knowing that now. But all I knew then was that I'd heard a voice and that it was full of special news for me. Some rich excitement. Possibly too rich. I decided it would be too rich, I mightn't survive it. I'm still not sure about that. *Let's go,* I said, and we grabbed each other's hand and we went. She—Frances! Frances McFaul! Jesus! That name's been lost for—I wonder—why, I—anyhow, *Frances,* I remember Frances looking up into my face as we almost ran away from there. I knew she was envying me. I knew she was thinking, why should the voice be calling *him, I* found the book first!"

Larry took a sip instead of a pull. He then gazed out over the darkish irregular pattern of our fellow drinkers' silhouetted heads. I gazed out there too.

"After all these years. Frances. What d'you know. Nice girl, I think. Although we never did . . ." And then he went on, "But what we saw in the workshop tonight"—he was still staring out there—"was a woman who's apparently given the keys to every room in her own little castle to an all-star jerk-off. Because why? Because why, Nik? Woman of some—in the light of what she just read to us—some apparent intelligence? Some modest gift?"

I had no answers to this. I was feeling confused, is the truth of it, which is probably why the word itself came up in what I then heard myself saying. "She's confused." And, "Maybe she's reading the wrong good books." And then, "She's confused her husband with I'm not sure who. With some demon sent to try her. Among the gods and the saints and the holy folk, a demon. I didn't know this until quite recently. Until right now," I said.

This seemed about enough for the time being. Larry waited, but not for long.

"I feel almost sorry for the kid, Nik," he said. "None of my business, though, thank God."

"Mine neither."

Demented exchange.

Of course, Marianne had filled me in on Sophie's background, what she knew of it. So when Teresa's castle cast its crenellated, I guess, shadow over our workshop, it was no surprise to me. Alone together on those Thursday afternoons of the husband's tutorial, the two women passed the time browsing the castle's inner rooms, those rooms Teresa calls mansions—paying an incidental attention, when a phrase or a thought lit up a book that had been quiet and ignored until then, to other spokespersons for the Single Path. Some of these have been mentioned here and some haven't.

Picture it like this. Marianne is sitting variously, Sophie is reading aloud from a chair by a window. The only light in the room comes from that window. "Pretty dark, some days," Marianne said to me, "for reading by."

"Well, I soon realized she usually wasn't *reading* at all, she knew almost everything by heart. Not to minimize this, nothing against memory work, but it couldn't have been hard. I mean, it was only the top of the tops, the heavy hitters I was listening to. The famous phrases. *'Morsels of dark contemplation.' 'Like shining from shook foil.' 'I saw Eternity the other night, Like a great ring of—something something— light.'* Good stuff, most of it at least a little familiar. But why the pretence of reading it? Why not just admit what she was doing? Such modesty, I thought. Big mistake, anyhow, because if she'd been willing to toss the books and just speak the lines like the Player King is told to speak them, then good old Marianne could have sat there enjoying the neat Swissli accent and wouldn't have had any excuse for noticing how dark it was getting. Because listening in the dark, far as I'm concerned, is a great place to listen in. As I know you know."

I knew.

"So. I hang about there minding my own listening business, but before long I realize that I'm trying, you know, perversely almost trying *not* to catch on. I'm trying not to understand why she would choose to read in such gloom, such—oh shoot, Nik, of course what I was realizing was that keeping the room dark had nothing to do with either modesty or memory work—"

"Gotcha."

"Thought you might."

Marianne waited.

"If the question was, 'Why is it so dark in here?'"—Marianne was still waiting—"and if I say that as explanations go, this one's really beyond the—this one's—" She nodded. "I wasn't there, Marianne, but I have a crude imagination, and since life is crude I often solve puzzles like this one pretty fast."

Big sigh from my beloved.

My beloved then said, not really slowly though more slowly than before, "So I tell her I want more light. To which Sophie says, 'Like Goethe.' 'Whatever,' I say. 'No,' she says, 'that's what Goethe said as he was dying. He said, *More light*.' 'Whatever,' I say again. 'Who cares,' I say.

Then I say, a boorish segue, 'Does that mean that where we are right now has got something to do with dying?' She understood I was going to be intransigent and said I could turn more lights on if I wanted to. If light was what I wanted, she said. Which I then did. It's not a big room, so the first switch was enough. I saw her in those couple of pot lights and I stopped saying 'whatever.' I'd have howled if howling wasn't by this time passé. I didn't howl. I just—I suppose my heart just sank. It just quietly sank."

"Liefste."

"I don't know," Marianne said. "I don't know."

I was going to go over to her, but she managed the sort of smile which kept me where I was.

"I do still have to tell you. Even in that uniform of hers, turtleneck, jeans, the whole bit, I have to tell you that on the one side of her mouth, the underside of her jaw, really—he must have been in a hurry the night before, so much of a hurry he didn't aim well, he forgot himself— well, she looked about sixty from that side. Oh, *Nik*. This is after all a young person still, and the sixty-year-old movements that this person made when she started to get up . . . My tact, seeing this, my tact didn't really hang in as it ought to've. I'm afraid I shouted at her, which startled her so she stood up, and then she kind of—well, she didn't fall, exactly—"

I couldn't help it. I don't know if I'd ever really interrupted this lady in the midst of a serious paragraph before, but— "It's immoral even to talk about this. You know? This isn't our thing. Not our thing to do, not our thing to talk about. This is for the—you know better than I who it's for, but how about welfare, how about police—I happen to know there's something called the At Risk Register—"

I wasn't turning away from Marianne, but with one hand I was scrabbling about behind me where I knew the phone was. And I was organizing my opening remarks in preparation for whoever would pick up when, in seconds, I would ring 911.

Marianne sat looking despairingly at me. "Won't work. She won't turn him in, won't complain, won't nothin'. If she would, I'd have done it, like, yesterday. This is one for the pros, I'd have said, you must know I'd have said that. Police, I don't care, SAS, Mossad, the pick of the local vigilantes . . ." And she added, "You don't know how she is." And added again, "It's not a police thing."

". . . What thing is it, then?"

"She thinks, Nik, she—she believes she has to go through with this. It's not a cause, exactly, but Goddamn it, Goddamn it . . . happiness isn't what she—I heard her say something like—not sure of this, but 'our Father lives only in secret,' that could be what I heard. She was explaining why she wouldn't talk about this. There's a confusion here which I need to get straight before I—in general I haven't got the Father stuff, the God stuff straight, that's the pitiful truth of it. And until I do, I think I should shut up. I should just shut up."

It seemed unlikely she'd really do this, but to my surprise—and, I think, hers too—she more or less did. We both stayed where we were for a minute, and then Marianne lifted up a large cushion that was handily on the floor by her chair and put her arms around it and pressed her face into it and after half a minute more she curled, cushion and all, into the farthest-back part of her large floppy chair and stopped moving. I waited for her to move and she didn't. I considered finding a blanket to drape over all of the chair

DOCTOR BLOOM'S STORY ~

and most of her but decided against it. I forget what I did, to be honest. I hung around, though.

Turned out it wasn't quite the end of our day. Late that night, after a walk over to Mount Pleasant and an entirely clear though unspoken agreement not to restart on the given topic until we'd survived the night, what did we do but, you know, restart. I believe the idea was to cheer each other up.

The topic of choice was suffering.

Good choice.

"See, Nik," said Marianne, "that's what all this is about. If you really think about it." We were sitting at the kitchen table. I say this although I don't believe it matters where we were sitting. We'd decided to close the day down with a saucepanful of hot chocolate, and after this had been brought to the almost-boil and decanted into two bowls, we were sitting at the table inhaling the good chocolatey vapours, each from her or his bowl, and it was then that I was given a severalness of quotes on suffering. All of them borrowed by Marianne from her or our new friend. Who had them from a variety of sources starting, I learned, with the Gospels. And all making the point that although our culture has decided that suffering is shameful, is to be avoided, and *can* be avoided if we're both good and lucky—that when it shows itself, it's only a misstep in the predestined march of humanity towards happiness—the Bible's view is different. As different as can be.

"Jesus never said he came to end suffering. Neither did Paul. None of those guys. Did you know this?"

"Uh-uh."

"Me neither. Learn from it, acknowledge it, almost *welcome* it, they all say. Don't say you're fine when you're not. Don't say things are great when you're perishing of sadness. When the neighbour calls on the phone, say, *Well, since you ask, I'm sad, we're all sad over here.* Suffering, sadness, loneliness, it's all part of being human and very likely the *deepest* part. So says Sophie. Quoting, of course. Not saying it as if she owns the tablets. And as for you know who, the dear dead mentor—wait a sec, I tried making sense of it in my journal."

And comes back with it, finding the page en route. "*All those human beings for whom I have made it easy to hurt me through my friendship have done so. When any human being speaks to me without*—I missed getting the next word here, I was scribbling in the damn dark, of course—the word was 'cruelty' or 'violence,' I think—*speaks to me without cruelty, I can't help believing there must be some mistake.* You'll know who that's from. You'll have recognized the fine Provençal hand."

"Doesn't really give the world a passing grade, does she? Simone, I mean. I don't mean Sophie."

"Don't forget, though, that all this comes through Sophie. I have a sneaking suspicion that Simone Weil is, was, a sort of genius of the holy. Must have been, too many people say so. Your friend—not friend but, you know, the novelist, you love her, what's her name—"

"Female novelist? George El—"

"Iris. That one. She says so too. 'Cording to Sophie. Sophie's reading Iris now because you love her, she said. Sophie—well, it seems Sophie likes you and, um, wants to read everything you've ever read. *Everything!* she says.

Good luck, I thought, but I let it pass. I'm not making that up, by the way. I hope you can deal with it."

I said, "Woo." I wasn't trying to be funny. It was my first step in trying to deal with it.

"Only thing is, Sophie's had no help in understanding either Iris or Simone. Sophie takes what she thinks is there, and maybe it is and maybe it isn't. Maybe something else is there instead. There's a condition people like me call ecstatic, or call rapture, nothing to do with a pill by the way, and we call it this without ever catching more than a quick glimpse, an unusable brief sighting, of it—and my guess is that Simone was often inside it and it carried her through those other—you know, through the rest of it. The *stuff*. Stuff she didn't need, stuff she wasn't good at. For Iris, stop me if I'm wrong here, it couldn't have been the same thing, could it? Of course it couldn't. No way. Nik? It couldn't. For Iris it has to have been the, you know, the roads, the series of roads—all those books—towards this condition. Which isn't the same thing. It's different and it probably, my guess is, it probably allows you to live longer. Allows you or forces you. I'm not sure Sophie's got this straight. This difference. This . . . difference. You know?"

"Kind of."

"Yeah. Kind of. Most of us don't get it. All we get from the far side are sights. Glimpses in passing that might show us lots of old stories starting to stir. Old really short stories. Interesting, we say, or think—must remember this, get back to it later, but, oh well, gotta go, we say. Which is only right. Like I said, I don't know enough about it all, this has become very clear to me, to be able to—for me to . . . OK?"

All at once, or possibly not all at once but I just hadn't been observant enough, Marianne was looking tired. That had been a long walk. She looked at me out of her kind, tired face, and said, the abrupt shift in topic making it plain that her mind had suddenly had enough of pretending to be anywhere else but here, "Hitting somebody like her must be like—I mean, what sort of satisfaction can it bring? Huh? Tell me."

And seconds later, taking my two hands in hers and putting her face against my face and whispering directly into one of my two ears, the left one, "I'm sorry, Nik, I'm so sorry. How dare I ask you that?"

"Has our man ever come home when you were at their place with her?"

Damn, I then soliloquized. *Why ask that? Why ask anything? Take her to bed.*

She sat back, not quickly. "Once. It was before— before last night. He came up the stairs very fast, we heard his footsteps, of course, also his breathing. The bedroom door was open and I—I didn't know what to expect. So, hearing him so close, I began talking loudly. I didn't want to surprise him. I also didn't want to hear what I was afraid he'd start shouting at Sophie before he even got to the room. Maybe he wouldn't have, maybe he's subtler than that, OK, who knows. But at the time I was afraid he would. So I was probably almost shouting, and he certainly heard me before he reached the landing. I don't know why, but even after that he waited a minute, easily a full minute, before he came in. It was like—do you know what it was like? It was like a children's game. When you're hiding and everybody knows *where* you're hiding but they pretend they don't know, otherwise the game's over too soon. Obviously we knew he was there. Obviously he knew we knew. We could hear his breathing slowing down, but he wasn't moving. When he came in, it was almost a relief. He came in—how shall I describe it? No, actually it's easy to describe. He came in at normal speed, and smiling."

"Then what? Marianne—" I was trying to hurry this up.

Marianne wasn't ready to hurry. She was tired, all right, but now she was back in that bedroom with Sophie and one other person. "Then nothing. I left."

"Sorry."

Pause. "He introduced himself—no, he asked Sophie to introduce him to me. Smiled at me while he asked her to do the introductions, meaning, *Silly girl doesn't know how civilized grown-ups like you and me behave, does she?* Stretched out his hand to me, too, but, oh Nik, I remembered your story of looking away and I did that too, I just bent away to pick up my bag. So no handshake, no hand-grazing. And then I left."

"Didn't kiss Sophie goodbye?"

"Kissed Sophie goodbye."

"Right on."

Marianne sat staring down into her two hands, one of which looked as if it might be hurting the other one. I was relieved when she looked up. In that moment, for that moment, nothing was clearer than that she had decided not to exclude me from this polar waste she'd talked herself into. *Still wilderness where no one is at home.* I walked over to her and crouched down directly in front of her, and she let me have her two hands again.

Still looking at me she said, "I have nothing left to say, Nik. Isn't that—isn't that terrible? To have nothing left to say?"

How to interrupt nothing? Best not to.

"I mean," she said, "how do you press language out of grief?"

After a while she came out of the polar waste. And the still wilderness. And not long after that we decided to take that week on a warm island.

It wasn't what we had started out thinking we'd do. Last thing, really. Running away hadn't been on our minds.

But how often can you put yourself through . . . well, what does *that* signify, Blomski? Because *you're* not the one who's being "put through" anything, are you?

No I wasn't. Well, I was, a little. But Marianne—that was another story.

A bit of cheerfulness had to break in somewhere.

So off we went. One of us quite a lot less sure that this was the right thing to do than the other was.

"As I write this, the noises in my head are so loud that I am beginning to wonder what is going on in it. They are making it almost impossible for me to obey those who commanded me to write."

If my darling Teresa could stand these noises and still obey those commands, there is no excuse for me! Anyway, I have begun to glimpse patches of light and this is surely a sign that I am going in a good direction. The clearing I must reach may form itself out of those patches of light. They will merge more and more rapidly, defeating the dark, which is such a source of pain and confusion.

He is the puzzling part of this. I know he is a special kind of emissary. The history of these special emissaries is that of persons who do not know what message they carry, or even if they carry any message. Think of Rosencrantz and Guildenstern on the ship bound for England, think of the pilot of the *Enola Gay,* think of the Son of Man. If they did know, their mission would be compromised, they would become self-conscious, frightened of their role and of themselves. They would hurl themselves out of the world and their message would be lost.

Here is his problem. To complete his studies and get the degree he wants, and at the same time not to abandon his role with me. A role which I cannot judge him for, how could I do that? He is in such darkness! For three nights in a row he has ignored me. My body rejoices, my soul is confused.

not read to our group

s.f.

"Normally, this is just not on, Mr. Wewak—have I got your name right? No? Oh, right, I remember now, friend of mine told me. You see, I'd always thought it was your brother's given name, so when you said . . . never mind. Back to the question at hand. It's such a vulnerable situation, you see, to be in a workshop like this. Their short stories are often straight autobiography, so it's delicate. They've become used to one another over the past six months, so the delicacy bit is, you know, it's OK now, problem pretty well gone. But to now have a total stranger present while they read their work—it could worry them. I guess Wew—I guess your brother didn't warn you. I'll have to ask the group. You know, if they wouldn't object to you sitting in. Up to them."

~ 169

"Don't trouble to ask them, Mr. Logan. Simply tell my brother I'll be waiting downstairs until you are finished. And please don't hurry. I bought my weekly paper just before leaving Heathrow, providentially."

"May I ask—no, never mind."

"Please."

"I just—Wewak, I, um, your brother, he's often spoken of you, of course, and he told me that his brother, you, that is, might be coming—but I had no idea that—"

"That I would not show up in a loincloth? Or less! Whacking great appendage tolling the hours?"

"Ha ha. Well, no, of course not, I never—but you see, for one thing, his command of the language isn't, you know, isn't what you'd call—whereas yours—"

"Surely. My brother left Papua too soon. I am fifteen years younger, and by the time I was twenty my contemporaries and I were picking and choosing among scholarships and grants from every state in the U.S. Also from Australia, of course. I was an anomaly, choosing the U.K. Who knows whether that was wise?"

"Great. Great. Really great."

"I'm keeping you, though. Nice to meet, Professor Logan. Happy workshopping!"

"Thanks. And sorry!"

"Really, not to worry. Now that I think of it, my brother warned me that observers were not encouraged. Warned me in our own tongue, which he speaks rather better than I. Perhaps you know of it. Motu? No? Here is a little-known fact, Professor, and one which I guarantee will be of no conceivable use to you. There are 817 variants of Motu spoken in our country, of which my brother mastered eleven during his adolescence. I have always been in awe of him. What I intended to say is that I was entirely prepared to sit outside and wait. Hence my *Statesman*, as you see!"

The worst of it wasn't the state of the court, although that, what with the rain they'd had all week prior to our arrival, was bad enough. Worst was the pro, a portly middle-aged Puerto Rican. He had seemed perfectly likeable before we got on court and, promisingly, was a foot shorter than I am, so everything had augured well—but once out there it was drop-shot lob, drop-shot lob, drop-shot lob until I headed off, no longer running, for the pool.

I knew Marianne wouldn't be interested in hearing about José's tactics or, come to that, the game scores of our two sets. I did mention the state of the court. "Red clay like that soaks up the rain, as you probably know. Just soaks it up. Within minutes I was carrying about a pound of the stuff in the interstices of my Adidas . . ."

"Poor Nico. Come here."

We walked a little, swam up and down the pool, ate crab and lobster and a sluice of their tiny nameless relatives every night, ignored the tours and basically lay on the sun-warmed clamped-together chaises longues on our balcony, reading, for about half the hours of every day. I hadn't intended it to be exactly like this, but with José being no fun, I just imitated the booklady I'd come with. Marianne had brought along her own copy, a gift from Sophie, of the collection of letters and essays called *Waiting for God*, a book of which you may feel you've heard enough by now; and was studying this as part of her project in positioning herself a little closer to wherever Sophie's mind might be guessed to be. I also noticed her riffling the pages of an anthology of essays on Jung by various hands. She was looking for clues, she briefly explained, on "the *Ungeheuer*"—German for "monster," a noun she'd looked up and checked the pronunciation of so that she would have it ready for Maggione should the right occasion ever present itself. Which it never would, she knew, unless and until the *Ungeheuer* was so far removed from his wife as never to be able to come within reach of her again. Marianne hoped that that day would come, she hoped that he would hear this noun that she was carrying like a loaded gun just for him, hoped that he would bend before its fury on that day—but any reference on my part to such a finalizing of accounts was likely to be met with a shrug, a shake of the head, a silence. Even here, behind our beach's high dunes and a thousand miles of tilting ocean, where I'd hoped that both of us, or, failing that, one of us, the needier one, would find her way towards a respite of some kind, no respite seemed near. The unguarded week just beginning for Sophie back there in Toronto was what Marianne couldn't get out of her mind. I wasn't immune from that worry but because Marianne seemed, now and then, so unsettled, so restive (e.g., the pre-breakfast phone call from our Toronto travel agent which I wasn't meant to answer but did, the agent obviously responding to a message from one of us, not me, enquiring about a same-day flight home), I concentrated on behaving in orderly and boring, no problem there, ways. Reassuring ways, as I intended. In this regard the sea did, I think, eventually, begin to play a role, the omnipresent, continuous sea; there began to be times, when silence had fallen and wasn't getting up again, when I thought wave-watching helped.

Those miles-long rollers took, we established—or *I* tried to establish, one very still noon hour—exactly nine seconds to succeed one another in their arrivings-at and passings-by a sailboat anchored way out there, all on its own. Whether the noticing and then the notifying of this sort of statistic was of any real interest or help to either of us I've no idea, but that sailboat's brief spasms of lifting, rocking, resettling, as each wave passed, seem now as secure in my memory as anything else in these pages.

Fending off vertigo was the main aim.

Mostly, though, when things were peaceable, we read, and periodically read aloud *from,* our books, and talked about what we had just read, a series of actions which adds up to, in my view, one of the best things in the world to do. It *is* this, anyhow, if you're with somebody of whom you are really fond and who is in possession of a mind. Both of which things, recurrent anxieties notwithstanding, kept on being the case.

Since my role was as I've described it, it didn't hurt that my book of choice was as remote from anything conscience-harassing or spiritually badgering as could be. What I'd brought was the memoirs of an eighteenth-century English rake named Benjamin Haydon, a boastful and mendacious fellow but really very, as I told Marianne, who seemed doubtful, likeable. As you'll see, there were parts of it one could warm to.

You may not see that but why rule the possibility out.

It was near the end of one of our last afternoons, an afternoon during which we were not, I admit—in spite of a really sweltering heat—using the full breadth of our clamped-tight-together chaises longues, that I came across a sentence in that eighteenth-century memoir which would have left me gloom-ridden if I had read it at almost any other time in the preceding decade of my mostly solitary, dismally so in fact, life. Now, however, it seemed to offer the lightest of yokes, it struck what I couldn't resist feeling was an unusually apposite note. Towards the end of one of many score-keeping paragraphs Benjamin Haydon wrote, "If I did not perpetually struggle against it, I might do nothing else but doze on lovely bosoms."

You will have noticed that my story verges on the prim. Time for one of the white bits.

A few less-frivolous lines also survive from that time.

Handwritten by Marianne and passed to me to read in the plane en route back to Canada: two short sentences from Elias Canetti. Marianne found these while browsing in an island bookshop, and borrowed paper and pen from the bookshop assistant to write them down. I think she must then have forgotten about that small sheet of paper torn by the assistant from a counter-pad and given to her, because flying back to Toronto she found the folded page in a pocket of the long mauve-patterned skirt which she had also been wearing that afternoon on our bookshop walk—and now reread what she had, seated at the shop assistant's desk there, copied out. This was halfway through our flight, and until then we had been as light of heart as at any time during that week. Now, reading the Canetti lines, Marianne became very still. She looked away from me out into the very close-up flowing whiteness of the clouds through which we'd been flying ever since take-off, watched that ragged flypast of whiteness for some while, and then turned back and, with a shrug, handed me the page.

We are never sad enough to improve the world, one of the sentences read. And the other one was, *We are hungry again too soon.*

This seemed very unfair. I knew that the two short sentences were beautiful and that for us they might be too much. I sat there thinking about this. At least I knew what not to do. "I know what you're thinking," I said to Marianne.

"You do?"

"You're thinking you'll not sleep in my house tonight." Her serious profile against the passing clouds. It didn't turn away but not towards me either. Long pause. "But I want you to."

After just a few seconds the profile's time was up. Marianne turned towards me and said, slowly, "You're right. Everything you said. Pretty good thing to say." A small smile. "I guess I want to too." And then, after a few more seconds, "Not just a guess, Nik." Her neat head, its sweet-smelling dark curls, joining up with my bony shoulder.

It was a long time after that that we had the confidence to confess to each other that if there had been one perilous minute in our relationship, a minute where everything might have begun to unravel—might have started heading off towards those Thousand and One Nights, as they're apparently known to people in Marianne's line of work, meaning the reassuring tales, comforting lies, that women and men in myth and legend and the next-door house tell each other late at night in order to win a few more months or years under the same life-deadening roof—this had been it.

Not that I count on that perilous minute never return-ing! But keep it off, you Fates, Gods, and all other potent and secret Night-Drifting Powers, is what I say.

And I say, anything I can do to help . . . you know?

The touchdown at Pearson was the last untroubled experi-ence we were to have for a while. The Tarmac was a rink and the 401 a blur of swirling snow as the cab took us east to the Yonge exit and so home. Marianne phoned her own house, expecting to hear Larry's voice, which is how they'd arranged it, but Clarissa answered and said he'd been gone all weekend. "It's OK, Mommy," she said, "he was going to be here, but at the last minute he had to be with Arlene. Everything's cool."

"Oh, well"—irony totally botching its effort to dis-guise anger— "as long as it's Arlene. What a relief that it's Arlene." And then, "Clary. Who in the name of heaven is— No . . . Would you please ask him to call me when he gets in? As soon as he gets in?" Pause. "Yes, Nik's." Pause. "Where else indeed, Clarissa? It's my favourite place in all the world. Go to bed, dear." Another pause. "OK, I'll see you tomorrow. Unless what's-his-name, sorry, unless Daddy doesn't come at all tonight, in which case I'll—"

Marianne lowered the phone from her ear and stood looking at it. ". . . I'll just shoot him," she finished. Then she turned to me and said, "She hung up. What d'you know?"

I was pretending to unpack, but in the same room. My house has small rooms. Enough of them, but small.

"I oughtn't to have said what I said, ought I," Marianne said.

I knew what she meant. I'd loved hearing it, but she was right, she oughtn't to've. She sat down on the bed for a bit, idly sliding the cordless phone about on the duvet, and then got up and walked swiftly into the hallway and I heard her go downstairs. In addition to having small rooms, this house is narrow, I may never have mentioned that but it is, so there's a good deal of up-or-down-stairs when you leave any room for any other room. Exactly like a *gracht*, canal, house in Amsterdam, only five hundred years newer. I heard Marianne punching in a new set of numbers. I heard her speaking, but quietly enough that that was all I heard.

Then, "What?" This was a different sound altogether. "Where did you say? OK, OK, OK."

Up the stairs, running. "Nik, I'm off. This is it, you know? This is *it*!"

"Was that about——?"

"She's in Sunnybrook. Maybe intensive care, the woman at her place wasn't sure. Cleaning woman, I intuit, doesn't have much English. You want to——?"

"Course."

And we drove off, me trying to keep in mind that I was driving on hard-packed snow instead of sleepy Antiguan cowpath, east to Bayview and north to Sunnybrook and then down into the parking garage, and running across those ill-lit low-ceilinged underground expanses, sometimes hand in hand and sometimes freewheeling, ducking my head which hates these places with their murderous steel girders waiting for any skull that's more than six feet above sea level . . . and so on until we came to where she was. Which was, bless the mark, not Intensive C. She was still in Emerg.

———

So I had a lot of thinking time at my disposal, walking up and down in a corridor close to the ER. I was out in the corridor instead of in the ER because it was obvious that only one of us ought to claim to be Sophie's near kin, and it was equally obvious which of us that should be. After a while I gave up on thinking about Sophie. Marianne was with her and if Marianne's eye and intuition weren't good enough for her, then Sophie was already dead. Which she was not, otherwise Marianne would have come back to say so. As you can tell from the aimless prolixity here, I was close to falling asleep. Being corpse-tired (delayed departure from island, intense wakefulness in plane, iced-up 401 to house, instant departure from house to here in Sunnybrook) my thinking time didn't lead to much, although while I was at it, it interested me. I found an unguarded chair and slumped in it. I moved on from blurry thoughts about Sophie to recalling our run through the underground parking garage, and from that to establishing to my own satisfaction that missiles like those low-flying girders in the parking garage wouldn't be permitted in Holland. Not a chance. Not in Amsterdam, anyway. Half the populace would take to the streets in protest, crying slogans out of mouths located an average 180 to 200 centimetres from the ground. To show you how tall they all are in Amsterdam, let me say that when I'd walk down Kalverstraat on a Saturday evening, my 195 centimetres, a.k.a. 6'5", *might* make me the tallest visible moving object, but it would often *not* make me that, either. The Dutch must be the tallest people in the world. Once I'd realized this, I mean as a very young person of the mentioned height, I was very impressed. Tallest in the world outside of the Masai, that is, and the Masai live on cow's blood straight from an artery, which gives them an unfair advantage. When I first went from Amsterdam to the U.K., then all over again when I came to Toronto, I used to dream about those late Saturday promenades on the Kalverstraat, and more often than was reasonable I would dream of a few minutes in my adolescent life which really did happen and which I know I will never forget, no matter what other good or ill things may befall me. Those few minutes changed my life. Up until those minutes I'd thought my height verged on the grotesque: when would I stop growing, was there some pill I could take, why were all the doorways so low, how could I have been so unlucky, would dumb-ass kids ever stop asking me how the air was up there, who could ever love such a freak—all those thoughts and more. The life-altering scene which I'm about to delineate, a scene which, yes, really happened and which afterwards recurred often and with much intensity in my dreams, daydreams and nightdreams both, always shows the same tall fair-haired girl wheeling her cycle towards me, I wheeling mine towards her, each of us probably fifteen years old but each of us already a mile high, higher than anybody else on Kalverstraat in that particular minute of that particular Saturday afternoon. I was devouring her more or less with my staring as we got closer, and already I'd changed my mind about being too tall, changed it permanently, being tall felt just entirely OK now that I'd seen this stunning apparition—not that she was as tall as I was, she wasn't, which was good, but not far below me either, also good—and then of course I lost my nerve and didn't look directly at her at all as we reached each other and went past each other, so I don't know if she was looking at me or not—and then I went on pushing my cycle for another ten metres or so until, feeling a total dickhead, feeling I was the world champion slaughterer of any chance of future happiness forever and ever, I stopped and turned to look back and, *Jesu,* she had halted too and was standing holding her cycle and looking back too. And what did I do? In the dream I always smile and wave, and so does she, and we both turn and head back towards each other smiling, and there's this landscape of tremendous expectancy coming up like a huge and glorious daybreak, nothing so grand before or since, and I wake up. I wake up because there's a limit to the lies the dream will tolerate and the intolerable truth is that there was no smile or wave, there was just this looking back for a few seconds, both of us standing and looking, before I turned and walked on away from her, happiness-slaughtering at every step.

Going back there the ten next Saturdays at the exact same time but never seeing her again. No shortage of incredibly botched shapes and faces to scowl at on my way along the crowded Kalverstraat—*didn't they get it?*—but never her.

Hello! Where are you, beautiful long-legged fifteen-year-old girl wheeling your cycle so often, all these years, up the Kalverstraat? Again and again and again and again?

Hello! Hello!

"Nik! Nik! Hello? Is that you Nik? Time to go."

". . . What—?"

"We can go. It's OK. Up you get."

On the way home Marianne told me she had cajoled her way into the curtained-off rectangle where Sophie was, and Sophie had been sleeping and so she had sat beside her for a while, listening to her breathing and, Marianne said, conjecturing now frantically and now methodically as to what she would say when Sophie awoke. Later, although pretty well sedated, Sophie had been awake for a half-hour or so. Her murmurs had been both audible and understandable. She was explaining why she was in a hospital bed in an emergency room. At home, at the top of the staircase leading down to the front door, she'd stepped on something, she said, and fallen all the way down. "What was it, Sophie?" "Pardon?" "What was it? That you stepped on?" "Oh . . . a piece of something." "OK. Sure. Go on, please."

So Sophie had gone on. Walter (she never called him Rollo, a story for a more leisurely time) had not been at home. "You see, Marianne? He was not at home."

"Wouldn't you know."

"Wouldn't you—?"

"Sorry. Please go on."

Lying in the entrance hall, she hadn't been able to get up, there was too much pain. The people in the ground-floor flat apparently weren't home. She didn't know how long she had lain there.

"Where was he—your husband—all this time?"

"Well . . . Haven't you seen him?"

"No, Sophie. Hasn't he been with you? I mean—"

"But . . . Marianne. He's here. He must be here still."

"Here?" Looking around suddenly. Was Maggione behind the curtain, listening to all this?

Nobody in sight, thank God. "He's not here, Sophie."

"No. Not . . . not *here* here. There, somewhere. Down . . . at the end? Somewhere in this room." And she retrieved one hand from its hidden place and moved it a very little, though Marianne couldn't divine any direction.

So Marianne got up from her position leaning over Sophie's bed, opened the curtain enough to re-enter the large ceiling-lit room with its five or six curtained-off ER

beds, and walked over to whisper to a nurse who was checking patient charts at a table in the middle of the room.

The nurse whispered back and pointed, and Marianne,
"heart in mouth," as she said when she was telling me all
this, walked as quietly as she could to a corner cell and
twitched the curtain enough to have a peek.

"And there he was, Nik. Lying on his back with his eyes
wide open. Staring at the ceiling. Hooked up, IVs, etc.
Monitor blipping away. Spiking away. I wanted to look at
the spikes—heck, I wanted the spikes to flatten right out, a
trace-line without a tremor is what I wanted to see. I didn't
watch him long, be assured. Twitch of the curtain, then
twitch again, I was gone. I'm certain he didn't know anybody was there, let alone meddlesome hateful me."

"Christ, Marianne—you know what this sounds like,
don't you."

"Not really. But you probably would have known. So
tell me. I promise not to think it's showing off."

"On second thought, forget it."

"Oh, but I want to—"

"No, I mean it. I was going to diagnose myocardial
infarction, a.k.a. heart attack. But based on what? Based on
a twitching curtain. Not exactly an infallible test. Which is
why you should forget it."

"Him, of course? The heart attack? Not her."

"Him."

"Well, come to think of it, the nurse said something
like that. She didn't actually say—"

"No no, she wouldn't. Well—but—he fell down the
stairs too? I don't think so."

We were both thinking uncomplicated thoughts.

——

Saskia was in my dream that night. I think Sophie was there too. Not sure about Marianne. Physically, Marianne was not in my bed, she had gone home. "So much awfulness around," she'd said, "and none of it in your house, and— and Nik, I keep on finding this dumb smile on my inward-directed face when I think of us, and do I deserve it, no, and—and I remember that line about never being sad enough to, you know, whatever. To improve things. God, as if there's any sign of me improving anything." And so she phoned to tell Clarissa and Martin she was coming to collect them, whether Larry came back or not. She needed to have them with her, she acknowledged before driving off, because of this "malaise, I suppose. Know any stronger French words, Nik?" She looked pale and tired. She'd be seeing Sophie in the morning, she said, and if I were to come along, we could have a bagel and coffee together in the hospital cafeteria.

That's if either of us thought we could manage food, she said.

Though it might be easier than improving the world, she said.

As for Saskia being in the dream, some news came with her. I think of Saskia about once a day, but the news I awoke into was that almost all of those thoughts had been counterfeit, perfunctory. What I'd glimpsed in the dream showed me that I'd been "thinking" the same images, rerunning the same scenes so often in my mind that they'd lost whatever edge and awkwardness and possibility-for-surprise they'd surely once had. Ragged imagery-wisps from the dream persisted into my wakening; they showed me our two silhouettes in known rooms in Amsterdam and, even more, in Cambridge, everything safely familiar for the first few seconds, until, stepping to one side or the other in order to see around those silhouettes, I saw . . . other things.

A kind of clarification, I knew it to be. Scenes from a marriage near its end. Plus one more scene, more nearly final than those. Saskia roaming the tidy rooms of a house she was too much alone in. Schoolchildren going by, always their voices and calls, every morning and every late afternoon, reminding. Saskia looking for the chair she would sit down in to write that economical last note, deciding where to keep that note for the next day or several days and then deciding where, when the right day was come, she would put it—into which discreet inevitable place it would go, a place I would not see too soon but would see before anyone else would see it. Her face, hunting around for these things, chair, first hiding-place, last inevitable place, was a face I hardly knew. Concentrated, drawn, older than any face I'd assigned to her in all these years of daily thoughts about her. I wanted to interrupt that face, remind it of things, but I knew that whatever came would come from too far back, it wouldn't be about either of us as we were now or as we'd been for a long while. After that I knew I had nothing to say that could stave off the darkness that must, or so I imagined, be racing towards this face I was now seeing, rushing upon it like an eclipse racing over the fields, cancelling everything, bringing black night to everything, closing off what she was, as she would have been realizing—realizing with a unique amazement, a totally new sense of the kaleidoscope of her life—about to be all done with, *finished with,* obliterating even the final half-motion of her mind, the half-formed last thought that perhaps, as the massive dark reached her, had just started to seem precious.

I found myself straining forward anyway, in case there was something I could change...

Ik heb nergens zin meer in.
Oh, right.

Hard to restart anything after that. Conversations, or anything.

As for Sophie being in the dream, she seemed all right in there. There seemed to be nothing that needed my attention, not for the moment.

I didn't have to take that as a good sign.
I didn't take it as any kind of sign at all.

Larry stayed over in Orangeville that night, apparently phoning about midnight to find out if Marianne had indeed come back when she'd said she would. He didn't actually stay in Orangeville, I learned later, but in a motel outside a nearby village called Palgrave. It turned out he had given a reading from his soon-to-be-published latest novel in Barrie the week before, and the convenor was a woman who'd read every one of his books and had brought them all along to the reading for his signature. That latest novel, by the way, you may have read it, is called *A Door in the River*. It's the one about a Canadian architect who misuses his early fame and drops out in Italy and—well, never mind, if you haven't read it, you've read something close. After Larry's reading most of the audience had gone to the convenor's house for coffee and sandwiches. Very well-read woman, the convenor, Larry told me. She and he had decided to continue their talk a couple of days later over dinner in a country restaurant which the woman thought was outstanding for that region, in Nobleton, which was where Larry had been when Marianne had tried to phone him that night. By the time Marianne called, he wasn't actually in Nobleton any more, he was in the motel outside Palgrave. It had probably been a mistake on his part, he said, both the dinner and the motel, because Arlene had found out he wasn't at home that night as she had thought he would be. Clarissa had in fact been wrong to tell Marianne that Larry had been with Arlene. Arlene had also assumed that when he left his home that night it would be to meet her, later on, in a bistro on Queen West they were both fond of, and at one point he had intended to do that, but it hadn't panned out, he said. What had panned out had been that dinner in Nobleton. And whatever had gone on just outside Palgrave. I found this Baedeker of north-of-Toronto towns and villages confusing but not really worth sorting out. At that point Larry was very low on my sorting-out list.

———

So we met in the Sunnybrook cafeteria for breakfast. It was 7 A.M., and with two exceptions everyone present was in some kind of hospital livery and looked much more hopeful about what would happen later on in the day than did the excepted two. I had more energy now than I'd had the night before, though, and after clearing this with Marianne, I o'erleapt the kinship business and used my hospital accreditation to go in to see Sophie with her.

Sophie was still in Emergency. The in-charge nurse told us she didn't need to be there, it was just that they had failed to find a room for her so far, but there ought to be a room before noon. I hope, the nurse said.

Sophie was not exactly sitting up but was tilted upwards. She smiled at us when we came in. Her face was pale but unmarked. Her hair was even tighter to her head than usual. (She looked like that Irish singer, can't think of her name, the one who kept on cutting her hair off, always doing her best to stop being beautiful. Always failing.)

She looked seventeen. Half her real age.

(*Sinead* something.)

"You are up so early," she said.

"And you—you are only a little up," Marianne said. Her voice was so steady and even that only a fool could have been fooled into thinking she was calm.

I said, "Hi, Sophie. Been thinking of you. Marianne's told me—you know—" My voice was neither steady nor even. Stupid voice, really.

"Have you been meeting? The workshop?"

I'd been hearing so much about her from Marianne that I'd forgotten that my own connections with Sophie were still almost entirely workshop. So her question, though natural, was unexpected.

"Yes. Well, *they* have. Been meeting, I mean. I've been away, as you know. I'm sure they've been meeting, though. Yes. They've been meeting, no doubt about it." I couldn't stop. "I'm sure they've been having a good time. Larry was away a few days, but, let's see, no, he wouldn't have been away the Thursday, so—so they'd have had their session all right. I'm sure they did."

They were both looking at me now. Patiently. Sophie with her hanging-in-there smile, Marianne still wearing her steady/even face.

"They probably missed us both," I added. I nodded a few times, corroborating the probability.

A short silence ensued. I was trying to stop myself from asking if she would like a newspaper, which, I would then say, I would happily get for her. I could then expand on that by mentioning that I had noticed, and made a mental note about, a *Globe and Mail* box not more than three miles down the corridor, which I could lope to in an hour or so.

There was, however, a limit to this behaviour, and by then I had reached it.

"Sophie," I said. "Sophie. I think I may never have spoken your name before. To you, that is. Just to Marianne. But now," I said, "I would like, if it's all right, to say—oh, a couple of things to you. If that's all right. Sophie."

I stole, as they say, a glance at Marianne. She seemed to be OK'ing whatever I might say next. I'd had a quick look at the attending doctor's chart at the foot of the bed, so I knew more than I was letting on; for instance I now knew that doctor's name, so if I chose to I could ask for a consult, but I just wanted to go on for a bit. Make myself faintly known.

"You know I'm a doctor." A nod. Might have been an anxious nod, I couldn't assess that, didn't know her well enough. "I'm not your doctor, though, and I'll not cross any lines. But if you felt able to tell me—or, you know, depending who your doctor is, if I know him—"

"Or her." No prize for guessing who said that.

"Yes. Well." I took a break.

"Excuse me a minute. I'll be back." The plastic curtain whispered as Marianne went out. Marianne hates it when she catches herself being didactic. It's possible that I grow fonder of her every time I catch her catching herself.

"I am grateful, Dr. Bloom. I have bruising in the kidney area, they have told me. And bruising, also, beneath the ribs on my left side. A little pain. They are taking X-rays of these—parts—this morning, but they do not think this will show anything."

"Could you call me Nicolaas? Or Nik. Marianne calls me Nik."

"Nicolaas. What a beautiful name. Yes, I will call you Nicolaas."

What a soft voice. What a me-seeking light in her eyes, even though her head could scarcely lift off its pillows. Business, Nicolaas. "May I know your doctor's name?"

"Mark."

"Mark—?"

"Oh, I don't know his other name. Surname. I am to call him Mark."

"Don't know him. Sophie—Marianne cares for you more than she cares for almost anyone. Her two children, no one else."

"You, I think, Nicolaas."

"Marianne, and I too, think you have been hurt quite a lot. You fall down, well, sometimes. We ask ourselves, how can we help Sophie with these things?"

The plastic curtain whispered.

"Oh Marianne. I am so glad to learn to know Nicolaas." She tried to sit up, and let herself slip down again. Neck pain, back pain? Rib pain? But I'd said about enough now. I had a clear impression that this had been a not-bad first meeting but that I should soon leave these two women alone together. Right now, why not.

"Goodbye, Sophie," I said. But then I couldn't leave off after all. "A social worker," I said, "can also advise you about all this. Can help you prevent some of these injuries. They are familiar with such things. If you like, I will arrange for someone to visit you. And if the social worker thinks it a good idea, then an officer, a woman police officer, you know, they could send one in. She could call on you here. Soon. Any time. This afternoon, if you like."

It was as if all the lights in a luminous room were flickering out in sequence. The eyes died last. Sophie's mouth opened and shut again. She again tried, as unsuccessfully as before, to raise her head. Failing, she turned it slightly to one side, away from me. An indecipherable sound came from her.

"Marianne—" she then murmured. A hand waved weakly and returned under the white sheet.

Marianne shook her head, either at me or out of a more general despair. I said a goodbye which no one acknowledged, and was back in the corridor.

Two hours later we were heading for Marianne's office, me driving. Marianne had stayed most of those two hours with Sophie while I had done nothing at all in a variety of corridors; and alone with Marianne, Sophie had, not always audibly, talked.

An edited version of that talk:

Yes, she had told a lie. She had *not* fallen down any staircase. Two things, however, she wished to add. Walter was not to be blamed, and she would never leave him.

Marianne to me: "I felt as if she were my patient. Easy to feel so, because I've been there before. Any family counsellor, mind-dabbler under whatever rubric, gets to hear the direst things when spousal abuse is what's on the table. I mean, no piece of fiction takes *dire* any further than . . . Anyway, Dear Abby told her it was OK, Abby would understand, just go on."

And Sophie had gone on.

M. to me: "Variations on a theme, Nik. The musical tinklings of Sophie of Küsnacht. Today for our listening pleasure the distinguished Swiss masochist presents her signature work, entitled, as who doesn't know it by now, *SUFFERING, a Tone Poem*—"

The stage setting: Marianne sitting on a fold-up metal chair and saying not much, Sophie pausing often to locate a less familiar, fresher-feeling position on the tilted bed, meanwhile talking at times disjointedly, at times ingenuously, the fluctuatingly audible, windblown voice. "I was ready to go home, let her sleep. I mean, come on. She'd endured the one-sided bout, she'd survived—look, here she was, still alive!—but let her now breathe some unthreatening air for a bit, OK? That's what I was advising myself. But here's the thing. Mark came in. You know Mark? You don't, do you. Edson, Mark Edson. Young guy. Doctor on call. Said he was going to do something about the pain but he didn't want her to go to sleep just yet, needed to have her awake so he could talk with her, so he could get a few things straight. Said there were aspects of her situation he was legally, not to mention morally, bound to get straight. Said he had stuff to do elsewhere first but I'd do him a favour if I'd stay and keep her awake. Gave her a pill. Not a sedative, he said. A bit the reverse, he said. Said he'd be back in an hour, hour and a half maybe, and she'd be talking her little head off."

"Oh boy."

"You bet. Well, it didn't seem the right time to set him straight on little heads. Anyhow—"

Anyhow, and all credit to the young doctor's little pill, within minutes of its ingestion Sophie had cut loose.

Me to M.: "Cut loose? Sophie?"

M. to me: "Well, yes. Unlikely, I agree. I heard more sheer *words* in the next ten or so minutes than I'd heard from her ever. *Ever.* And here's the original bit, Nik. Original, what am I saying? Surely not original. Nevertheless, for me, interesting. Just when I was thinking that this young woman, in spite of being one of the people I love best in all the world, was beginning to sound like just another wannabe penitent, Teresa-yearner, martyrdom-huntress—just when I was beginning to, oh, back off a little, modify certain thoughts and get back on track into my own life—well, right about then, what do you suppose she says?"

Sophie to M. (not a verbatim transcript for a while here, more a spasmodic précis): "People who—I don't know if I am one of these people, Marianne, but—people who feel they have a task, who believe that there is a journey to be taken and that somehow here they are, they are the ones, they are on this journey . . . Marianne?"

M. to S.: "Yes, Sophie. *Ich bin hier.*"*

S. to M. (small giggle) *"Gut dass du da bist.*† Well then, everything I know about this—everything I have read—tells me that there is a Single Path. And it tells me that this Path, which is single, is also a path to be travelled singly. Whatever it is that you experience on the way, from which understanding may come—it must be *unbemerkt.* If it is not *unbemerkt* it may be spoiled. Its purity may be lost."

"Unbemarked?"

"*Unbemerkt.* It's like 'unnoticed.'"

"Unremarked. OK, sorry, go on."

(M. to me: "She seemed quite willing to continue without further input from me. No interlocutor needed, thanks. That little pill she'd swallowed was chugging away in her bloodstream very nicely.")

". . . So what I must do about this, this singleness, this aloneness, which the books I am reading tell me I must cling to—" (distractedly, suddenly)—"Oh, Marianne! If you say you are all right, or fine, they just think you are being brave. And if sometimes you *know,* however, that you are *not* fine—no, no, that's not what I want to say. What was I saying—?"

"Unbemerkt."

"Teresa writes that if a pure stream changes into a torrent, then it becomes something less, the purity is lost. It does not become more, in spite of its larger noise and its volume of water. It becomes less."

"OK . . . ?"

"To bring other people into this *unbemerkt* thing that is happening—this is what Nicolaas said we must do, Marianne,

---

* I am here.

† Good that you are there.

remember? Nicolaas said we must ask other people, whom I have not met, whom I cannot trust to understand what is happening to me . . . Who did Nicolaas say must be brought in? *Die Polizei?* Whatever it is that I, however unworthy, am now a part of, if it is to find its way towards me or I my way towards it, it must be done quietly, on its own. I must not permit, I cannot allow, other people to come into this, to enter into it and join it. If I do, they will surely—"

"But Sophie, Nik only wants—"

"They are the torrent, you see."

M. to me:

"I remember her mentioning his name, *Walter,* she always calls him Walter, and saying, *Even if he is my only real task, as I more and more believe he may be*—and then suddenly calling out, 'Ah, but I don't know anything. I don't know *anything!*" And looking so puzzled! So that I felt like taking her in my arms, Nik, a child, she seemed, a little girl who happens to be taller than me and who was suddenly realizing how far away she was from anything she really understood. But then she shifted ground on me."

S. to M. (quietly): "If only some *Klarheit* could come. If some clarity would come into this. And into his mind. Not so that we could be closer together, I have realized that this may not ever be. But so that God could smile."

"Dear Sophie."

"This is what Simone Weil did. That book you borrowed, you know?"

"Of course I know, dear. I did read it!"

"Did you love it?"

"Well, I . . . I think I may have. Parts."

"Marianne, if you love that book, I should have said nothing all this time. Just to name it would have been better.

DOCTOR BLOOM'S STORY ~

To call out its title. At great, great length this morning
I have managed to say nothing of—of similar worth. You
know? Nothing."

Demurrals from Marianne.

"But you see, this is why Simone behaved as she did.
In the factory. The Renault factory where she had a job.
Working and then talking quietly to those who worked
near her. And not wishing to be known beyond them. Not
wishing to have anyone else listening. Not giving
speeches. Do you remember what she says? How she
reminds us that when the Bible says, *Where two or three are
gathered together in My name, there am I in the midst of
them*, it really *means* this? It doesn't just mean 'people.'
'Two or three' does not stand in for 'many.' It means *only*
two or three. You know?"

"Well, yes, although I thought—you know, I always
thought . . ."

Sophie waited. "The two or three—so you really think
that was intended literally?"

"I think Simone lived as she did so that what she would
know and what she would say would be the pure water, and
not the torrent."

". . . Was Simone a saint?"

"Oh . . ."

"Because she's not called a saint, is she? Though I suppose that could still come. That could still be in the works."

"I don't know these things, Marianne."

"Course not."

"I think there are saints. But to be *called* a saint . . . even
Teresa never called herself a saint. Others did that. And
Simone not either. It's no one's fault if he is called so."

"Or she. Course not."

"If there is a saint, good. Let him be so. What occurs has its own *Klarheit*. Clearness. If nothing else is present then it is accepted."

"Who accepts it, Sophie? God again?"

"What a stupid thing I have said. If nothing interferes, then it *may* be accepted. It is like—well, I know Mr. Logan understands about this."

"Who's—? Larry? *Larry?*"

"Oh Marianne. I forgot, I forgot. How stupid, I forgot that he was—"

"Sophie, omit 'stupid,' please. I was just surprised that you might think that Larry—I mean, Larry's as little involved in certain sorts of metaphysical or spiritual states of mind as anybody I . . ."

Long pause. Until Sophie said, "I was thinking of poetry. Of literature."

Marianne looking at her. Getting ready to be knocked sideways by this person's unguessable next sentence.

"Mr. Logan always says, when you have a good image, a good phrase, keep it as bare as you can. You know, Marianne, how he says that? It's like a tree, or even just a stick, that you've put on your page. You have written this word on your page, he says, you have presented this stick, but now you have to keep the underground—that's not right—that's not the word he said—you have to keep other things away. Keep other words off."

"Underbrush?"

"Underbrush! Underbrush. Stupid girl."

" . . . !"

"Yes, sorry, OK. But now you understand? A word may not wish to be mixed in with another word. It may require to be alone. It may require its aloneness, in order that it may be—may be purely seen. May be of the most use possible. Inside the sentence. Inside the poem. The purest use."

So it went during those two hours.

"I hate saints, Nik, always have. I know I love Sophie, I quite intensely love her. The generosity of her thoughts and, oh, more than that. Possibly, you know, possibly something that's noble is trying to work itself out there. Odd old word, isn't it. Noble. And yet I'm almost sure of it. It might still lead me to, who knows, the sunlit heights of myself—what a revolting way of putting it. But I don't love *this*. Also, I can't love Simone Weil. I find Simone Weil admirable and profound and uniquely fucked up, all at the same time. I mean, her humility is every bit as marvellous as her arrogance, and she does, OK, write mesmerizingly about the value of paying attention, of *waiting*—she *was* brilliant, Nik, and her life is as moving as can be, and in spite of the title they gave her little book when she was too dead to object, it's clear that you don't just *wait* 'for God'—she knows very well that if you're a writer, for instance, then what you must 'wait' for is your next line. And she did get to talk to God and all, she says she did and therefore she did, I do believe her. I don't believe in God but I do believe she talked to Him. Or to Her. Or to some other pronoun nobody's ever heard of. Yes, that'd be it. But her bourgeois parents, you know, her poor bourgeois parents had to keep on rescuing her from her shiny deeds in the sinful world, did you know that? And I think about them, those two harmless, apparently well-meaning, apparently loving people, year after year, coping with their strange daughter's pleurisy and her self-imposed malnutrition, which last, by the way, coincides pretty interestingly with some of her major God-talks. Which makes good medical sense, as who knows better than you. And there's also, I suspect, a good deal of personal incompetence on file somewhere here, people like Simone are often not the sharpest when it comes to life's tedious little tasks. For instance, she burnt herself so badly with cooking oil when she was in Spain trying to help the Loyalists during the Civil War that her parents had to hop into the family Citroën and go looking for her and eventually find her and bring her home. Burns and all. So I think that, you know, if there's any saintliness to be found in that neck of the *bois,* maybe it's with them, that bourgeois couple who just hung in. And what does 'saint' mean, anyway? In any context that boring old me takes her breath in? I have no problem admiring the usual stuff, the self-denial, the striving, or, which applies to Simone, the sheer blazing fire-in-the-mind, I mean they're trying a special route, aren't they, saints, they're not content to be just like the rest of us, eating and screwing and sleeping and mildly trying to be good. But I think—I think life has to be, what, *acknowledged,* you know? I mean, consider the lilies of the field—no, don't, but consider the uncelebrated millions who live far off the main roads and do whatever they do but who don't prate about it and who above all don't *write* about it. Them I praise almost to the heavens.

"My rant," Marianne said, "is done."

I was awake most of that night. Not unusual for me, hence not worth recording except for this one difference—my mind was tracking over high-up and never-visited terrains for hours and hours instead of, as is its wont, trying to abandon its place inside my head and fade into the forest dim. My mind was busying itself with our late talk, was keeping an eye open for passing or pausing saints, was reflecting on exemplary acts, at one stage was briefly considering Sophies and Mariannes as archetypes of humanity—in short, my mind was distinguishing itself even beyond its usual pre-dawn anarchy. Out of this babel there emerged at some point what has for a long while now been, for me, a kind of proven schematic method for coping with dishevelled or rumpled thoughts about others and myself—known and unknown others and selves. I'm not sure you'll find my schemata useful but it'll be quick. It involves dividing us all into two standard sorts of beings, two types, hence it is, yes, simplistic, but it's the sort of cartoon view which has always attracted O'Blomov. The types have names. The first are hedgehogs and the second, foxes. Most of that night I spent trying to remind myself of everything I had ever known about these pseudo-heraldic animals, doing this because I knew that when morning came I would be explaining it all to Marianne, who just now was so confidingly asleep beside me. Hedgehogs, foxes. I'd known them well once. Now, merging them into last night's talk, I was deciding that they were very like saints and non-saints—non-saints, for purposes of this debate, being run-of-the-mill neighbourly folks, the sort of persons who, glimpsed now and then jokily aproned beside their patio barbecues, do not immediately strike you as quest-oriented or grace-seeking. In this duality, "the fox" (in case you don't know this, and just patter on by if you do) "knows many things, but the hedgehog knows just one big thing."

Original script by a Greek poet named Archilochus, but I'd met it in a book about Tolstoy by Isaiah Berlin, the Oxford all-rounder. Isaiah Berlin widened the cartoon's usefulness by complicating it—Tolstoy, he declared, was a fox who believed in being a hedgehog. Which, when I was in my twenties and first read this, was to the prancing young igno-ramus Blom an irresistibly seductive thought. Of course, I at once knew, this is how I have always felt! Not about Tolstoy, about whom I had superbly few thoughts, but about myself. I too, I knew right away, was a fox—and I too longed to be a hedgehog. I had never known this about myself before, but it was wonderful learning it now. Rather Pascal than—let's see, whom did I resemble?—of course, Albert Camus. Rather Dante than Shakespeare—a couple of averagely good names there, Bloom. Rather Cruijff than the entire varied rest of the Ajax *elfta** (finally, something I was an authority on).

Starry comparisons, and I felt myself to be somewhere among them. As the first patches of pre-dawn undarkness were littering our bed and Marianne was showing her eyes just above the top of the duvet, I observed to her that since what she had said just before going to sleep was—wasn't it?—that she "hated" saints, this must therefore mean that she wasn't really, really enthusiastic about hedgehogs. There followed a pause and then Marianne murmured, "I thought you just said the word 'hedgehogs.'" A brief run-down of what you have just read regarding Archilochus's two animals ensued. Dear Marianne attended to this run-down without complaint, to be honest without any word at all, her eyes still barely visible above the duvet, those eyes

* eleven (as in "the eleven" of a football/soccer team)

closing sometimes for a few seconds but always, out of her deep courtesy, opening again. It might be true, she eventually, haltingly, said, that she did not feel comfortable with hedgehogs. Was she feeling comfortable at all, I had the sense to ask. She was getting there, she replied, although it was pretty early, wasn't it? She then said that hedgehogs and saints, hmm, well, yes, probably they *were* one, a unity—in fact, yes, no problem with that, they definitely seemed to be what I'd said they were. I wasn't saying that *all* hedgehogs were saints, though, was I? No, I'd never said that. But all saints were—? Yes, they were all hedgehogs.

She had a point to make here, however, Marianne said. She would never be able to live with a hedgehog. She was glad I was not one. Even if I had once, as I had said, longed to be one. She hoped this wouldn't hurt my feelings. If it did, well, she might not be thinking clearly yet, she said. It was still pretty early, wasn't it?

All the same, she said, those hedgehogs—I often admire the hell out of them. And shrugged. I could see the shrug, even under the duvet. I shrugged too. So, two shrugs.

Two days later, thanks to a former student of hers now attached to the psychotherapy unit at Sunnybrook, Marianne read a copy of the report on that Tuesday night arrival at the Sunnybrook emergency unit of both members of the Maggione/Führ family. The event had become a briefly celebrated *cause* in the hospital's emergency unit because of its rarity—a husband and wife with radically differing injuries (not, e.g., joint smoke-inhalation or car-crash victims) both entering Emerg at the same time.

According to the report, the wife had been the one to call 911, although once arrived at the entrance "patient could barely speak." The report noted that she was injected with 75 mg of Demerol, put into an ER bed behind a curtain, and had slept. Indicated follow-up schedule: continued Demerol, X-rays, abdominal ultrasound, blood work, interview. The final comment: "Visit from social worker strongly indicated."

The husband, whom the paramedics on arrival at his home had found to be "ashen, sweating, moving his right hand erratically about on his chest, belly . . . ," was, by the time he reached the ER, protesting against the need for any treatment at all. Somebody had written "query angina" on his sheet, but by the time an ECG was taken, there was no indication of this. He had spent the night on a heart monitor, and the following morning, after blood work showed normal, he had been permitted to leave.

The only further comment on the report sheet was that before leaving hospital, this patient had demanded to see his wife. He would not, he had said, "abandon" her here. Why should she not leave with him, he had asked, no one knew better than he what must be done for her. But since the wife had been asleep and was scheduled for a series of appointments later that day—since, also, there was that concern regarding the nature and the extent and the source of her injuries—the demand had been denied.

All this was interesting. Those worried hand movements, the pale face, the sweating—knowing what I knew of the events that had led up to this episode and these symptoms, the odds were that Maggione had had an incipient angina attack. To the on-duty people in the ER, however, enough time having elapsed between attack and examina-

tion for the patient's heart rate to first quieten and subse-
quently re-establish itself, no such diagnosis had been obvious. So there was no angina notification on his record.

Why go into all this? The fact that I knew more about it
than I was telling anybody just seemed worth mentioning.

Like an unsmiling child proud of a clandestine triumph:
"I told her I had fallen in my frenzied—frenzied, yes?—
running downstairs to ask the people for help for Walter's
frightening collapse. Marianne, *yes*, I did. She said she suspected my injuries were—that there had been previous
injuries. She said she must report this. I said not. She should
not report what no one had complained of, I said. She told
me she would find the medical records. Somewhere there
must exist records of previous hospital visits, she said.
However, it would save us both time if I would tell her, she
said. But I suppose, Marianne, that no records were found,
for she didn't come back. And how *could* they have been
found, since no such things have happened?"

"This is me, Sophie. *Me*. Remember?"

"I meant that no *hospital* had . . . happened. Not here.
Not one."

"And in Zürich?"

"I write a lot and take a lot of time over it. I've ordered the
doctor's sign taken down for the time being."

He was only twenty-six years old when he wrote this to
one of those young women who hung around the edges of

his life and whom everybody called his *antonovkas*. And here I was, as good as sixty, or as bad, also wanting to write, and my doctor's sign was still creaking in the wind. So what was going on here? The answer was, something was going on, but it wasn't writing.

Oh, come on, O'Bloomov, how about all those prescriptions?

There were plenty of differences between Chekhov and Bloom, and aside from the obvious one, our ages—we all know there's another one too—aside, also, from the fact that even at that stage of his life there were a dozen or more of those amorous *antonovkas*, some beautiful, some wealthy, a few both, all fainting with ecstasy whenever they received one of his typically unsentimental, even dismissive postcards—

—While *Nota Bene*, as my eighth-grade teacher once called out, intending thereby to summon me to the front of the room to be handed back a class assignment (too subtle a summons for Nicolaas Blom, that *N.B.*, I was still staring blankly about when he resignedly Frisbee'd my assignment down the row of desks to land dead centre on mine), had no groupies at all—

(How A.C. would have enjoyed that description of his devotees!)

—Aside from these considerations, it may have been true that in just this year of my life, the one you're reading about, I was happier about some things than Anton ever was about anything—

—*Except, obviously, in those moments when he could see a perfect thing appearing beneath the nib as his hand moved his pen*—

—*I can hardly imagine how that must have felt! Anton's*

*"perfect things" being of a different order than almost anybody
else's perfect things ever have been, those moments must have
felt—must have felt—*

—Ah, how must they have felt!—

—Pretty good.

(I am sorely tempted to list several of those moments
for you; what a leap in my mind's pleasure level it always is
to remind myself of them! I'll list only one—in addition,
that is, to those already mentioned antelopes running
through the woods. Near the beginning of *The Three
Sisters*, when the long-absent Vershinin has just entered the
living room of the sisters' home, Masha, who remembers
him from years before, when she was a little girl, cries out,
"You have grown older! (Through her tears) You have
grown older!"

How my world grows still when I read and, reading, see
and hear that scene!—when I watch Vershinin as he hears
Masha say this and in the same instant sees himself through
her eyes and remembers her as a little girl and remembers,
too, himself as the young lieutenant she is now remembering. I watch Vershinin who, now paunchy and, in his own
eyes, morally damaged and aware of everything, is standing
still and saying not a word. It is a holy moment in art.)

Who would have believed that a day like this would come?
On this day a man who in my imagination was still sweating from beating his wife savagely enough to hospitalize
her, and who routinely, no imagination required here, paid
for the privilege of misusing other women, was en route to
our clinic and, within our clinic, to my consulting room.

Yes, he'd been here before, but I had known less about him then. Now I knew more, or thought I did. Out of all the many cubicles available to patients here, our labyrinth of miniature destinations, he was on his way to *mine*. I could have forestalled this, of course, people in my profession have buffer systems in place. I could have instructed my receptionist to tell him . . . something or other. Go away. Off limits to brutes. Fuck off.

Endless variants, obviously. At the very least I could have readied myself for this approaching unpleasantness by following Chamfort's advice, my favourite among the many entries in his much-thumbed *Maximes et Pensées*: "It is best to start every morning by eating a live toad, following which nothing more disgusting can happen to you that day."

But I let Maggione come.

A mere week after his collapse, he seemed in every respect normal. Colour, abrupt movements, confident smile, all was in place. "Doctor! How good of you to see me. Such dedication. But we patients expect it of you. We know how *privilegiert* we are."

I'd thought I was prepared for him, but apparently not. I looked at him and could not speak.

I nodded instead. I told him I had had a report from the Sunnybrook ER. Not true, I'd had it from Marianne. "A Dr. Edson. He makes various suggestions as to what is to be done. But first tell me how you feel."

"Free of symptoms, if I may put it so. A great deal was made of a very small event. However, I felt it necessary to visit you. That Doctor—how is he called?"

"Edson."

"Yes. That Edson. May I ask—he is not a close colleague of yours?" My shrug meant *I've no thoughts on this,* but he took it differently. "Ah, *bene*. I must say I felt he was excessive in his diagnosis, and impatient also. You know, Doctor, I have no clinical understanding of the condition in which I, so *poco tempo fa*, so little time ago, found myself— nevertheless I know when I am being treated inconsiderately. This Edson! I am after all a person of—my accomplishments may appear minor to the ignorant, but . . . however much the female underlings in that emergency room conspire to make him feel powerful, he should not feel superior to me, his patient. Doctor? You say nothing."

"Dr. Maggione, please understand that I can have nothing to say about anyone in the Sunnybrook ER."

"Nothing to say?" He shook his head slowly, staring at me. "I lie before him on my stretcher bed and he treats me with—he shows me no respect. He looks away during my explanations. He taps with his pencil. He does not respond to my questions."

"He was probably overworked. It was very late." Or he may have had another reason, I then thought. Would I mention it? I would. "I believe this doctor also saw your wife that night?"

He stared at me for ten, eleven seconds. His lower lip tightened. We had had a moment not unlike this before, he and I, in this office. I'd been, that time, aware that the moment might turn unpleasant, even violent. This time I thought only of a bedroom in his house, and of a woman who, that night, with no one to hear but him, had surely cried out there. How often might she have cried out?

I forced the sound away.

"I must tell you, you may have had a heart attack. May not, but may. Extensive tests are needed. This afternoon, if they can fit you in, otherwise tomorrow. Blood tests, a

series of them, another ECG, a stress test. It won't be a
repeat of the one you've had. I'll speak to my nurse about
it. Meantime, your shirt, please."

Still staring, he began unbuttoning his shirt. "ECG. But
you have done this. And I had such a test at Sunnybrook.
That fool of an Edson ordered it—"

"The fool of a Bloom is now reordering it. Deep breath."

Nothing new.

"On second thought—since you think things were not
well done at the hospital, I will do these tests myself. Right
now, if you can stay."

"*Sehr liebenswurdig.*"*

I went out, checked the treadmill, which was free, asked
to have the electrocardiograph machine wheeled in, surprised Auriele by telling her I would handle both these
myself, and drank two plastic cornets of very cold water.

Drinking the cold water, I was aware that this was still
feeling interesting. Unpleasant but interesting.

What made it interesting was the realization that if the
clinic with its many consulting rooms was, indeed, a kind of
labyrinth, then I was not your usual adventurer making his
way towards its centre—towards whatever impatient creature the adventurer might find waiting there.

I was at its centre. *I* was what was waiting.

Giorgio was chief organizer in the campaign to save
Larry's job. Not the job itself, that was safe, Larry had
tenure. It was his position as director of the creative writing

---

* Very kind.

workshop that needed saving. In a way it was no surprise that Giorgio had assumed this role. He was simply moving on from his position as number one pest in the workshop to the same digit pest in the eyes of the university *nomenklatura*.

This was how Larry viewed it, anyway.

He was sitting in my living room and Marianne and I were lounging about.

"You want me to thank the big dumb peckerhead, is that it? I could care less about their workshop, if you want to know. Screw 'em. If the workshop's killed, I have that much more time for better things. I'll teach the rest of my courses and Thursday nights I'll stay home and write. I'm way past deadline on my book as it is. If the only way I were to keep this workshop going was because that dipshit—because *Giorgio* took up my case . . !"

"I do so adore your tact, Larry."

"What's tact? That oversized Sicilian strutter has screwed so many decent moments in the class this year—"

"Not referring to your chief or only defender. I've never met Giorgio and haven't a thing either for or against him. I was thinking of Nicolaas. For a, no, not dwarfish but, let's be kind, average-length person like yourself, Larry, to refer to anyone at all as a big or oversized anything is droll. I mean, here we have Nik, sitting here drinking his own wine, as you are also drinking his wine, enduring stoically your beguiling comments about bigness, although it's entirely clear who is big around here—and I'll go no further with that one, old ex-roomie, although if I'm pushed, I'll—"

I stirred my slow length. "Ding-a-ling. Back to your corners, both. Marianne, the creative-writing prof and I have to be on our way. Please stay. I'll be back you know when."

"Mm, wish I could. Stuff to do. Kids. Bye, dear Nik."

We kissed, Larry observing us with his crinkled-up gaze. He got a much swifter one. "Bye, ace."

My heart surged towards her, that small curly-mopped person, watching her go. So brisk and *sui generis* in here a half-minute ago, and now so anonymous and vulnerable walking off. I watched her heading west towards Yonge. So blessed, I said to myself, wishing I would say it aloud. Larry was watching her too. I've no idea what went on in his head at such times, I mean when his ex and I were in the room. I'd had no practice at that myself. I had seen my wife with a lover exactly once, and only after that lover had lost his privileges. The rest of them had stayed out of sight. Out of my sight, anyway.

The workshop, denied college space until its future was decided, was meeting for the second straight week in Larry's house. When he and I got there, a breath or two after leaving my place, four of them were already inside and working on a poster designed to assist Larry's beleaguered status in this confrontation with the department. They meant to run the poster off and paste it plentifully about the college to greet the morrow's incoming students. *TWO FEET GOOD, THREE FEET BAD*, the poster blared. This was a reference, Giorgio explained, to the fact that whereas Larry walked unaided, his principal enemy, who was the department head, walked with a cane. It was believed that the cane bore a Gucci logo and was in no way orthopaedically indicated, nevertheless Larry expressed instant reservations. There was a brief debate and then the chief draughtsperson, a major in graphic arts, cheerfully said she would work on a new design all night long if that's how long it took. The workshop then took place without incident and the participants left, swearing fealty. Larry brought in two premium-size cans of Heineken Gold.

"They're good kids," he said. "Only trouble is, they're not kids any more, most of 'em. They're my age or even, God help them, verging on yours. And yet a certain want of *fin de siècle* sophistication at times peeps forth. Am I right?"

"Can't argue with that."

"Loved that Sophocles touch, though. Two feet, etc. A new take on the Sphinx's conundrum. Only problem, every Ryerson halfwit would be able to unravel it."

"I was thinking Orwell."

"Short and humiliating life of the Ryerson Sphinx. Crouches over the university's main entrance chortling over the big question she's been primed to ask, and the first asshole to come by for his early lecture answers it correctly. Sphinx topples into Victoria Street."

"I was thinking Orwell."

"Sphinx kaput."

Silence for about two minutes. The two-minute silence felt a little, though only a little, like Remembrance Day. Which we have in Holland too, by the way. Which *they* have in Holland.

Different ambience, I admit.

"Sophie didn't make it, I noticed," Larry said.

"Obviously not." For some reason I was a little ticked off.

"She coming along?"

"Coming along?"

"Getting better. At Sunnybrook."

"Yup."

"I mean, you seem to be there all the time. I phoned you at the clinic, that's *your* clinic, not Sunnybrook's, remember?—*your* clinic? And they said they hadn't seen you much lately. They said you'd probably be at—whatever her Sunnybrook room number is. I forget what they said it is."

"They were probably right."

"Well, what is it, for Christ's sake?"

"What is what?"

"Holy shit . . . what'd I do? You sit here bridling at something I said and drinking my Heineken, not Château d'Yquem it is true but a soothing potion nonetheless, and entirely appropriate, one would think, for a po-faced Dutchman of no particular provenance, and words emerge from between your puffy overkissed lips like—"

"Ah . . ." My chin happened to be in my hand and, instead of moving it out, I left it there and just sat staring at him. I was thinking how all this time he'd kept on showing that bless-you-my-children face to Marianne and me and meantime, what was more natural, he hadn't always liked it.

"OK," I said. "Time to part." I tilted my glass for its last bit of amberish colour.

"Are you feeling quite normal? Nik? What? Eh?"

"We have to have a talk one of these days, I see. Maybe Marianne too. Maybe not Marianne. Kind of late right now, though, so—"

"Bloomster! You—this has got nothing to do with Marianne. All right?"

"Good that it doesn't. Do I believe that it doesn't? No. It's still late."

"Nik—fuck's sake. For the love of whoever. I admit that I—I confess to a kind of initial, a formal—but no, not really. Not really at all. With all her intolerable habits I still admire Marianne. With very little strain I can recall experiencing random clusters of pleasant days with her. I eschew any mention of nights. But I am relieved out of my mind not to be her boyfriend any more. Prison gates have opened, the released prisoner's a little puzzled occasionally but is mostly breathing deep gusts of amazingly refreshing air. Long-forgotten-type air. That I am still Marianne's husband is an anomaly we shall soon put right. You got all that? I only ask because until now I was sure you already had it."

This was true on both counts. I said so.

"OK. Is it all right if we now become at least transiently untruculent?"

"You start."

"I was asking you something which you wilfully—*wilfully*, bloody Nik—misunderstood, and did not answer."

This also was true. "Sorry."

"So?"

So I told him Sophie's room number.

He thanked me.

Puffylips went home.

I was walking down Bayview, heading for a bus stop and staring as usual at the sidewalk, which was more wet than frozen, soon be slush, when I heard my name called. I turned to find Sherin looking solemnly at me. He was a youngish fellow, forties probably, but youth was not the first thought I had, seeing him up close. Sharp-nosed and grey-faced.

"Bloom," he said again.

Well, small talk had never been his forte. We shook hands and he asked if I had lunched. I had not, so we headed further south and found a fish-and-chips shop with an unoccupied table just inside. We sat down and ordered. Haddock and chips for Sherin, cod and chips for me. The Dutch have always been loyal to cod. Ever since the time when, as one of our sixteenth-century mariners reported, you could lower a bucket into the waters off the Grand Banks and bring it up "foaming with fish" (cod).

Sherin asked why I was strolling along Bayview at this hour.

"Visiting a friend in Sunnybrook. And it's a nice day."

"I guess it is." The rejoinder was sufficiently gloomy that I felt I was being invited to ask how things were, which I did. Things were not good. Sherin had moved to Orangeville where he had not, in fact, opened an office on his own but had joined a three-person practice. The partners were OK, but his wife was "suffering," he said, from "civic deprivation. There's only one street you can shop on in Orangeville, Bloom, for Christ's sake. Doris is going nuts." There had also, he was sorry to tell me, already been whispers floating around Orangeville concerning the death, a year before, of a patient of Sherin's back in Toronto—and where could that story have come from, if not from our clinic? Plainly one of his ex-colleagues had blabbed about "all that Salvioni crap," Sherin would stake his life on that. "Probably Adams, natural back-stabber that he is. Got that shifty look, ever notice that? Awful turd. Knew it the minute I met him." He picked up a fry and bit off half of it, suddenly thoughtful. "Wait a sec, not Adams. Adams is OK. Who was that SOB lived in the Beaches and used to chomp celery all the way through the monthly meetings?"

"Gibson."

"Worst breath in Metro. Spite of the celery."

It turned out that Sherin had disliked Gibson from day one, meaning for twelve years. He had even, it was disconcerting to be told, come close to taking, or considering taking, extreme measures about his dislike. "Well, I wondered about it. Course I wouldn't have done anything, but God damn, it was tempting. Awful reeking esophagus to have to keep edging past in that narrow corridor all day long. Anyhow, here's the thing. Fellow had a wonky heart, angina no doubt, and used nitro as if it was popcorn. I was once in his office, can't think why, maybe I wanted a total change from inhaling the fresh-type air of the rest of the building—and he went off for, he said, a minute, and stayed away for ten. Was I pissed or what? I had patients that day too! Anyhow, I started looking around, way one does, checking out the untabulatable small items, you know, things people leave lying around that they're never going to miss, and there was his little brown Nitrostat bottle on his desk. Open, too, he must've just popped one. Anyhow, Christ, you know what?—I actually thought about messing with it. With his nitro. Switching things around. Salt pills occurred to me—you know? How they look almost identical? If I'd had any in my pocket I honestly don't know. I mean, I've never killed anybody or anything, not deliberately, plus he could have tasted the difference—or, something else, too—some other reason why he'd have—oh yeah, there's no fizz in salt pills, putting one of those in his mouth, he could have wondered about that. If I'd substituted them, I mean. So OK, it'd need more thought, I realized. Still, it was an interesting moment."

I thought I'd smile at him, perk him up, also show that I was a friend, in case I had to go to the washroom and leave my unguarded cod there with him for a bit. So I smiled. We got on to other subjects. When we'd finished our fish, he asked where I was going and it turned out he wanted to go that same way and it was still nice out, so we skipped the bus and walked on down to Eglinton and all the way over to Yonge. We said goodbye at the subway and I was partway down the escalator when I heard my name again. I looked back and he called out, "Keep on with the salt pills, Bloom, OK? Know what I mean? Eh? Eh?" I think the point he wanted to make was that the nitro story had just been his idea of a joke. Little joke, Bloom. Best not to mention it, somebody could take it the wrong way. He'd never killed anybody, after all. Not deliberately.

Saskia's father had died of a brain tumour, sad to say, at just my present age. Plump and prosperous farmer, dress him in a brown leather jerkin and he'd have danced in a Breughelian *kermesse* with the best of them. We had little in common but I had liked him for his obstinate good nature and was sorry when he outlived our marriage by only a year. His widow was a sour woman whom Saskia visited just once, and reluctantly even then, in the ten years after his death. I was allowed not to accompany her on that visit.

She's still alive, my ex-mother-in-law. She'd be the one leaning out from an upper window emptying a piss-pot onto the *kermesse*.

So as far as family goes, except for my wife I have had almost no close-up experience of an intimate dying. More than enough dyings, but patients, not relatives. My own parents, who as you may have noticed have played almost no role in this narrative, have been of little help in this regard. This is because my Scots mother died so early and my father remarried more or less instantly, the funeral meats still edible, etc.—and he and my stepmother are both still alive, both still inhabiting the four-storey Leidsegracht house, both over ninety now, both probably as healthy as seventy-year-olds. And both still entirely content never to see me again. I prefer not to mention or think of them either. I do so now only because not to do at least the first of these (see: "mention") would surely raise more eyebrows than anyone could want to be responsible for. This coolness between us, understatement of the book, this icefield, dates from the minute they learned that Saskia and I were in trouble. That we weren't getting along. That we were trial-separating and behaving accordingly. What I'm saying is that they began feeling this way well before Saskia fell ill, before the start of her long dying. They loved Saskia—so did most people—and assumed without further question that I was *de enige schuldiger* (I remember the phrase from the letter they jointly sent me when they had read my careful, I'd thought, explanation of what was going on. Translation, "the sole guilty one"). I don't accept that this was so, but although I've never really blamed them for their initial use of the phrase, I did eventually grow tired of seeing it again and again; no matter how brief their later notes were, they always found room for it. *De enige schuldiger.* People who have it in for other people should mellow a half-centimetre every decade or so, is my position on this.

Also, they have given little thought to the possibility that if they loved Saskia, I loved her more.

I mention all this because dying, the act of it, was by now getting my serious attention. Nothing arcane about this. Obviously the world would feel better about itself if Walter Rollo Maggione left it. On the other hand, I was not sure I wanted to murder him. It was necessary for me to use that word, "murder" when thinking about it, because its sheer bluntness was, so far, preventing me from taking these airy fancies any further. If I could have accepted a less violent word, say "damage," or, better still, an abstraction like "program" or "needful action" I might have gone farther and acted sooner. But abstractions have got a bad name lately.

Nevertheless, here was the situation. In my more or less professionally correct fashion, I loved Sophie. Marianne loved Sophie too, which proved that Sophie deserved to be loved. Larry was aware of Sophie and had not uttered a single cynical syllable about her for a couple of months—who knows what that meant. And the workshop also liked her, perhaps loved her in its fashion, because it kept on sending get-well cards with awful doggerel improvements hand-printed below the doggerel already in situ. Meanwhile, Sophie herself was at home again. That is, with Maggione. She was not attending the workshop, and I had not seen her since she'd left Sunnybrook. The only fully-paid-up human being who *was* seeing her was therefore Marianne. And Marianne was in that flat only once a week, during Maggione's Wednesday afternoon sessions with his thesis-adviser, a man called Hagauer.

"She's OK, I think," Marianne reported, after her first visit there. "Writing, she tells me. Won't tell me what. Her desk's covered with mystical-type texts, though. There's Teresa, who I gather used to be the star attraction. Of course S. Weil's in plain view, and then there's Jakob Boehme, a quondam shoemaker. Boehme's book looked to be in German. I think I saw Teilhard de Chardin there too. Which last was like old times."

"You and Teilhard were close?"

"I read him quite a lot once."

"And?"

"Hmm. Anyhow, who knows what's really going on. She won't go out. I thought this was an understandable cautiousness. A generalized insecurity, I thought. Now I think it's because walking on pavement's difficult for her. Any uncarpeted surface. Isn't that the—gosh, I'm about to use an expression my mother still uses, last person in the world to do so—isn't that the limit? The bloody limit? *Bloody*'s my own improvement on my mother's usage, by the way."

What could we do about this, Marianne wanted to know. Hope, I replied. She said she needed to hear something better. We stay on the qui vive, I said. Something better in English, Marianne said.

At breakfast she said, "From now on could he just be Maggione? I'm not sure about Walter, but Rollo strikes me as an innocent name. Ergo, let's scratch it. Until such time as we meet somebody else of the same name, which with any luck we never will. That all right?"

Of course Maggione, formerly Rollo, showed up on time.

"Well, Doctor Bloom. Here I am, you see. Anxious to be given your consoling news."

"Let's do this first."

"But of course." Shirt off, torso tensed. Welterweight champ of one or another Swiss canton. A few post-champ inches around the middle.

Shirt on again. "We need to get something straight. You do wish me to follow up on your episode of a week ago?"

"Excuse me? Episode?"

"Sunnybrook. The hospitalization."

"Yes, yes. That Edson, *wissen Sie*—"

"You told me. Sit over here, please."

Within fifteen minutes it was done. I was now formally in charge of this man's body. An unprofessional description, but accurate. The only problematic part of the quarter-hour came when I had to harry him into acknowledging the grounds for his ER night. From "It was nothing, a needless precaution" to "A certain irregularity within my chest. Had I been more patient, I should have enjoyed an undisturbed night in my own bed" to "Yes, pain, of course pain! Had there been no pain, would I have allowed my wife to telephone the hospital as she did?" This took half of our total time. By the end it was clear that my patient (the possessive pronoun there, the mere writing of it, is bothersome, yes; but it showed me that I had a role here, and the one thing I wanted never again to notice myself doing was standing on the touchline of these two people's lives making tiny impotent noises and wringing my very clean hands) had had a fright that night. He had felt "like a— what is this called, this thing, you place a piece of wood, let us say, in it, you then tighten—"

"Vise."

"Vise, yes. Vise. And this tightness, you see, went on. It just went on. I confess I was worried. I have several times had a sensation, a tightness, but this vise, no, this was different. For me, who has always been at a level of fitness which few other men—"

"What do you think brought this on?"

"This vise?" He had made the word his own. "I have no idea. You asked me this before. We were having a discussion concerning I know not what, let me think—"

"You were at home. And your wife was there also."

Impatiently. "Yes, of course. Where else would she be?" He was about to continue but seemed to be struck by a late-arriving thought. A comical thought, apparently. "Where else would she be, Doctor?" He was smiling ungenially. "We are speaking of a late night hour, *ja*?"

"All I meant was that Sophie—your wife—she might have stayed late with a friend, mightn't she? Or even stayed over? Or seen a late movie? Nothing criminal."

"Never. I would never—my wife has no interest in such things. If she were to wish—it is folly even to speak of this. A late movie." He shook his head pityingly. "Such an interesting scene this makes. I am at home, working on my thesis, some solemn involvement with the world of thought"—he smiled again, perhaps ironically—"and my wife is out at 'a late movie.' Which movie might this be, to attract my wife away from my house so late in the night? Who might one find, would you please inform me, sitting next to her at this, as you call it, movie? Would you tell me this?"

I was beginning to weigh fresh insight (value of) against several things: my overdue next appointment, a generalized rising irritation, and the possibility of some rash move on the part of this patient. I said, "We're done, for now. I'll want to see you in a few days. We'll do your chart—"

"Just one point, Doctor . . . Bloom. You are my doctor. *My* doctor, yes?" He was standing now, gathering his black overcoat. "Not my wife's doctor, I think. My wife—there is no requirement that she be discussed on these occasions. She is no concern of this clinic. Is this agreed?"

Big glare now, pointed upwards, recent smile gone far off. Glare pointed at me. I nodded, a cowardly nod. I told him the date and time of our next meeting. He started away, paused, there was a half-turn of his head back towards me. I'm almost sure he was going to insist on some verbal acknowledgment of his last remarks, but his head didn't complete its turn, and he went off.

My next patient was an elderly chap with a fibrillating heart come to discuss a recently adjusted prescription for his flecainide acetate, up from 100 mg twice daily to 125 mg twice daily. "You can't split those 50 mg tablets in two, Doc, have you ever tried to do that? In order to get down to a 25? I mean, it's never exact. Some mornings I'm getting 33 mg, I'm sure, others 15. This can't be good, can it? I don't want to make a nuisance of myself, but my wife particularly insisted that I consult you about this. She's at her wit's end . . ." As he went off again, calmed and as grateful for nothing as patients so often and so touchingly are, I noticed my own heart bumping about just a little.

Fellow feeling, Bloomovitch. With one or other of the day's patients.

Angina isn't exactly a funny thing but it's elusive. It signals itself as a pain, a weight, a "clenchedness," I've heard patients say. It could be in the chest or arm or elsewhere. At this point it's a narrowed artery through which the blood is trying to force its way. The forcing hurts. If the medical event that's called angina happens, it's because the blood does eventually get through.

If, for a long enough period of time, the blood's not getting through at all, other Latinate words tend to appear. Words like *morire*, and *de mortuis*.

Why I said angina is "elusive" is because the symptoms are so varied. Also because by the time a doctor, let alone a cardiologist, is on the scene, the pain has normally faded off and has left few or no signs behind to show it passed this way. No signs at all unless special investigative procedures are invoked. Which they very often are not. So it's often missed, it's not listed in the diagnosis, and probably just as often it's diagnosed when it didn't happen.

"Elusive" seems about right.

There was no doubt in my mind that Maggione had experienced an angina; both the medical evidence and the "history" supported that view. The stress test I had put him through had shown ECG changes strongly suggestive of serious ischemia—heart muscle oxygen starvation, if you're interested. Point is, I had not entered this result into Maggione's chart. That formal record, the kind of thing that would be available to anyone checking this patient's clinical history, showed only his "resting" ECG, a different configuration altogether. Why I was doing and not doing these things is something I was not always conscious of, but at other times I had an inkling. The inkling was that I was pacing off for myself a certain area. An area of a possibility. For what, who knew.

And one other thing I was doing. I was simplifying my *Weltanschauung*.

(I was not simplifying my four-syllable Germanisms yet, but one of these days.)

("World view.")

And having done so, I realized that in this simplified world view or outlook there was no longer anything I would not do for Sophie, if she would allow me. And there was, I was also realizing, nothing I would not do *to* Walter Rollo Maggione. Allowed or not.

Hippocrates. The famous oath. Away with it.

Parables, forget them.

Maggione lying in seriously damaged condition by the roadside and perceived there by passerby Nicolaas Bloom, MD?

No problem. Bloom trucks on by. Bloom gives a small wave to the gathering crows, *Go for it.*

When I had my next and as it turned out penultimate session with Maggione, I told him that his condition was unthreatening, that what he had experienced had been more fear than a physiological event, that there was no imperative reason for him to change his lifestyle. There was a faint haze of truth in all that.

Since, however, I said, blood tests showed there could be a degree of plaque buildup in the arteries, I was prescribing for him a low-level dosage—0.3 mg, to be exact—of nitroglycerine. Brand name Nitrostat.

This was orthodox procedure. Placed under his tongue during a moment of sharp pain, the Nitrostat would, as I told him, dilate the offending artery and allow a temporarily freer blood flow. This might stave off the blockage or stacking-up of blood which causes a stroke.

I gave him a very small number of the tiny Nitrostat

tablets. This was because, I explained, the dosage level had to be tested. I would call him in for a repeat or altered prescription soon.

This was a one-on-one interview with nothing entered into the patient's chart. It was not a complete diagnosis. Maggione's BP was up, and together with the enzyme results this pointed to the probability that an angina had taken place. He was now a bona fide heart attack candidate, not too far off, in fact, from the head of the queue.

This is not to say that if he behaved well, did not fly into rages, did not crank his emotions up into the Swiss Alpine (or any other thin or mountainous) air, he wouldn't survive for a good while.

Particularly if he had his nitro always at hand.

And if his doctor was on his side.

Sophie was coming to the workshop again, but now her husband was both bringing her there and waiting to take her home. He'd done this before but less methodically. There was now, too, nothing equivocal about his feelings concerning the group—arriving or departing, he looked at no one and spoke not a word. We were meeting in Ryerson again, Larry having won a grudging extension as workshop director, so for the three hours of the workshop Maggione did whatever he did but would be back again outside our third-floor room punctually at ten to ten. The minute the door opened, there he was, standing aside with evident impatience while the first leavers went by; then making straight for where Sophie was either still seated or standing to accept, from her classmates, the various sets of pages for next week's session. He'd reach for her bookbag—I saw her hesitate the first time this happened, but that was the last of her hesitations—then for her hand, and off they'd go.

Wordless, all this.

The second time this happened, a few eyes were rolled, but these were eyes which hadn't been in regular attendance. No other eyes seemed amused.

As for the workshop leader, "amused" was not the word.

"What do they call these people nowadays, the cleaners, sweepers, lockers-up? Used to be content to be called janitors."

"Custodians? Executive custodians?"

"Sure. How if I slip the boss executive custodian a—some bribe—to keep that fuckwit entirely out of the building?"

"Bribe him with our poems."

"Or we could go back to meeting at my house."

"The fuckwit would then be outside your door."

"I'd set the dog on him."

"You don't have a dog, Larry."

"Come on, Nik. This is an in-house European matter, you should be right at home with it. Although now that I think of it, are the Dutch really considered to be a part of—? . . . Anyway, work on it. Find a solution. I feel like throwing up every time I see his mug, and I see it twice every Thursday night now."

The following Thursday, Larry had the class take a break halfway through. A month before, with everybody enjoying things and jealous of the passing hours, we had voted to skip the breaks, but what we heard now was a straightforward undemocratic pronouncement. Nobody objected, although several people blinked around a few times. We should all head down to the coffee shop, Larry advised, where he would join us in a minute. Sophie got up, but I noticed her glance at Larry and noticed, also, his glance in return. If I were to describe it, which I'm about to do, I'd say it was an imperative glance. She hesitated, neither of them moved, and by now I was the only other one still hanging about. That's what narrators have to do, it's how they find out things. Eventually I too left and went downstairs, leaving the two of them alone. I'd no intention of showing up in the coffee shop anyhow. I thought I'd step outside for a look up at the stars if there were any.

When I opened the door to the street, there he was, the constant husband, so heavily there he almost stumbled in past me. It was as if he'd been leaning against the entire college. He turned a furious face to me, who knows what he was about to say—and now, because of who it was, important Bloom instead of some nobody, it was merely awkward.

"Oh," he said. Gasped. "It's—"

I was considering stepping backwards and letting the door fall shut, anything to end this. He forestalled that by stepping backwards himself, down the two steps to side-walk level, where he turned on his heel and went off down the dark street.

Standing very still I could hear his footsteps for a while. I took a look up above. There were, yes, some stars, and they had their usual effect on me. I've never gone along with Pascal, I've never been frightened by stars. Not by their eternal silences either. I always find that no matter what turmoil I bring to them, and I have brought plenty, they calm it, they seem to me to represent a wisdom that eases all human perplexity, shows it to be distant and unthreatening. I always feel they are the best sight I've had for months. So why don't I look up there every few minutes, I occasionally ask myself. And I reply, well, if you looked up that often they'd get used to you looking. They wouldn't come through for you the same way.

Still. They always make me feel I will have better thoughts now, for a while.

"Don't know," Larry said. "No idea. Of course I asked her. Well, she said, it was kind of her husband to wait there for her as he now always did. He was simply concerned about her, she said, surely I would understand that. He worried about Toronto at night, she said. He would worry about this break we are taking right now if he found out about it, she said. I said I knew more than she thought I knew about his kind of concern and his kind of worryings. I didn't describe him to her as a rotten cowardly shitbird reptile, that would not have been cool. Didn't matter, I got nothing more from her. Sort of a smile is all. By the way, does she have a hearing problem, do you know?"

"Why? Did she say she did?"

"No. Does she?"

Not that I knew, I said. He scowled into the night street.

And a week later, on the day following the next class, which I missed, I got the sequel. At the half-time break Sophie had unhesitatingly gone down to the coffee shop with the others, and Larry, who had hoped to repeat the one-on-one talk of the week before, had in frustration followed them. Once there, he had sat down without a word but had "blocked her off," he admitted, when the others had started back. She asked him to let her pass. He asked for one minute. She stood silently. He demanded to know whether she was under orders not to speak with him. "Of course I am," she said. This directness impressed and, at some level, pleased him. She added, "You must understand why this is so, Mr. Logan."

"What have I done? I wish to be your friend. Nothing more."

"You are a man, you have no wife, you—"

"I have a wife, actually."

"You live in your house alone. My husband believes that you have special thoughts about me. You and I know this is not so, but he cannot be blamed for this. We must go up, what will the others think."

Regarding the "hearing problem." Marianne noticed it and Sophie said, yes, she had noticed it too. It was recent, she didn't know how recent. Marianne then said she'd made an appointment to see her doctor that afternoon and could Sophie possibly accompany her—that way they wouldn't miss their usual talk and could have a coffee later. Sophie was fine with this.

Before leaving, Marianne phoned her doctor, a woman named Celia Coomaraswamy who, over ten years and what with patients in common and shared professional interests, had become a confidante, and told her what she had in mind.

Dr. C. took extraordinary measures and her waiting room was empty when the two women arrived.

"I must apologize, Doctor," Marianne then said ("burst out, not unidiotically," is how she described it to me)— "here you have cleared a time for me and, checking my book, I find I overlooked an appointment. I must be at my office in minutes. I do feel badly about this."

"Well," was Celia's cool reply, "how inconvenient. For us both, of course."

Marianne: "Sophie, dear, you could not—let me ask you, you could save me much embarrassment—" and Sophie was drawn away into a corner of the waiting room to listen to a brief series of premeditated lies. Marianne then mentioned to the hovering doctor her friend's hearing problem. Might it be possible that Dr. Coomaraswamy would be willing, since no one else seemed to be waiting, to, very briefly of course—?

Not that it went off smoothly. There was a "remarkably sulky" look from Sophie as she entered the consulting room. Still, into that room she and the doctor went. And off went Marianne to cruise the Annex streets waiting for the reluctant patient and press-ganged physician to accomplish whatever they might accomplish. "I was feeling way below clever about setting Sophie up. As for the suspicious stares I was getting from the Forest Hill doggie-walkers as I drove slowly by them, again, and again, and again . . ."

But a purpose was served. The diagnosis was that pressure of some sort had affected the middle ear, left side, but the doctor guessed that this would be temporary. The real value of Marianne's way-below-clever move would plainly be if patient and doctor happened to get on. In this regard

Marianne had counted on Sophie's innate courtesy as her best ally—and so it was. After the middle ear had been looked to, Dr. C., remembering that her waiting room had been cleared, initiated a conversation with her patient by mentioning how useful it would be if she might take a few notes on the family's medical history. This was agreed to, and led to the desired end: an obvious decision on Sophie's part to like this unjudgmental listener, and appointments for a series of tests beginning in the next week.

"I don't know if the doc'll tell me what she finds, though, Nik. Depends whether she'll feel bound to bring in the law."

We'd been through that already. The police option still looked, to us, unworkable. Also slow. The problem with slow was obvious. Sophie was not a minor, was not incoherent, was adequately compos mentis. And therefore couldn't be rescued unless she herself sent up a flare.

Which seemed, as a possibility, not worth anybody's sitting up late to watch for. Sophie was, after all, still the stalwart defender of her husband.

"Stalwart"?

Come on, Blomski, do better.

In his hands I saw a long golden spear and at the end of the iron tip I seemed to see a point of fire. With this he pierced my heart several times so that it penetrated to my entrails. When he drew it out I thought he was drawing them with it . . .

This is what Teresa says she endured in her journey towards becoming what she joyously calls "a slave of God."

There is a sort of humiliation involved here, I think. (Nothing original in thinking this, Sophie! Yes, I know.) My question is this: what if the golden spear kills you before you have passed even the earliest stages of the journey?

I once saw a movie of which this reminds me. It was a Canadian film. I cannot remember what it was called. But a young woman, younger than I now am, fell in love with God and at the same time with a priest who had a strong and grave voice and was also handsome. Both loves were pure, but she felt she must decide between them and could not. It must be said that she also wanted to change the world. At the end she poured gasoline over herself and set herself alight.

It's the certainty that I am at such a beginning of my journey, whether the journey will be along a straight road or through the many mansions of Teresa's Castle, that causes me such worry. I have begun to believe that Teresa's metaphor is the correct one. Surely there can be no straight road! To think now only of last Thursday, that embarrassing moment during our break from the work-shop when he came to me in the cafeteria—what could I have done? or said? How could he have behaved so? And yet the great happiness I felt, and the humiliation of feel-ing it! Think of my efforts to wean my husband away from his terrible though often understandable hatreds. Whichever direction one turns there is another mansion and, at least at the moment of entry, another darkness. My thoughts crowd one another to death. At least one night each week there will always be bodily pain to remind me of the necessary singleness of purpose, but sometimes the pain is so severe I cannot think or feel. And unless both of these are well, there can be no growth. This is what I am confused by. "I wish only to hug my pain," Teresa writes, and adds that this caused her to feel "great bliss." If I could feel this bliss! And sometimes I do. But sometimes I feel only blinding pain.

As she burned, what did the young woman in the film feel? Watching, all I saw was her body toppling into the smoke.

(journal entry, *s.f.*)

It wasn't my intention to abandon Sophie so abruptly back there. Leaving her alone with that doctor like that. A brand new undescribed character and all.

Celia Coomaraswamy is a tall and energetic and, it would be perverse not to acknowledge this, gorgeous Tamil. Eyes pre-eminently and other parts merely eminently worth mentioning. She's also a good listener and the only one of Marianne's pals whom Marianne guesses to be swifter of mind than herself. Another of Sophie's quick conquests, it turned out. (I never know what to think about this: many women's unimpeded marches into mutual fondness. Elective affinities. *Look how simple it is!* they seem to say.) Because of the special circumstances (I mean Marianne's confiding to Dr. C., one professional to another, what she knew of Sophie's history) the doctor had no scruples about returning the favour, and before long a shadowy Identikit began to make outlines that you could, if you wanted, put a name to. Sometime after that the two doctors let a third member of the profession into their parleying. Which is how I learned what close bonds can form between people all three of whom have, for even a short while, been facing up to the same abhorrent possibility.

What the two women cajoled or beguiled out of this unregistered patient of theirs was not the entire history of Sophie Führ's life and times, but it was a beginning.

A beginning at the family address in Küsnacht, which is a settlement of rambling large homes on what's known as Zürich's "gold coast," overlooking the slate-grey wrinkles of the Zürichsee a hundred feet below. Marianne and I already knew that Sophie's forebears had played host to James and Nora Joyce way back when. Thanks to Celia ("CC") we now got confirmation that it had been a *significant* friendship and one that assisted the Joyces through those marooned-in-Switzerland World War I years, the years of the many redraftings of *Ulysses*. Between then and Sophie's birth an unremarked generation had interposed itself, but the awareness of those touching-the-mantle days had plainly never died out of the Küsnacht house. "When I was little," Sophie recalled for CC, "Klaus and I used to visit the Fluntern cemetery where they are buried.

"They were one grave apart from each other—somebody was in between them, isn't that curious? We used to try to imagine what that in-between person was overhearing all those years. Lying there and listening to the two voices through the earth, one from each side. Nothing writer-ish, we thought. We thought it would be 'Your shirt needs mending,' or 'Please read me the *Herald-Trib*'s rugby scores, my eyes are bad.'"

Such were Sophie's circumstances through adolescence up to that day when—a topic Celia Coomaraswamy innocently introduced—the Geneva art gallery had failed to open.

"Geneva art gallery?"

"Well . . . yes. You don't mind me knowing this? Marianne told me. How you met your husband. Doctor.

Bloom, Nik, I should say, told Marianne the whole story, and—if I should not have mentioned this, forgive me, I—"

OK to mention, but wrong whole story, it turned out. Not Geneva had been the place of meeting for those two, but Munich; not an art gallery, but a gathering of interested persons on a sidewalk outside a travel bureau in that Bavarian city; not a doctoral candidate on a study mission, but a tour guide, a.k.a. courier, meeting the youngest member of this Munich group, all of whom were booked into a tour called Great Cathedrals of the East. The Wall had just come down and it was the first time since the war that the East German cathedrals, some old and bejewelled, some new-risen out of the bombed-flat rubble, some unrisen—Dresden, Leipzig, Magdeburg—had been accessible to the "Wessies," the West German tourists. "Walter was our guide, our cicerone. He arranged everything, he *did* everything. He knew every stone of every building. He was . . . wonderful. Everybody said so. But he and I—at that time we were not, you know, we were not—"

An encouraging nod from CC—

"Only after a while, we—you see, Dr. Coomaraswamy, the others were so different—"

"I know. Older. *My* age, the others were. It's OK to say so."

"We never talked about ages. But they all seemed older. Perhaps they were not, but they seemed so."

They would retrace their steps in the late afternoons, she and Walter, during nap time for the generality, back to re-examine what they'd been sorry to leave when the rest of the group had insisted. A half-blackened stone figure meditating in a side altar, a full-scale poster of a Dresden window that had, of course, not survived the searing heat. On their own they could look at these unhurriedly, without the surf of questions, the babble. And in the evening, when the waiters had abandoned them and the generality stayed on and on in the hotel dining room lamenting *die verlorenen Länder,* the lost German provinces lying even further to the east, full of towns with names that no longer sounded right, that would never sound right again, Polish, Lithuanian, Russian names—

"Walter could tell how I hated all that. I would say I was going to bed, but I wouldn't, I would wait outside and he would come as soon as he could. If the cathedral was closed, we would just walk. Several times we walked until late at night. Talking, talking. He knew everything. If you could have heard him . . .

"We never talked about before or after, about ourselves, families, any of that. Only once he mentioned this, just a little. About being a *Kurier.* About the ignorance of everybody. The way they treated him, like a servant, he said. Like a menial. Oh, and—" She stopped, her mouth tightening.

Celia said nothing, waited.

"The—the invitations women would send to him late at night. The same women, Doctor, can you imagine, who during the day—"

"Celia. My name's Celia. You can call me CC—Sissi."

"Sissi. A bell-person—what are those people called?"

"Bellhop. Bellboy. Bell-person."

"A bell-person would come to his room late at night. To tell him a room number and hand him a key. Smiling and smiling."

———

"Nice man, brother Klaus, I bet," said Marianne, putting her head into my workroom after her latest *telephonisch* update from Celia. "But you know what? There are people, they're called intellectuals, we may even know one or two of them, who are more frightened of actually speaking out to save a loved one from what with all the wonderful clarity of their multi-degreed minds they can plainly see is a disaster in the making than . . . than I don't know what. They need time to reflect, they tell themselves. And meanwhile . . ." Head withdrawn.

Klaus, when intimations of the relationship reached him, had been puzzled but passive, this was how he had always been with his gentle but determined sister, so curious in her likes and dislikes, so "different." When the relationship became an engagement, he went so far as to mention the recent death of their adored father. Might this not, he wondered aloud to his sister, have some bearing on her feelings concerning this sudden fiancé, especially if one considered the similarity in ages of those two men—

But insistence wasn't Klaus's way.

The ceremony, *privat*. Resignation of a *Kurier* and enrolment of a mature student in pre-doctoral courses at the University of Zürich. The ex-*Kurier* had been randomly accumulating course credits for several years; it wasn't long before he was admitted to a graduate program. The newlyweds took an apartment in a Zürich suburb. The husband had grants and a tutorial assistantship, the wife a modest income from the Führ estate. The former studied unremittingly, the latter kept the apartment tidy and supervised the big house in Küsnacht which Klaus, with her encouragement, was staying on in. Things marched, more or less. One walked by the lake, one fed the pigeons, sometimes two walked by the lake and fed the pigeons. The ice on the lake came and went. There were no signs of what was ahead. Well, no, that wasn't true. There *were* disagreements now and then. There was, once, something, Sophie forgot just what, which was penalized by the student-husband through the imposition of two days of absolute silence. *Kein Wort*— not a word—was the sentence. But that was all, Sophie said.

"*All*, Sophie? You call that *all*?" said Celia, shivering. The domestic tactic wasn't new to her.

"Well, not quite all," said Sophie, who had misunderstood.

"I don't know what to call it, it was just—it changed so many things. For me and for him. For both of us. I don't know what to call it."

"It" took place not long after the posting, one May morning on a wall outside the University of Zürich's Graduate School, of the date for her husband's thesis defence. Hour, room number, names of examiners, all listed. And Klaus, who held a chair in Psychology and was by fifteen years Maggione's junior, found himself scheduled to sit on his new brother-in-law's examining committee.

"*Natürlich ist Klaus zuruckgetreten*—sorry, Sissi—naturally Klaus withdrew. What else should he do? The next day his place on the committee was taken by Professor Moosbrugger. Well, we all knew Professor-Doktor Moosbrugger. I had known him since I was a child. He and my parents played music together, my mother was the pianist and he the violinist, my father sang or turned the pages for her. . . ."

The news of Moosbrugger's appointment—he was a former department chairman, now retired, an austere man from whom Maggione had, years before, received a low course-grade which he had appealed, successfully, to a dean's committee—had caused her husband "terrible nervousness." And when, a few days after the defence, he learned that he had been failed ("It was not so bad. It was not a unanimous decision. They gave him a full year to resubmit") was when "it" happened. Late that night, on their way home from what was to have been a celebratory dinner in Küsnacht with some of Sophie's late parents' friends, elderly folk who had for a long while wanted to meet this prodigy, oddity, apparition, this unknown husband of their dear friends' adored daughter, a dinner that had initially been cancelled at news of the academic disaster and then reinstated and then, near the end of the evening, stalked angrily away from—

"There was a misunderstanding. A coffee cup was upturned. The coffee spilled across the table and some of it went on a carpet. It was a carpet my grandfather had brought back from Islamabad. It was old, impossible to tell how much had been spilled on it before. Of course there was no need to apologize. Walter was trying to explain how it had happened, and Klaus was saying, please, please, all that matters is that we refill your cup. And then Klaus added something funny, he was always doing that—some remark to turn attention away from—from this, everyone understood that. I can't remember what he said. Perhaps it was about the pattern and the coffee stain, that the carpet was now improved, that he had often observed a lack in just that area. . . . Nothing special. But Walter didn't know how Klaus talked and felt he was being, you know, felt he was being—"

"Patronized?"

"Yes. Well, you see, he blamed me. First of all for Klaus withdrawing from the committee. If Klaus had stayed he would have been able, Walter thought, discreetly able to change the voting. To change the result. Walter thought that because our marriage had been so quiet, there was no real reason for Klaus to resign from the committee. No one would have noticed, Walter said. Especially, he said, if I had agreed to change my surname, as he said he had wanted me to, if my name had no longer been Führ, then *certainly* nobody would have made the connection. But he had not *asked* me to change my name. Of course I would have if he had asked. But you see, Doctor—*Sissi*—it just wasn't true, about nobody noticing. Klaus was—Klaus was well known, and not just in Zürich, in all of Switzerland. He was Swiss under-21 finalist already when he was seventeen. In the Swiss Closed he got as far as a tiebreak with Jakob Hlasek!"

"I beg your pardon? Under-21? The Swiss Closed? Jakob—?"

"Sorry! Klaus played tennis wonderfully well. And his full professorship had been granted when he was only thirty-nine. This never happens in Switzerland. Never! Even at fifty it is unusual. And I, just for being his sister, was a little known. People would have noticed. They would. Even if I *had* changed my name."

"They *would*," Sophie said again.

("Obvious who she was speaking to there," said Celia, telling us all this. "It wasn't you or me," she said.)

"So what happened next, Sophie?"

"Oh . . . not so much."

"Nevertheless."

"I thought at first it was playing. Playful. It was that night, the one I was telling you about. And we now had left home, the Küsnacht house, the guests were all in dismay, but— and we were driving towards our apartment, along the lake road back to Zürich. We weren't saying anything. I was watching the road and I was wondering what I would say when we reached our apartment. I knew Walter was upset. Would I be able to explain what Klaus had meant? This is what I was wondering. Klaus is much funnier than any of us. I was wondering if I could make what he had said sound as funny as . . . Then I realized we were going too fast and I began to say so. I asked Walter if he knew we were going so fast and I was leaning a little towards him and—but then . . . what happened then was—Walter reached across and hit me in the side. Twice. Two hits, both together, really. He wasn't looking, he didn't turn his head. He was driving, so he didn't turn his head. I thought he'd meant to miss me, meant to punch the air, people do that, don't they—I thought he had not judged the distance well—you know, just hitting out but not being able to look. But it hurt and I cried out. Then he was *surely* going too fast and I said so and said he must stop. After a few seconds he did stop. There was a space, it's called a lay-by, yes?—at one side of the road and he stopped there. He— I had no idea that he. . . . He stared ahead where the side of the road was lit by our headlights and I knew he was upset because of everything, because of leaving the dinner and his thesis and everything. So I reached out to touch his face. He lifted his right arm and pushed the hand I was reaching out with up against the car's roof. I was so surprised! I think I began to say something, how unexpected or how careless of him this was—and then he turned and slapped my face very, very hard, no one had ever hit me before like that, no one had even hit me in the face in any way at all, even playing with Klaus when I was little, never, never, no one . . ."

CC wasn't about to say a word. She risked a glance at Sophie and saw a tense and pale face. She had, she told us, "an absolutely palpable sense of that slap. Good God, it was—it seemed as newly arrived a slap as anything I'd ever heard or even heard *about*. I *heard* that slap, and the sound of it took my breath away for a second. So much so that I remember looking—again—at Sophie to find out how she was taking it. How could she still be sitting up straight in her chair in my office after such a slap—"

Celia had stood up and considered what to say or do next. Sophie had looked as though she wasn't about to alter anything in her expression or her posture ever. "Well, so I sat down again and smiled at her. Why do we do this, Marianne? Nik? Make a happy face when we—? To what end?" Neither she nor Sophie had been sure what to do next, but more time had gone by than they had realized, and they heard voices in the waiting room. In the same moment the intercom buzzed to remind Celia—a second reminder, she realized—of those waiting patients. Alone in the inner office, the two women kissed. Sophie then left.

And that was Dr. Coomaraswamy's story.

So many doctors' stories!

Initial consultation and interim physical examination of this patient shows the following. Locally concentrated internal bruising, some of it probably dating back months, some recent. Primary area of bruising: kidneys and spleen.

"To generalize," Celia amplified, "soft tissue areas, mostly in the lower body. A particularly noticeable aspect here," she continued, still being professional, "is the orderliness. This lady could do a runway number wearing what your typical supermodel wears or doesn't wear and nobody'd be the wiser."

Long sigh from Marianne.

CC wasn't done. She said, steadily, "I picture him labouring over her."

Neither Marianne nor I said a word.

"A kind of artist," Celia said.

One of us, either Marianne or I, said, "I have no idea what you mean."

"Me neither," Celia said.

She got up from her chair and gathered her things. She walked to the door and had almost left but then turned and said, "Thanks, I guess, for letting me in on this, you two. Bye, Nik. Bye, Marianne. If I can . . . you know."

"Nobody can, Celia. See, that's it." Marianne was anxious to go too. It was the middle of a weekday afternoon, a working day for her. She sounded tired already, though, when she said, "Nobody can help because nobody's read the book on this. Which they haven't done because there *isn't* any book on this. As I expect you know. There's never been any identifiable pathology for the brute/batterer. Just guesses floating about. Maybe he wants control and . . . oh, fuck, fuck, it's all so obscene—so obscene and *human*. Sometimes he knows other people behave abominably, but he's sure he's different, and he's always got some specious ground for thinking this. *His* victim is still alive, see, there's a distinction, plus he hasn't been caught yet, so on both those grounds he can't possibly be like . . . whoever, some other spiritually opaque unclassifiable shit he's read about in the tabloids. My language is dying on me. I think *I'm* . . . no, I'm not, I'm still alive and still here. Still maundering on. Whereas Sophie—Sophie'll never say *anything*. Nik, what was it she called herself, that reading she did to your group?"

"It's not my group. Larry's group. Slave of God, you're thinking of. That what you're thinking of?"

"Yes."

"St. Teresa said it first."

"And a billion other people have said it since."

"And how many of those got punched for their trouble!" This was Dr. C., who'd lingered, maybe so she could learn about the Slaves of God. "Do you know—I said I was leaving, but here I still am—most of one summer I did a locum for a village doctor, little place outside Madras. I was still in med school. I was the first woman doctor the village had seen, the first woman almost-doctor, I'd better say. Three of the village women came in. They didn't mind talking, it poured out of them, nobody'd ever asked before. Walking through their god-damned villages with their darker than usual faces and newly squashed noses once or twice every month of their married lives. On and on until they'd had enough and died. Well, one of them died. I can't speak about the other two, didn't stay long enough. Missed the last act. But one of them, yes. God, to adapt your phrase, took her home. Took his slave home."

"Christ." That was me. I.

"Happens here too, you know, right here. It's not just us subcontinental darkies."

"Go to work, Celia."

"Gone."

". . . You see, Nik? You *see*?"

"He will, too, you know. I don't just mean God, although He might have a vested interest here too. I mean the other guy—can't bring myself to say his name. Not the first time I've choked on it. He too. It's kind of a race, you know? And he'll win it. He'll take his slave home, take her back to *Schweizer*-land. Back to his mountain fastness. Way up high, the King of the Golden River, so high that nobody will ever be able to see what's going on. Or hear. The only people in the whole world who'll know'll be us. And the worst of it is, she'll go."

This was the evening of the afternoon I've just been describing, and Marianne wasn't finished yet.

"And that'll be the last of it, 'cause nobody'll be able to hear her calls in the high thin air."

She was wandering over towards my book wall. She loved that book wall. She pulled out a book. I was twenty feet away, but I knew that book better than I knew her. Odd thought.

"What would *she* think of all this?" The book was *Middlemarch*.

"What do you mean, 'it's kind of a race'?"

"Just being melodramatic. C'mon, Nik, what would this lady say? I know you know."

"Oh, well . . ." What did I know? Half as much as that lady had known? On a good day, possibly. "I know she'd think about it a long time."

"Yes?"

"She'd try to reason it out."

"And?"

"You're badgering, Marianne."

"Yes."

"Don't."

"Nik—when you're perfectly content to know stuff other people don't know, to know it and not *tell* them what it is you know, they *have* to badger you. That's assuming they want to learn some of the stuff." Replacing the book where it belonged, standing there looking down and then turning towards me. Amazing smile. "Doesn't hurt if they also love you."

Well, I'd known that. That last bit. Thing is, though, there'd never been anything half as fine inside my chest, head, other places too, as there was right then, even though right then it had to fight for space in there with abomination. How had I managed to keep breathing for almost fifty-nine years before finding my way to this generous— why not call it what I really think, this *noble*—spirit? I couldn't get over it. Hoped never to get over it.

And meanwhile, what was it we'd been talking about? There'd been some question of—oh, right.

"She would—she would act, finally."

"What do you mean, 'finally'? Why 'finally'?"

"Because first of all she would ask herself who might be more suited to act than she herself. Not passing the buck, but because she didn't always trust herself—trust herself to be the best at something, you know? But then often she would have to be the one. Like it or not. She would realize that she was the one."

"The best one."

"Well—"

"The one who had to act."

"Yes."

"That's what I was wondering. Because—it'd be hard, wouldn't it. I mean, you go out looking for somebody to do this difficult thing that needs doing, hoping that some custom-made face will show up. And nothing does, none of them compares, really, with what you feel inside your own—" Marianne's face suddenly had a stricken look. "Gosh," she said. "What a thing to think of."

"What's that?"

"When I was in grade two—have I ever even *thought* of this before? *Ever?* Since it happened? Nik, I don't think I've ever . . . One morning the teacher asked me to stand up and then she told me to go up and down between the rows of desks and tell her who had incised the deepest and inkiest initials and stuff onto the top of her desk. Or his desk. We had these reddish wooden desks. I went up and down those rows with my heart getting heavier all the while, because I was afraid it was me, *my* desk was the worst, *my* initials palimpsested over and over in that weird hieroglyphic tilt kids come up with when they're using a ballpoint or a compass leg instead of any better tool. And I kept on feeling the teacher knew this and that's why she'd picked me to do this inspection, but I wasn't totally sure that this was so. And I didn't want to say anything in case it wasn't so. When I'd done all the rows, walking slower all the time, and got back to my own desk, she said, 'Well, Annie, who is it?' And I started to turn a half-degree towards somebody way over on the other side of the room and I know I got so far as to say, well, maybe it's—and then she took mercy on me and she said, 'It's you, isn't it, Annie?'"

Marianne sat still for a few seconds.

"And then?"

"And then I started to cry." She turned to me and said, "The word 'wimp' wasn't in general use at the time."

"You were just in grade two," I said.

"Yes."

There was a short pause. I understood that this sad little march among the desks, and Marianne's remembering it, might have something to do with what was going on with us here—with, I guessed, the business of having something asked of you, of having to decide whether to say yes to some task or responsibility that maybe you could avoid if you . . . but that was as far as I wanted to go with it just at present. The pause had to be dealt with, though, so I said, "What did you mean, 'race'?"

Marianne lifted her eyes, which had become unlifted. "It's not important," she said.

"OK," I said.

"No," she said. "Honestly, Nik, I—I just meant, you know, between God and him. *That* race. To find out which home the slave ends up in."

In which minute it became apparent to us both that we'd had enough. Marianne remembered an appointment she could still manage to keep, and went off to keep it.

The next few days were a matter of going to the clinic, seeing my patients, walking all the way home in order to tire myself for sleep, and going to bed wide awake with what I was reading at the time. Which was Ivan Goncharov's story of a few days in the life of a man whose archetypal indolence I have loved and honoured so much over the years that I have been mangling his name, as you may have noticed, mangling it and jamming it together with my own name, on just about every tenth page of this story. This story of my own indolence.

"There, that's enough lying in bed!" Oblomov said. "I must get up."

Eventually, round about three or four o'clock, I tended to go to sleep.

And, sometime after that, I would know that I must get up.

On one of the days I also got the final report on Sophie's condition from Celia. Needless to say, I wasn't formally a consultant on the case and therefore had no right to the data, but Celia couldn't, she wrote on a yellow stickum, care less. *Here it is,* she wrote, and she wrote *I don't want to be the only one who knows this!* An ultrasound had shown hematomas and a sufficient number of other bruisings to the extent that, if she had not known better, Celia's note said, she'd have surmised a high-speed car crash. Since she did know better, it had to be, the note said, not a high-speed crash but a regularly time-tabled series of low-speed crashes. *How many words are there,* a second and larger yellow stickum went on to wonder, *for this kind of thing?*

On the very most recent of these several days, Marianne had been on the line with a social worker attached to the Metro Toronto Hospitals "At Risk" team (Celia was in her office with her, ready to offer backup testimony if required) just when Sophie unexpectedly walked in on them. End of "At Risk" phone conversation. The three of them had had to talk the whole business of legal intervention through all over again and Sophie had accused them, Marianne in particular, of bad faith and had then run out weeping. Marianne had felt sure that everything she had gained was now lost, but had decided against weeping. The two learned women had pursued Sophie down a sidewalk and all three had entered the first door they could open, which was a Second Cup door, and coffees had been sipped and a sort of compromise had been reached. Dr. Coomaraswamy, a.k.a. Celia, a.k.a. CC and Sissi, had, with Sophie's consent, set up a watching brief with "uncancellable, agreed?" appointments in her office every fortnight and a homemade safeguarding routine involving two-rings-and-hang-up phone calls, this routine to be checked and refined depending on developments. The doctor was unhappy with this because she feared, she said, saying this not to Sophie or Marianne but to me on another yellow stickum, that this patient could die or be crippled for life if another such scene as the one that had hospitalized her were to take place; but if this was all she was going to be allowed to set in motion here, then this is what she would set in motion. I agreed with everything and was relieved to be one of two witch doctors involved here and not, as in a sense I'd felt I was before, the only one.

I also went to the workshop on Thursday. I was in a sort of daze, but a directed daze, an aimed daze. Twice somebody asked for my views on a paragraph or stanza which someone else had just read aloud, both times I must have responded not to the workshop lines at all but to some query or concern in my ongoing internal Sophie-centred debate. I got blank stares the first time, noisy gratitude the second. I'd said something no one else had thought of, no wonder.

What the aimed daze was about was killing Walter Rollo Maggione.

Well, it had been inevitable all along, hadn't it. Just not inevitable to me. There'd always been one last semi-diaphanous screen left between murder and me. In fact it was as inevitable as any of the elemental structures of the natural world, is more or less how I now regarded it. Here was a man abusing a woman I loved, loved chastely but much, an emotion the rightness of which it was impossible to doubt since, as I believe I've said before, I had ample objective grounds (see index under *Marianne, feelings for abused young Swiss-born woman*) to know her deserving of this emotion. This woman, who would not defend herself and wanted no defender, needed one in spite of herself.

Not a knight. There was no Field of the Cloth of Gold here. Nothing shiny or chivalrous. Just a dark deed when nobody was looking.

And having stared all round, I was now reporting back to myself that there was no one better suited than I to do this deed. Larry, no. Slaying with wit, even furious wit, wouldn't do it. Marianne would probably take it on *faute de mieux* but Marianne was as ill trained for this as her ex was. I thought of Klaus Führ up there in his watchtower over the Zürichsee, I got so far as to think of making a transatlantic phone call, but how would the conversation go? At that point I stopped considering him. Nice guy, probably in possession of the sort of hi-jinking second serve to his opponent's backhand that even in his dreams Bloom would never be able to handle. But no use here.

Nobody else.

Just me.

There was still one unanswered question, of course. How to do it. But one sleep-deprived night I thought of James Sherin and a fish-and-chips place on Bayview, and recalled a weird minute or two there. Death mutterings, I recalled. Mutterings that had never been intended seriously. *Keep on taking the salt pills, Bloom!*

I could feel my forehead wrinkling. Always a sure sign O'Bloomov was staring down into thought caverns.

It was a day later that Larry came by to advise me of a new chapter in his erratic saga. Erotic saga. He'd been invited to spend six weeks in Banff in May as senior fiction editor for what was called "the May studio at the Banff Centre for the Fine Arts." The phrase rolled off his tongue impressively.

"Sounds terrific. What is it?"

"I know what you mean, but this is on the level. I get a suite of rooms, all meals and a thousand a week. Not Stephen King rates, but what am I, a superstar?"

"And you lounge about and stare at mountains." I was already envious. I didn't have a single credential for the job, but envy can always o'erleap blunt truths like that.

"Forgot that part. I work with five writers on their manuscripts. Advice, edits. It's not even a workshop, it's one on one. Heaven."

"Crikey."

"*Crikey.* What is it about that word for you? Not the first time I've heard it from you. It's out of date, it's obsolete, this entire country was only a rumour to you when the last wrinklies went around gumming it."

"OK, OK."

"You still had your thumb in the goddamned dike."

"Larry, it's terrific. As I said."

Who knew if it was terrific, really. Maybe it was terrific.

"So it's Banff ahoy starting the last week of this month. You'll have to look after things. Y'know? Things." Nodding meaningfully.

Nods from me too.

"Just one little matter, Nik. I get to choose my five writers. The ones I'll work with. Whose pages I'll be doctoring."

"Yes?"

"So I thought I'd ask if—you know. If she'd come." Silence from me. "If she'd like to come."

Phew from me.

"Question I have for you is, is she well enough? That's what I don't know. Mountain air, great, cafeteria meals, apparently they're OK, but . . . you know her better than I do."

I was thinking at a seldom-achieved rate. Seldom by me. I was blitzing. Sophie goes to Banff for six weeks, which keeps her away from her husband all that time, good. Keeps her away from Marianne and Celia Coomaraswamy and, dare I say, me—not so good. On the other hand, probably OK. None of our business, really. Yes, it is our business. On the one hand, Celia was on the case, and Sophie trusted Celia, a huge plus. So, to be without Celia for six weeks, not so great. On the other hand, if Celia thought this was OK, it would probably be OK. Possibly much better than OK. On the eighteenth hand—

"I have an idea she'll go, and yes, she'll probably be OK. Some stuff to be worked out first, is all. You know."

Did he know? I'd no idea.

Larry nodded, telling me he didn't know. "I haven't even seen a decent-sized manuscript of hers, to be honest. Not sure where her strengths qua writer are, either. But I've read a whole bunch of thirty-page portfolio applications to

the program so far and aside from one, a guy who's been in
the quarterlies a lot, too smooth but if I can rough him up a
bit . . . aside from him, nobody's a lock. I can get her in if I
want, simple as that. Just *moi,* no committee, thank God.
I have to be sure, of course, that . . ." He was nodding his
head again, confirming something to himself.

I found myself nodding too, not at myself but at him.
Asinine, it must have looked.

Saskia once attended a fortnight's so-called studio in Wales,
a big farmhouse-cum-outbuildings near Merthyr Tydfil.
This was also in May, and was also what's called an art
colony, which is why it came into my mind after I'd heard
Larry's Banff news. That was the year Saskia had decided
she was a painter—"visual artist," the Merthyr Tydfil
brochure called it. She'd attended some art classes for a few
months in Cambridge at the Fitzwilliam, where the students
had copied still-life masterpieces upstairs as well as working
at their own fruit-and-veg images at home. I'd thought
Saskia's interest in this had, like several previous interests,
petered out, because when the Fitzbilly course ended, her
paraphernalia (paints, brushes, canvases, palette, linseed
oil, easel, liquefying tomatoes, fuzzy oranges) went into
the shed and stayed there. But in May off she went for two
weeks in Wales. Point is that although she phoned me
every morning to say how much she missed me and how it
was still raining and all, about two days after she got
home, her Merthyr Tydfil instructor, not a Welshman at
all by the way, from St. Albans I think he was,
Hertfordshire, yes, showed up, and the staring-in-the-face

fact was that he was at our door because he was awash with passion for Saskia.

How did I feel about this? Unsurprised is how I felt, why should I have been surprised. It wasn't the first time. Hard to remember in any more detail how I felt. In this regard I had almost attained to the wisdom of Pushkin, a claim I don't often make: "Domestic sadnesses do not astonish me. They have entered into my calculations." I do remember sitting in my usual chair in our living room and Saskia in her usual chair and this guy, the instructor, who oddly enough did not look like a rugby player even though he had come so freshly from Wales, who was maybe thirty-five and whose name was Glen, which seemed quite Welsh to me (I remember trying to recall, as I sat there looking at him, my brain in a kind of stasis but needing something off-topic to occupy itself with, hence trying to recall where Glendower fit into the cast list of *Henry IV Part I*—*Owen* Glendower was the full name, I remembered that much)—anyway, Glen was also sitting there, not in his usual chair, of course, since he couldn't be said to have one, but on our four-seater chesterfield. And everybody except Saskia was doing what he could to behave naturally. Glen explained that there was a show of Flemish prints at the Fitzwilliam which he'd just learned about and which was due to close soon and which he just had to see, hence his unexpected and unforewarned arrival in our town. He kept looking at me while he talked, you would have thought no one else was in the room.

After seven or eight minutes of desultory sophistries like that, I said I would make coffee or get drinks, which was really a question, but I didn't end it on any kind of up-note, so nobody felt they were being consulted. I went out to the kitchen. I was upset, don't suppose I wasn't, we are not talking about any complaisant husband here, but I was dispirited. Why not go out to the kitchen, I told myself—things are not going to get worse because you go out to the kitchen. And if they do get worse, that will probably make them better.

So I stayed out in the kitchen for longer than I needed, not making coffee, by the way, but opening a can of Watney's brown ale for myself. Eventually I returned to the living room with my Watney's but I didn't sit down. I just stood in the doorway to sip my Watney's and keep an eye on things.

Nothing had changed. Glen was not sitting out of breath in some different place on the long chesterfield nor was Saskia looking pink and rumpled in her usual chair. They looked as if they were themselves a still life, two very still lives, and so still they had also abandoned speech. Saskia then got up and said she was going up to bed. And what she said to Glen was not good night but goodbye. Unbelievable. True, though.

If I were a different person than I am I would be able to add that at this development I suddenly felt a kind of male kinship with Glen and went back to get him a can of Watney's brown ale and we stayed down there and finished the carton and drank *Bruderschaft* together and so on.

However, this is not what happened. I knew pretty well what had gone on in Wales between these two, no details but the larger picture, and nothing about that pleased me, but I was pleased that it was over. I did feel pretty sure that it was over. Glen seemed very depressed. I'm not sure why. I mean, in a way I was sure why, but in another way not. Because after all, what was so surprising here? What had he expected? Playing Tristan and Iseult in an art colony in

Wales with Tristan, a.k.a. Glen, telling everybody that there's no beating pig's bristle for a really super brush is one thing, but away from the easel crowd the plot was no longer under guarantee, surely that was obvious. I almost told Glen this. Didn't, though. Truth was that Saskia could be Iseult wherever and whenever she felt like it, and nobody would object, everybody would instantly know that she was right for the part—but most people couldn't follow her there, or only very rare people. Me, who knows. For a while, probably. I mean, once upon a time. Glen, only in Merthyr Tydfil. This is probably what was depressing him.

That's more flashback than digression. Point is that my experience of art colonies was limited and in its origin distressing, so I needed time to make up my mind about Banff and Sophie. Banff and Larry and Sophie. But once I'd done that, I was for it and I said so to Marianne, who listened and was serious. I'd thought she might be sardonic, but she was not. "Larry's not a complete jerk, Nik. He's an incomplete jerk. This'll be fine."

The next stage was like this. Sophie got an official-looking letter from Banff informing her that she had been selected, on the basis of a recommendation from a faculty member, to participate in the writing program, known as the May Studio, at the Banff Centre for the Fine Arts from April 26 to June 2. Board and lodging gratis, no-fee instruction, double room all to herself, use of computer facilities on the house. Her only expense would be her return fare. She was to acknowledge her ability to attend ASAP.

She had been warned by a phone call two days earlier from an admin person at the Centre that this was in the cards. This had caused her to look, Marianne said, pensive. At least she hadn't said no.

Fact is, Marianne was terrified about it. How would Maggione react? Marianne was sure that Sophie had kept all this, the advance tip and everything, to herself. But the arrival of the Banff acceptance letter must surely signal a more critical stage.

"This is your cue, Nik. I don't know how or what you'll do, but it's critical. Dearest Nik, I know you care as much—do you?—as I do."

And of course she was right. My turn.

So the morning of my date with Black Fate, which is how, in the terrific Mahabharatan legend, Krishna identifies himself to Arjuna before a battle—"I am Black Fate, come to annihilate everything"—the chill that always runs up my spine when I think of that self-identification!—anyway, that morning I was standing at the window of the little unused room at the top of my house staring down at the neat row of 0.6 mg glyceryl Trinitrate (nitroglycerine) tablets I had counted out onto the sill there several days earlier. Twenty-four tiny white pills lying innocuously in the sunlight. By now they had undoubtedly been there long enough. Long enough under the gentle but in this context "annihilating" rays of the sun to have lost all effectiveness. Long enough to have become no better than placebos.

How obediently they all lay there!

And how strange, their mission. Little negative bullets is what they were now. Tiny messengers with obliterated messages.

I put one of them under my tongue. If it fizzed, it could still have some life. Some worth.

No fizz.

"I am Black Fate, come to annihilate everything."

And now I was putting them back into their little brown Nitrostat bottle. Maggione's appointment was for mid-afternoon, and he was coming for this little bottle. His earlier prescription medication had reached its sell-by date a week ago, and, methodical as ever, he had called to advise me of this. Bring what's left, I had said. I'll replace them.

Sell-by date or not, they would be of more value to his next angina than these were going to be.

How did I feel about this? Shaky as hell.

With every fibre of my being I wished a man dead. For good reason. A man who, allowed to go on living, would sooner or later blunder past his limits, pump his arm those several additional times, and—

Yes yes. I've been there, pictured it, I've brought that sight up on my screen—

And yet . . . shaky as hell.

To permit an unpermissible death or to assist . . . another sort.

Karl Kraus: *If I must choose the lesser of two evils, I will choose neither.*

I've never had any problem understanding and admiring that. Approving it. But not choosing, here, was choosing.

Easy does it, Bloom. These pills weren't going to kill him. They weren't cyanide. Or any of a hundred other devious compounds. Not poppy or mandragora or any other sweet and drowsy syrup.

All they would do, in their unspectacular way, having surrendered all of their healing powers to the warming rays of the sun, would be to fail to assist a heart, any heart, to survive any kind of assault. In particular, to survive another of the sort of assault a man well known to me had already experienced at least twice.

That "twice" almost guaranteeing that another such assault would sooner or later show up on his horizon. Guaranteeing, in fact, that it must already be waiting. And that it must be feeling pretty optimistic, you'd have to think, about its chances with this man, now that the odds had changed.

Nicolaas Bloom, odds-alterer.

Still. Shaky was the word.

I dreamed of my dying last night. In my dream I was in the very transition of moving from my life into my death. As I began to enter death I saw my daughter who was already there. She was Saskia's and my daughter, of course, the only child I have ever had, the child who died before she could be born. But now here she was, a little girl of perhaps eight or nine, and when I first saw her, she was looking towards some other little girls whom she must have been playing with but who had now moved a little way off, as if they knew this was not for them. She turned back towards me just as I approached. She had white-blond hair like Saskia and was wearing a little flowery dress and she saw me and smiled and said, "Daddy, why did you wait so long?"

I dream of my daughter too often, and too hard. I'm afraid that sometime without knowing it I may dream of her so hard that she will be dreamed into life. But since I won't know this has happened, I won't know enough to go looking for her.

And how will she possibly know where to look for me?

My final, as it turned out, date at the clinic with Maggione lacked drama. He was obviously preoccupied and made things easy for me by raising, early in our five minutes, the subject of Sophie's proposed flight to the West.

"If she wants to, why not? Not for the full period, of course. Six weeks! That is *sinnlos.* That is without sense. She is a married woman with responsibilities. She may go now because she is of no use to me at present. My thesis defence, which I am now preparing, brings with it the sort of pressure which you will understand but for which she has no comprehension. How should she? A series of ordeals such as I am facing is outside her experience. Her life, *sehen Sie,* has been entirely without pressure! I cannot blame her for this, it is the case with many women of the privileged classes . . ."

He had no doubt she would return whenever he signalled.

And in the meantime, at least his wife would not be in "that infantile writers' group" while she was at Banff. I realized that this was why he was allowing her to go. I realized also that he had no idea who the Banff fiction editor was.

I gave him his repeat order of Nitrostat pills. Bouncing the little brown bottle in his hand, he said that he would be "very unlikely to have recourse to these." With his constitution? Off he went, looking amused.

Anton writes in his journal that he yearns for the time when he will have his own wife and not somebody else's. It's a typically energy-buzzing Chekhov line, starting out with what looks like a maudlin wish but before you've had time to notice its banality there's the crackle of those last few words.

When I came across it last night, I was, of course, simply admiring it, its economy and speed—but an hour or two later, trying and as usual failing to sleep, I began to wonder how close Larry Logan's circumstances might be to Chekhov's. Ever since he and Marianne had gone their two ways, other men's wives had floated into Larry's orbit, not a lot of these drifting women, but some. And where he was at present, out there in the mountains, same drifting-past phenomena, it seemed likely. Now and then a passing glow up there in the night sky, probably slowing down when it saw him down below. Call it a pausing glow. And him down there on his little balcony, surveying his realm. Counting glows. Zbigniew Cybulski, after all. And a CanLit star into the bargain.

OK, not star. All the same.

That this kind of thing might be happening was so little my business that I'm really taken aback to notice myself on this page at all. I wasn't concerned about Larry/ Zbigniew's behaviour either way. I was truly not concerned about it.

It was only that with two of their six weeks gone, his weeks and Sophie's weeks, and not a postcard or phone call from either of them to any of us . . .

No. No way. Marianne had said not, ergo not.

One other thing, though, just as unlikely, did happen and did involve me, even if my involvement was inadvertent. I had a phone call one night, very late—according to my garishly luminous non-digital clock it was 2 A.M. Not a second's doubt who it was. He didn't introduce himself but seemed already in mid-sentence, and although I couldn't have been fully awake, I remember quite clearly the first words that I heard. They were ". . . archetypes in their only true home, the human unconscious." And the voice went on, a startling rant into which I could not break, although I tried. I eventually began to pick up a thread. He was evidently reading aloud a paragraph, several paragraphs, from some scholarly work, perhaps his own scholarly work. A draft of his thesis, I later decided.

Then silence, except for breathing noises. Then a quite different voice, no longer scripted. "So, Professor Doctor Hagauer. This is what I would have added had you not informed me my time was up. Your colleagues were entirely willing to let me continue, particularly Professor Doctor Leinsdorf was making notes and regarding me with a sympathetic eye. It was only you who insisted that the committee had heard quite enough, these were your very words, and then telling me you would now adjourn the meeting until my oral presentation, which you stated must be held on—"

"Hello," I said. "Hello. Dr. Maggione? Is this Dr. Maggione?"

Pause. "Yes."

"This is Nicolaas Bloom."

Longer pause. "No. You are Professor Doctor Hagauer."

He was referring to his thesis adviser, *that* Professor Doctor Hagauer.

"Don't you know my voice?"

He tried one more time, but his own voice faltered, by now he knew his mistake. "But I have a number here—where is it—yes, here—ah . . ."

The dial tone resumed, placid as always.

Sometime after that the pressure on Sophie to come home began. Or accelerated. Probably it began or accelerated the minute Maggione was advised that his oral defence had been set for mid-September, four months away. Probably it was the morning following the evening on which he had picked up the phone and reached me instead of his thesis adviser. The secretary to the program director at the Banff Centre came into her office that next morning to find five calls from the same Toronto number stacked up on her answering machine. The caller had disregarded time-zone differences, the first call having been received at 5 A.M. Banff time. Messages of expanding impatience. Each demanded a response from "the Program Head who is responsible for Mrs. Maggione, a participant in the Writing Program," and went on to demand that Mrs. Maggione return the call at once or, should this be impracticable, begin preparations for her return to Toronto. There was one message which began in English and concluded in a language the secretary didn't know.

On an aggressiveness scale rising from one to ten, the secretary reported, these were nines.

Fortunately, Larry came by the secretary's office on his way in to breakfast that morning, so he was the first to be told. He skipped breakfast and phoned his ex-wife. Well, not ex-wife yet but—you know. Marianne said let's think about this. She called CC. CC uttered the f-word several times in a controlled manner and then apologized for all several. "They have to tell her," she then said. "Have to give her the messages, I mean." Adding, "Don't they?"

Marianne agreed that they did. In a last-ditch try for even better advice she dropped by at my house, but I wasn't there. She scribbled a note on my desk pad, phoned Larry back, got him and asked how things were.

"Great. Twenty lengths in the pool every morning before brek. Believe it, Annie? I'm expecting to come home ripped like you haven't seen me since you welcomed me into your life way back when."

Marianne said, had Sophie been told about the phone calls?

"Can't do that, Annie," Larry's voice came briskly down the line. "Can't tell her. She'd go home if she knew he was calling. Can't have that. I only told you about this so you could set in motion some damage control at your end. Calm the guy down, whatever. She's doing so great here. Annie, it's spooky. I'm spooked. Her writing—hmm, won't go into that here. It's OK, it might be open to becoming much better than OK, but fiction isn't her thing, I'm thinking. Some other genre, why not, whatever swims into view. But listen to this—speaking of swimming, she's some kind of water baby, y'know? This morning she passed me a dozen times, so help me I reckon she was kicking up a special piece of splash as she blew past me the last time. I couldn't believe—yes, I could, I'm beginning to believe. That the dead shall quicken, that the dispossessed shall enter at last into their kingdom. That the downcast shall lift their weary faces into the sunlight and . . . You still there, Annie?"

"I'm here."

"Know what I'm saying?"

"I do, Larry. Yup. But she has to be told, at least. She's a grown-up. You're not *in loco* her dad. Or *in loco* anything else, by the way."

"Chrissake. I know that, Annie."

"I know you know that, Larry. But tell her. Pass the messages on to her."

"She needs a few more days. Three more weeks, actually. But a few more days minimum."

Neither of them spoke for a few seconds, until Marianne said, "I'll call you back," and went away from the phone. As it turned out, she never did call back.

This is how it was explained to us. Rollo—he's got his name back again, for reasons jogging slowly towards you—evidently decided that his messages to Banff weren't getting through and that there must be some other number he could punch in. Sorry about the verb. Seeking this better number, he hunted through the drawers of Sophie's desk, and although he did not find the better number, or anything else that was better, he did find something. This was a Banff brochure which listed, under *Fiction, Poetry*, etc., the names of the writing program's instructors, with a photo and potted bio for each one. Larry was looking quite solemn, even dignified, in his photo, but the disguise wasn't good enough. When Rollo came upon it, something in him may have ruptured, some micro-organism may have gone dark, blinked noiselessly a few times and gone out forever—hard to be sure of this, though, medicine has much to learn in this regard. It could be that nothing at all happened (and I wasn't there, neither was anyone else, so this entire sentence is guesswork), it's just that what Rollo did next left enough clues that the guessing's minimal. He must have decided to dispense with telephones and fly out without warning, surprise Larry and Sophie in whatever *flagrante* activity might be going on, and then—and then, he would see. They would all see. Being nothing if not methodical, he first called the university's Graduate Office, where he learned that his Ph.D. committee had suspended any decision on the date for his oral until the next week. He then booked a return flight to Calgary and took a cab to Pearson.

When I think of this, of Rollo sitting in his window seat or his wherever seat flying out over the Soo and then Superior and on over all the forests and flatlands en route to the Alberta foothills, and try to imagine what's in his mind, of course I can come up with speculations, but the odds are I'll be miles off what was really there. And who, anyhow, could want to have access to the tightened-to-bursting wires, as I think of them, inside that mind? My own wires have probably never been close to it, although there've been moments . . .

Supposing I'd driven off madly into Wales that time, and arrived in the very ecstasy of one of Glen and Saskia's couplings. What then? To me this conjures up Othelloish scenes involving goats and monkeys, toads living upon dungeon vapours, cranked-up adverbs and sweaty adjectives, and all of it a long, long way from any of the truly tragic scenes in the great rolling landscape of what humans

can be asked to endure. I'm not mocking jealousy! I know
that you can sicken of it, I myself have wandered about in
its ache for days. Still, if you do manage to go on living, as
most do, it fades off. Often it even becomes embarrassing to
remember, a source of real self-doubt. "Can I really trust
my own intelligence, granted that I felt that way about her,
about him? brought my serious life to a halt for all those
weeks because of X? because of, of all people, Y?"

Point I'm trying to make is, what did this man have in
mind, heading off towards a destination he'd never seen
and probably never thought about, and towards what must
have looked, to him, like a closed-ranks regiment of aliens,
this despised "art colony" that was conspiring against the
established pattern of his life?

I find myself half admiring his journey. First time for
such a feeling vis-à-vis this man. Perhaps not quite the last.

His arrival pattern must have been like this. He lands
in Calgary, and misses the first Brewster-line bus to Banff
because he doesn't take the time to check with an information booth and nobody tells him just how hair-trigger
the connections are. Gets the next one (his thoughts
unknown for those several hours up the Trans-Canada).
Is deposited at the foot of the wide flat-stoned walkway
up to Lloyd Hall, which his brochure, the one he found in
Sophie's desk, has informed him all the candidates have
their rooms in. And heads up to the Hall, thinking, *First
Floor, 144, First Floor, 144, First Floor, 144*. Or not thinking that.

What's clear is that Sophie was not in 144 when he
arrived. He certainly showed up in the downstairs office
and learned that most of the May studio group had gone
for a late afternoon walk up Tunnel Mountain. Tunnel

Mountain is more hill than mountain, with a wide track curling around it and an easily reachable summit, therefore not a long-lasting tramp, but Rollo was not to know this. He apparently stormed off wordlessly in the direction of that wide track. The group was coming back down and met him at the only faintly disturbing part of the walk, where there is a steep, vertiginous in fact, drop-off as you go round a wide bend. Rollo had stationed himself awkwardly, it seems, where they met, and at least one of the walkers remonstrated with him for forcing her to step nearer that dizzying drop than she liked. He moved aside, just enough.

Larry was not with the group, and neither was Sophie.

So he followed the others down and went again to 144. Sophie still wasn't there. He returned to the Lloyd office, which was closing for the day, and asked to know Larry's room number. The woman who gave it to him was sure, seconds after doing so, that giving it to him had been a bad idea. His face looked so weird, she said. Weird? "I don't know. Twitchy." And somebody watching her monitor farther back in the office chipped in, "Jumpy." This to Larry, the next morning.

I won't prolong this. Sophie must have been doing her lengths in the pool right then, having earlier been in the library with earphones on and listening to, she said, and of course I have no trouble remembering this, Kodály's *Háry János Suite*. Larry had gone to Calgary for the day to do a promotion/reading for a year-old book of his, a local bookstore owner being a fan and having learned of his proximity.

Maggione didn't find his wife until he walked into the cafeteria that evening for dinner, where he spied her sitting with a friend across the wide, cutlery-clattering, spiritedly conversing space.

They didn't see him until someone took a chair from an adjoining table, pulled it up to theirs and sat down. Smiling and genial. Taking Sophie's hand and kissing it.

"Walter! When did you—"

"I have been seeking you. Everywhere. Your room, the mountain, the reading room—"

"I am so sorry. If you had phoned me—"

"Ah. Telephoning you is not an easy matter, *Liebchen*."

"No, of course. I ought to have called you. I am so sorry. I have been so immersed in—in all these things—"

"Understandably, my Sophia. Understandably." He smiled at the companion and, half rising, offered his hand. "Maggione. Doctor."

"Erica, hi."

"What a shame, Walter, that you must waste your time looking for me. I was in the library most of the afternoon. I was listening to the most beautiful Hungarian music. It is surely based on folk songs. Walter, it was so— "

It was at this point that Erica, the companion, noticed a slight glitch in the amiability. Maggione was patting Sophie's hand, and now he took it into his own.

"Indeed you were not, my dear."

"Walter?"

"You were not in the library, let me assure you of that. I looked everywhere. Between every stack." Still smiling.

"You looked—?"

"Let me assure you, yes. My dear." His hand, the suddenly horrified Erica noticed, was white with the pressure it must have been exerting on Sophie's hand.

"Oh. I am so silly. Of course, I was not where you

would have seen me. There is a small music room in one corner, at the back, and the door may have been closed, yes, it was surely closed—"

He was nodding, Erica noticed. She also noticed his smile in her direction as he listened to his wife confess to her error in sitting behind a closed door listening to Kodály. "Fuck was he smiling at *me* for?" asked Erica later. Nobody knew. His smile was undisturbed as he nodded, listening to Sophie's continuing explanation, and his hand plainly, Erica saw, had not lessened its pressure. Erica was by now thoroughly frightened. She said bravely, "Sophie, shouldn't we go?"

Sophie looked at her "wildly," Erica reported.

"What should you go to?" Rollo/Walter then enquired, addressing them both. He looked from one to the other in a friendly fashion, then evidently lost interest in Erica.

"No, nothing," Sophie said. "Nowhere. Erica—Erica, don't wait. I—"

"Sophia. You are prevaricating, which is unfortunate. We have been through this so many times. I shall be very interested to learn of your evening engagement. Now, let us go back a little. Your friend was reminding you—"

Erica got up and, in "a stroke of unusual genius, for me," she was to say, extended her right hand to Maggione, who released Sophie's hand and grasped Erica's in the briefest handshake she had ever been given. That hand had, however, "a pulse, for God's sake," Erica remembered. She was still worried about Sophie but also a little for herself. Perhaps this man would now insist on her explaining what their totally unspecific plans had been. She went off quickly. Evidently she headed for the Sally Borden common room to find someone to talk to about all this, but no one was around, it was too early in the evening. She tried Larry's suite, but he wasn't yet back from Calgary. She looked about but eventually went to her room and took a long bath. This was, after all, a husband and wife.

The coda to the Banff episode was compact and swift—a few noisy chords and then an assortment of notes struck, mostly, offstage. Larry got in from Calgary very late that night, he's always claimed his lateness was due not to some oilwoman's, if that's a category, friendliness but only to the usual problems with an overbooked last bus, would they put a second bus on or not—and they finally had, but not quickly. Somebody was rapping at his door at seven in the morning, this being Erica. Erica was filled with guilt at having slept well in spite of everything. When he'd heard her story, Larry ran, not walked, to Sophie's room, he said he was buttoning his shirt as he ran. She wasn't there. He persuaded a chambermaid to let him into a facing room which looked out on the front of the building. From that window he could see the early morning bus to Calgary vibrating away in front of the Donald Cameron Building and a small knot of people unknotting its way into it. Having Erica's story freshly in mind, he did what he called one of the more self-renunciatory things of his life, meaning that he did *not* race down there; if Sophie and her husband were together by the bus, he insightfully surmised, then showing his face at that juncture might do Sophie no good. "Not that we'd been up to a damn thing," he added. Adding this much later, when he was back in Toronto. "I mean, c'mon—Sophie? Up to something? It's true we took a walk down by the Bow River a couple of mornings, so if you want to count that . . ." Nobody wanted to count it. "We talked about her biography. She's on the brink of writing one, did you know? Doesn't want to call it a biography, calls it a song of praise. About you know who, Frenchwoman, kind of a working priest, died during the war. Sounds like Sophie all right, eh? Sophie's illuminated chart of the world—an immense landscape with here and there a solitary little manikin shining in it. Or womanikin. Lighting it up with wordless faith. Might even be worth reading one day. Might not." Shrug. "As a title, *Song of Praise* has to go, that's for sure. Kiss of effing death, title like that."

Apparently almost everybody in the program was down by the bus, and they were there just for Sophie. Hugs, kisses, some tears. Erica's news had raced around. After what happened next, and after the bus had rumbled off, Larry was told, within seconds, five or six times, the whole story. Sophie had been pale and seemed subdued—this wouldn't have been noticed a couple of weeks before, she'd been "subdued" the whole time back then. But that was then and this was now, and now they'd become used to a woman who smiled often and laughed sometimes, so the difference was plain. Maggione had climbed into the bus and then come back out again, thin of lip and pale of cheek—he'd thought his wife was following him in, but she had been delayed by two women of about her own age who were talking earnestly to her just to one side of the bus. Maggione descended, took Sophie's arm, "shouted" or at least spoke loudly, sounding "slurred," somebody said, and then obviously wanted to regain his seat, pulling his wife up the step after him. This wasn't easy. Somebody who couldn't have been paying much attention to anything took Sophie's other arm, grinned in friendly fashion at Maggione and struck up the refrain to "Auld Lang Syne." A few of the others joined in. Meanwhile the bus driver was becoming restive. He left his seat and shouted at Maggione that their two bags, which he'd stowed in the bus's luggage compartment, would be unloaded if he and his wife weren't in their seats "like, five minutes ago."

Maggione waved at him, though whether he waved in sympathy or anger or was already losing touch with himself, nobody later was sure. The bus driver's take on this was, "Guy didn't seem to be looking at me at all. Seemed to be looking upstairs somewhere. Know what I mean?" Whatever the bus driver meant, Maggione then fell off the bus step into the arms of an alert member of the "Auld Lang Syne" chorus. He was unconscious when those arms stopped his fall.

So Sophie did not travel back to Toronto that day. It was almost instantly clear that she would not be travelling there the next day either. Within minutes of arriving in the Banff hospital's ER, her husband was diagnosed as having sustained a TIA, transient ischemic attack. In English, a mild or pre-stroke. A half-hour after his tumble he was talking animatedly to one of the nurses, but when Sophie was allowed in he reverted to *Schweizerdeutsch*, a Swiss approximation of German, and after that he rarely left that language. Two hours later he was being helicoptered to Calgary, together with a nurse and a doctor. There was no room for Sophie in the helicopter, so she went down that afternoon in one of the Centre's cars. A half-dozen of her fellow participants in the studio volunteered to keep her company, but she declined all these and arrived at Calgary's

Foothills Hospital on her own. And moved into the cardio ward in a room adjoining her husband's.

The rest of this I know partly because it's routine, partly because, fading though my expertise is, I still retain the odd piece of specialist wisdom in matters of the heart. And the rest of it is because somebody told me, Sophie or some anon at Sunnybrook. It's in any case not much.

At Foothills they did a CT scan, blood work, MRI, put him on a blood thinner and medicated him to lots of sleep. He was still functioning almost normally, bar the language preference, and in one of his more prolonged waking periods he succeeded, his wife interpreting, in making it clear he wanted to get back to Toronto without delay. He didn't succeed in making it clear *why* he wanted this so urgently. Perhaps it felt closer to Europe. What's significant is that he was or appeared to be sufficiently compos mentis that the Calgary clinicians couldn't deny him a voice in his immediate fate. Their objection to his travelling so soon was formally noted, but if he didn't want to stay, and if his wife wasn't insisting, and she wasn't, that was that. The odds were that he was giving body room to some sick arteries, heart or brain or both, but he wasn't about to die. The rest of the story could be Toronto's, the clinicians must have felt.

So as soon as he was stable enough, Maggione signed himself out and was put on a flight home, stretchered and with a private nurse in attendance. Sophie was in attendance too. En route, in their private alcove at the back, all was apparently well until, two and a half hours into the flight, a few miles perpendicular to Thunder Bay, the nurse took her patient's blood pressure. She'd been testing it throughout and it had been OK, she said, on the high side but, you know, not too bad—but she found it, now, off the scale, so far off she "knew" it must be her own error. In the very first seconds of her starting to redo the BP, the patient felt a severe pain in his chest. He tried to speak and pain crushed his voice so unanswerably he didn't try again.

This is where things get murky. Sophie had her husband's brown Nitrostat bottle, the one he had walked out of my office bouncing in his hand; the nurse had her own standard-issue nitro; and only I, ahead in Toronto, knew there was a difference between the two. Later, I asked Sophie about this moment in the flight, taking care not to insist on too exact an answer. This may have been because I didn't want an exact answer or simply that I didn't want to be noticed insisting. In any case it worked out all right since I didn't get an exact answer. As far as Sophie was concerned, what did it matter? She'd had nothing to do during the preceding several days except browse the cardio pamphlets, so by now she could recognize angina behaviour almost as well as the nurse could, and all that mattered was that the nitro was there when it was needed, which was instantly. Had she given her husband the nitro or had the nurse? Well, after not much thought, "the nurse," Sophie said. "OK," I said. Off the hook, I thought. I didn't even know if being off the hook was important, or good, or if I cared. My first reaction was, if anything, disappointment. So I hadn't done a thing here, had not moved off my sideline-observer-narrator role after all. Was this anything to feel good about?

Hippocrates was staring straight ahead, he hadn't seen a thing.

Sophie spoke up just as I was trying to come to terms with my neutered role. "I mean," she said, "she was the one who got him to hold it in his mouth. You know, not to swallow it, to let it dissolve. He didn't understand that right away, that he mustn't swallow it. But eventually he did."

"I see."

"It was funny—not funny but strange—because of course at home he'd known perfectly well that he wasn't to swallow it. It was—well, it was a kind of, a first sign, I think. You know."

"Of how things are with him now, yes."

"But I think we used Walter's own bottle."

"Oh." Not neutered after all.

"He was used to those, wasn't he. He saw the bottle, I had it right there. And I think he wanted it. He couldn't speak, but his hand opened up and he—I think he raised his chin towards it and then downwards again. As if he said, yes, that's it, hurry up. Anyway, even if he didn't, it was what he was used to, that bottle, wasn't it. It wouldn't have made any difference, but if he was even a little more comfortable that way . . ."

But she wasn't, couldn't be, not totally, she said, sure. Yes, she unscrewed the cap on the brown bottle. She shook a pill into her hand—didn't she? She thought she had done that. But did the nurse pluck that pill from her palm and give it to the patient? Or use one of her own?

Sophie couldn't be sure.

Well, yes, she said, after all, I do think that—

No, couldn't be sure.

Which was interesting, to me. Because during that flight to Toronto the minor or pre-stroke that Sophie's husband had experienced on the steps of the Brewster bus in Banff came looking for him again with unfinished business on its mind and found him, found him quite easily, you'd have to think, sitting up on his stretcher between his nurse and his wife in the alcove at the back of Air Canada 456, Calgary to Toronto. Only finding him so easily this time meant that it wasn't a minor attack or a pre-stroke, it was the central thing itself.

No, I don't mean the Distinguished Thing.* He didn't die, hasn't died yet. But a substantial thing all the same.

It will do.

How to continue here? A few things still to be said. Sophie's and her husband's arrangements in Toronto, the life rhythms of almost everyone this story has concerned itself with, all these changed—I won't say "irremediably," I will say *visibly*. Some of those ways can wait. One that needn't concerns the Marianne–Sophie connection. Latent and shadowy before, out in the unthreatening sunlight now.

They met almost every day. Met briefly or, as Marianne once said to me, and as Sophie, nearby and smiling, agreed, "interminably." I think of their meetings as, in a small-print way, more sociologically significant than anything that can be caught in the humble net of the word "conversation." They were the sort of encounters great persons in literature and history have always had with each other while the world eavesdrops—the world as a rule understanding hardly a word but staying with it, ear cupped, anyway, because even if it doesn't understand, it's moved by the gulf between its own habitual buzz and the luminous things it's now listening in on. These destined-to-be-remembered words. The comparison's overblown, of course (were these two friends "great persons"?—only one other person would say so). All I wish to suggest is that the

* "Here it comes at last, the Distinguished Thing."—H. James

two women's talks meant, for each of them, a sensibility at full stretch. How often have you sat with somebody and had that feeling?

Often, you say. Fine. My point's simply that you can't ask for better than that. Whether you throw a big shadow on the world or close to none.

This started quite soon after the Return, and got its special spark from Sophie's quantum-improved energies. She was still Sophie, still not quite eyeing the world's stage for a starring role, still best pleased as intent watcher. But the familiar silences, the deferrings to all the ignoramuses in the room before testing the occasional faltering syllable of her own—these were gone. Now her syllables entered the air lightly, easily, as everybody who cared about her had long wanted them to. As *we* had wanted them to, and as, just possibly, here's a stretch, a famous syllable-maker whose life had flukily drawn to a close up there over the Zürichsee might have had pleasure in knowing about and listening to too.

"To too" wouldn't have added to his pleasure, but let's get on.

In any case, it had to happen, all that. I mean, Sophie *had* to take charge of herself, contribute her share of words to the public air, otherwise Rollo, formerly Walter, latterly Maggione, would have had a very thin time of it, just sitting around. Watching the days go by. Waiting for Switzerland.

Which is what he was doing. It's what his every diminished sense was trained on.

So Sophie spoke up, she talked, and if I were to be asked what her conversations with Marianne were about, I'd say "many a bootless thing." And some unforgettable and to this day unforgotten things, also. But one of those things had to be, as anybody who knew Sophie's history and knew Marianne's skills at finding her way into shielded histories could have predicted, that private sorority of *religieuses* that Sophie had been silently conversing with, listening to, for quite a lot of her young and recent life.

These sometimes intense, sometimes desultory talks took place, as a rule, in the early afternoons, starting at one or two because Sophie had to get home to Rollo by five. Five was the hour at which the live-out nurse wanted to leave and was also, very reasonably, the hour at which Rollo expected to have a chapter of the current book read to him, whatever the current book was. Sometimes, if my house had been the venue for the two women's meeting and if, up there in my third-floor workroom, I had dotted the day's last *i,* and if in spite of all that dotting I was still awake enough, I would come downstairs and, mouse-still unless anybody encouraged me to speak up, sit through the last of their talk. Was it worth my time? When I could have been having my pre-dinner nap or my post-nap drink? Usually. Nobody's perfect, and no dialogue either, but usually. There was also an early evening, once, Sophie having departed homewards some hours before, when Marianne said, as the two of us were walking slowly back from the ravine, having run a bit too far for one of us—and no, not for me, although I know you thought it was—"You know what you told me once, about the attic in your house in Amsterdam?"

"My parents' house." (What a memory, though, *liefste.*)

"OK. This woman, you know who, Simone Weil, the one who waited for, you know—"

"Sure, Him."

"—attics were very big in her life too. Bigger than they were in yours, if you don't mind my saying so. I mean,

I much prefer thinking of you in your attic than of her in hers, and I bet your attic was a lot nicer as well as lonelier—"

"How would you feel about me calling you Annie?"

"I would feel unwell. Up in Simone Weil's attic, here's the thing, there was a lot more going on than dead flies on the windowsills. Guess who else was often up there?"

"Wouldn't be General de Gaulle?"

"God. God, that's who. He stayed up there for three days with her once, eating only bread and drinking only water. That's the boring part. But the great thing about that story, I just heard it a couple of hours ago, is this. Are you ready? . . . Don't just stare at me like that, Doctor dear, it's worrying. She says, I mean Simone Weil says this, not Sophie, Sophie's quoting it, however, and doing so with such pleasure—so fine it was, Nik, to hear her quoting this— 'There is a great difference between pain and affliction. Pain is merely physical'—NB, *merely* physical, Sophie obviously wasn't arguing with that—'whereas affliction is of the soul. And it's affliction, of those two, that brings one closer to God.'"

" . . . "

"Well, what about it?"

"It's good."

"That's it? That's your comment?"

"I'm turning it over."

"Darling Nik, it's not an egg."

"I've turned it over enough now. You're saying this is a good development. A step forward for Sophie. If pain is 'merely physical,' you're saying, then—well, then for Sophie that's obviously progress. Nobody's going to put up with pain if they think it's *merely* physical. Or *merely* any-thing. Am I getting warm?"

Encouraging smile. Hardly any irony in it.

"I'm not sure about affliction yet, though. Where affliction comes in, I mean. Obviously it's higher on the moral chart than pain, but—"

"Yes? "

"—but that word 'soul' . . . Hmm. Funny thing, Marianne. I used never to give 'soul' any space in my life. Lately, though—" In that split second I was close to, not quite on the brink of but close to, saying something to Marianne about a matter I had determined never to speak of to anybody. Never, no one, not a word. This matter being a row of small white pills lying in the sunlight on a window ledge in an unused room at the top of my house.

It was in the last few seconds, when I was already listening to my inner practice-voice starting to say it, that I told myself, *No.*

Inner head-shaking too. *No.*

No more brinks. Finished. Closed down.

Just me to commune with myself on this, forever.

"Lately—?"

"Lately, um, lately. . . . Lately I *have* thought about it. Soul. I'm still thinking about it. When I come to the end of the thought, I'll probably tell you."

"I'll wait."

"You probably studied far past any thought I will come up with when you were in second-year Psych."

"You wouldn't say that if you'd been in second-year Psych. But Nik, dear Nik, listen. Don't you think— don't you think this is pretty wonderful? I don't mean Simone Weil, even though she's pretty wonderful too— and she really is, you know, in spite of being seriously masochistic—"

"Lots of those around, Marianne. Masochists, I mean. Look down there, a whole gang of them. Still running in all this heat. Crazy. Instead of sensibly about to get drunk, like us."

Because by this time we were on the porch. It was truly hot but at least, this late in the summer, there were no small biting things flying around. Nothing afflicting. I was feeling unusually well, since I'd been the one who had wanted to go on running. I unstacked two of the plastic chairs on the porch and sat Marianne down in one of them. I then went in to get something cold. It was Sunday and it was August and it was two months since Sophie's husband had become somebody nobody minded having around, somebody called Rollo. An innocent name, and one he had earned.

What Rollo's and Sophie's days were like when they'd got to Toronto is simply told. The doctors did what they always do with heart-attacked/stroked people, what they do a dozen times a day in this town. Bedrest and blood work and scans, and afterwards days and days being wheeled about among the specialists. Sophie was always there, encouraging and watchful. The diagnosis, (which, as his quondam GP, I had regular reports on) was of unspecific brain damage (accidents on the neurovascular highways tend to deposit as much generalized, strewn-about litter, a.k.a. plaque, as the metaphor would suggest) and, secondarily, in a jargon-free phrase that Sophie overheard, "an exhausted heart." The latter is a phrase I've often used myself, finding it a useful description of a heart that can tire in minutes and is not to be relied upon to keep the faith throughout a long life. You could live ten years, or ten days. Once home, Rollo sat in his chair most of the daylight hours, watched as his medications were counted out, occasionally riffled through the pages of his dissertation. Or he would pick those pages up, squaring them thoroughly against the board that lay across his chair-arms, and put them down again. He watched a lot of television. Two months after he was back, the University of Toronto granted him his doctorate without requiring the oral. Whether this was a sympathy judgment affected by the department's awareness of the circumstances, who knows. Certainly that thought did not occur to Rollo, who was very pleased. As the weeks went on, his routine became invariable. A day-late issue of the *Neue Zürcher Zeitung* was read aloud to him every morning and always, this was essential, in the same sequence: listings of academic appointments first, local news second, editorials and letters third. Following this he went for accompanied short walks, and later, for a time, he walked short distances on his own. The unsupervised strolls were soon discontinued, it seems he returned in an agitated condition from one of them, no one knew why. In the beginning they had decided—Sophie had decided—against a night nurse, which meant Sophie was sole caregiver. After a while this was too much and a live-in person was found. Sometime after that the future began to be discussed.

She had as many hours of the day to herself as anyone could wish for, Sophie said. The rest of the day—

"Well, there's so much reading-aloud to be done, isn't there. It's wonderful, what he wants to learn about."

"Reading who aloud?" This was from me. I was interested. In his very old age, unsure of many things, Bertrand Russell had others read Wittgenstein to him. Somebody perhaps not quite as marvellously rich of mind but infinitely more beloved of me, Iris Murdoch, watched the Teletubbies from the blur of Alzheimer's. While she was, in her own words, "sailing into the dark." I bless her there.

"Well, Jung, these days."

"What of Jung?"

"The autobiographies. Such wonderful evocations of his childhood, Nicolaas! As a child he lived in a village near Basel. Near the end of his long life he remembered that he—this is so moving, I think—he remembered being carried outdoors by his father. It was in 1883. He was eight years old. He remembered his father carrying him outside to see the reflections in the night sky of the eruption of Krakatoa. Krakatoa! Such a famous event in history, that eruption! Thousands of miles away in Asia, imagine, an explosion occurs and its brightness is reflected in the sky over a little village in Europe. As an old man he wrote in his autobiography that the sky that night was, I have memorized these words, 'shimmering in the most glorious green.' Imagine, Nicolaas. How that green still shimmered in the sky for him when he was old! And shimmers now, a little, for us, do you agree? Because an old man remembered seeing it when he was a child, and wrote about it while he still could?"

Rollo had listened to Sophie's reading of this paragraph a dozen times. She thought he would ask for it again tomorrow.

When she was not actively caring for her husband, she walked and walked, or read and read. Yes, Rollo wanted to be read to, wanted it strenuously, but he would tire easily. Ten minutes might be enough, he would signal her to stop. Or tell her to stop, sometimes he could manage this, there'd be that flicker of *temps perdus.* Then he would sleep and she would read to herself, late, late. With the television off, there was nothing to remind her what time it was.

Being summer, there was no writing workshop. Sophie ran into Ms. Madell, though, one day in Edwards Gardens. Irma Madell was seated on a bench writing a poem. It was her third poem of that morning, and she called out to Sophie as she walked near. They spent the early part of the afternoon together. Irma told her how worried they had been at times during that last term, how they hadn't understood when Sophie didn't come down with them during that workshop break, and then when she did go with them, the next time, it had been so peculiar. The teacher had obviously been such a nuisance to her. Staying behind as he had, to talk to her when the rest of them went back upstairs.

"No, not a nuisance. He was being kind."

Irma was relieved to hear it. You could never be sure with that man. Of course he published, she had to admit that, and she'd borrowed a book of his from the library and still had it, as a matter of fact. She had put it aside for a while, but now that she was reminded of it she would start again, perhaps tonight. But he could be so strange. And so rude. For a teacher, a professor! Still, now that she had heard about his kindness to Sophie, she would think better of him. Perhaps she would even enrol again in September.

"And you, Sophie? Will you enrol too? I do hope so."

But Sophie would not be doing that. She would not be in Toronto. Her husband wanted to return to Europe.

"Ah. Your husband. Such a fine man. So devoted."

Afflicted souls. After that talk with Marianne I couldn't stop thinking about them, those afflictions. No, untrue. Truth is, I have never thought much at all about afflictions. I respect the word, is what I should say. It always conjures up for me one of the plagues of Egypt, a million winged insects zooming out of your wallpaper. I suppose I have always lived too comfortably to be intimate with a word like "affliction"; when it seemed near, I just got on a train. What I in fact was thinking about, much more than was usual with me, was simply the word "soul" on its own. Not an abstraction, nothing theoretical, and, to be honest, not Sophie's soul or Marianne's soul either. Just mine. My . . . soul.

Asked about it at any earlier time in my life, I might have said, lip-synching Thomas à Kempis, that insofar as "soul" exists at all, it must be in abeyance, off-screen somewhere, biding its time. Always reminding us of our daylight shallowness and hinting at its own crepuscular *profondeurs*. Waiting for its moment, the eruption of eternity's terrors. Reminiscent of phrases that ought to have lost all power but haven't lost a thing, e.g., *I commit my soul to the deep*. Reminiscent of the mantras my mother said in unison with me at my bedtime for as long as we had each other. *Keep my little soul tonight, Close to thine till morning light.*

But lately, a change of heart. I have an idea why this is so: it's to be found under *Guilt:* see *early awareness of,* or *brushes with.* The word "soul" now does seem present and distinct, it seems important. We have one, we tend to ignore it, but it will wait. Someday we might want it. Why? *What can I do with my soul, which dwells within me like an unsolved riddle?*

That's it? My final whispery thought on this is a question? Not good enough, Bloomski, do better!

OK. The word feels infinitely pure and, not sure about this, but—does it *shimmer?* It almost shimmers. I'm sure that that word reaches my page via Sophie's story of Krakatoa, *that* shimmering. How would Dante feel about "shimmer"? He would turn to whoever was there, Virgil, who else, and lift his arms, palms of his hands upturned, and shrug. He's Italian, after all. *Cosa fare?* he'd say. What's to be done?

Shimmering, it has hung in, this word, this oddity, "soul," through the many years of many, many unkempt lives, mine and others'. A reminder of who we were meant to be.

Meant to be? Chrissakes, O'Bloomov!

Who's all this in aid of? Me, perhaps. Do I need aid? Why? The sunlit pills? What is this, do I wish I'd done nothing? Would I rather that Rollo, formerly Walter, alternately Maggione, was back again in all his power and with all his corrupt, vicious needs?

Course not.

What arrogance, though, talking about soul.

Well, it was on my mind.

Your fault, Sophie. Also yours, Rollo. What afflictions you both are.

———

Here's where we are now. Sophie's taken the new-baked double-Doctor back home. They're living in the big house in Küsnacht, which they share with Sophie's unmarried brother Klaus. There's a very large outdoor patio, the floor of which is made of large flat stones of various colours and extends outwards from a sitting room's glass doors towards a concrete-and-stone railing, from just this side of which you can sit in your wheelchair or any chair of your choice and watch the sunlight glint off the changing surface and small irregular wavelets of the Zürichsee quite a long way below. I intuit all this from a picture postcard that came yesterday. We know that Klaus lectures most days at the university, so in the daylight hours Sophie and Rollo have the place to themselves. That's when the readings-aloud happen. There's also a small stream on the property and, in an interesting development, Rollo has taken to spending an hour every morning working by the stream, moving small stones about on the muddy bank, making forts and houses and unspecified additional buildings. He hasn't said why he's doing this and Sophie hasn't pressed him on it, she doesn't want to meddle with what is obviously a dedicated time. Klaus, though, mentioned it at lunchtime with Psych Department colleagues and somebody had a plausible explanation. It could be a kind of homage to the chosen father, to Carl Jung, the lunching academics think. Unconscious, perhaps, but all the same. Turns out that Jung, although sixty years old and world-famous, used to do the same thing, stream and stones and mud. He called it playing, and said that in playing like this he had regained access to endless sequences of forgotten childhood feelings.

At the same time as she keeps an eye on these activities, Sophie has plenty of energy for her research project, which centres on the late seventeenth-century Pietist movement in Germany, a movement which had ripple effects in Switzerland. Sophie has a half-completed manuscript which a publisher in Frankfurt has shown interest in. I've been glad to notice that in writing to tell us about the publisher's interest, Sophie omits to say that she is amazed or incredulous that this interest should exist, nor does she say that it will surely lead nowhere because, well, who could possibly be interested in anything *she* is doing, etc.

I should add that she also visits a physiotherapist several times a week. This was mentioned in one of her e-mails and was at once seized upon by guess who, and after numerous e-mailed threats and badgerings by that person, more information finally forthcame. It seems that the physio had, and still has, no explanation for two distinct concentrations, "clusters," she calls them, of tiny hardened areas, subcutaneous, in her patient's lower body, but has come to believe that her own treatment plus, any day now, a program of massage may heal these. *Will* would be better, but *may* is what we've got.

We also find in the mail, now and then, old-style picture postcards, all of which, although they are obviously on sale to the public in Switzerland, are in fact photographs of the Führ house and land. I've taken the point. Sophie's former and now again current home is the sort of locally illustrious place you'd chauffeur your visiting tourist friends to see, if you had such friends and were chauffeuring them. You'd slow down while driving past so you could sketch in one or more of the various folkloric tales about this house that everybody who lives along the lake has heard a hundred times.

I refer, of course, to the Nora-and-James tales that just seem to keep on showing up in the pages of the world's press, and especially, it makes sense to suppose, in the weekend edition of the *Neue Zürcher Zeitung.* In that edition Nora and James will obviously long ago have outlasted any lingering references to that other twosome, Klaus and Jakob.

That's Klaus Führ and Jakob Hlasek and their tiebreak in the Swiss Closed.

Not outlasted. Out-rallied. I knew I shouldn't have rushed that sentence.

Marianne will soon have more details about all this. She's flying over in May for two weeks. She wants to take Clarissa with her, if Clarissa can get off school.

I continue to go along most Thursday nights to the Larry Logan Show at Ryerson. All new faces with, counting me, three exceptions. The others are Ms. Madell and Mac, the retired school principal. Most of last year's group signed up for a workshop that's solely devoted to poetry and is directed by a young woman poet whose first book got a really breathless review in the Ryerson newsletter a while ago. I was walking out one Saturday morning with thoughts of buying the book when I ran into Larry, who informed me that he had shared a reading with this poet and that she was the least talented human being he had ever met. I kept on walking but with diminished enthusiasm, and bought, instead, a novella by one of my ex-countrymen, a man called Nooteboom. First name Cees. Most talented living Dutch writer in any genre, his blurb says. I think I agree. Unless, of course, you want to count . . . no.

Wewak has gone to London, where he has a job with the Papua New Guinea trade commission. His brother had something to do with this.

Giorgio, although he didn't re-sign with Larry, was accepted for part two of that "Bloomsbury" seminar given by Dr. Suresh Kilachand. Who did, by the way, get tenure.

Larry has applied for a sabbatical next year. Not sure where he'll spend it, he told me, and says it depends to some extent on the ex-children—will Clarissa and/or Martin go with him wherever he goes, or will they stay with Marianne? However that works out, what's certain is that he has agreed to give papers at conferences in Basel and Grenoble in October of that sabbatical year. Both conferences will focus on the question, "Is Creative Writing a Teachable Subject?" There'll be big-name *conférenciers* from Iowa, East Anglia and Toronto—these are, according to Larry, the three major bad addresses on the wall maps of the uptight wankers of orthodox academe, most of whom think all the best writers are either dead or at the very least harmlessly stapled into their required-reading lists. When I pointed out, since I wasn't sure how closely acquainted Larry was with continental Europe, that both Basel and Grenoble are within an easy train ride of Zürich, and hence of Küsnacht, Larry first nodded, as if this was a given, and then showed belated surprise. Is that so? Bless my soul! and so on. Naturally I then enquired as to how long it was since he'd decided to drop in on the Führs/Maggiones, and he explained that it was a quite recent decision. The talk then became more general until Larry regained his composure. At that point he said, as earnestly as I have ever heard him say anything, that I could put my Dutch-housewife suspicions to rest—he was not going to go there to behave like a four-star asshole.

On the other hand, he said, nobody could stop him from thinking certain thoughts, or from glimpsing, now and then, metaphorically speaking, distant images of a happy life. And he hoped Sophie knew this.

Marianne continues to find me irresistible. She herself is resistible every second or third day for an hour or so. We run in the ravine three afternoons a week, though we've given up talking while we're running. This is because we are living together most of the time, hence any unuttered running-type thought can be confident its hour will come.

Marianne has not sold her own house, however. As she says, these days many splendid couples are in the same two boats.

As for the really private matter, Hippocrates was, of course, right. The true physician endeavours to keep his patients alive; he doesn't set out to kill them. I could say, though, and I will say, that that lawmaker and general table-setter of our profession cannot have been a subtle thinker. If he had been, if his canons 'gainst self-slaughter and also against other, very rare but needful, kinds of deaths had been subtler, had opened a very small door here and there to actions demonstrably of value to a few good people, people helpless to help themselves, people trapped in a terrible grief or pain or humiliation that will just go on and on unless a death, or something like a death, intervenes, then I would admire him more.

Still, we're on unsure ground now, and I'm as unsure as the ground. Point is, after all the *son et lumière* that's been flashing on and off around here, I knew I must give up doctoring, and that's what I have done. As far as anybody knows, I have simply had enough. This is independently true. I am no loss to the profession, and I do not miss the profession.

I'm testing another one.

Acknowledgments

I have specific debts to acknowledge to two people. They are Gabrielle Guenther, a poet and translator living in Amsterdam, who vetted all of Dr. Bloom's use of the Dutch language; and Richard Heinzl, a doctor and writer (formerly with *Médecins Sans Frontières*), who checked and rechecked the medical data so essential to this story.

Thanks also to Sarah Coles and Luke Coles, both of whom read and critiqued an early draft of *Doctor B.* And to Heidi Coles, who did the same and then, at the last minute and for the last draft, healed the German.

DON COLES is one of Canada's most successful poets. He studied at the University of Toronto and Cambridge University and has spent more than a decade on the continent in France, Germany, Switzerland and Scandinavia. He taught at York University for many years and was for ten years Senior Poetry Editor at the Banff Centre for the Arts. He has published ten books of poetry and is the recipient of a Governor General's Award, a Trillium Award and the John Glassco Prize for Translation. Don Coles lives in Toronto.